SAFE & SOUND

THE LOST & FOUND TRILOGY BOOK THREE

VM RHEAULT

Safe & Sound
The Lost & Found Trilogy Book Three

Re-edited and republished November 2023

Published by Coffee & Kisses Press

Cover design by Vania Rheault via Canva.com
Pictures purchased and used with permission from depositphotos.com
City Background: Contributor, @ dell640;
Photo ID, 35619901
Handsome Man: Contributor, @ depositedhar
Photo ID, 187814218
Baby Carriage Vector: Contributor, branchecarica
Photo ID, 34646559

Cover fonts: Playfair Display
Author name font: Cinzel Decorative
Interior text font: Fanwood

Coffee & Kisses Press logo designed by
David Willis and Drake Rheault
Coffee & Kisses Press owned and operated by
Vania Rheault
Printed in the United States of America

Paperback ISBN: 978-1-956431-35-3
E-Book ISBN: 978-1-956431-34-6

❀ Created with Vellum

ABOUT THE BOOK

I won't let her break my heart again.

Roman

I have nowhere else to go, and I fall to my knees in front of my ex-wife, begging for help.

My daughter's life depends on it.

I'm a suspect in a murder investigation, and I'm trapped until I can find out who killed my daughter's mother.

Nothing has changed since Claire and I divorced, and I have to get out of here before she breaks my heart all over again.

Claire

I don't want them here. Felicity is going to steal my heart.

Roman always had it.

I still love him, even after all this time, but I know the moment he clears his name, he's going to leave.

Unless I can move beyond what my parents' mistakes did to me. I want to, but I grew up believing I wasn't worthy of love.

And that's all Roman ever did . . . love me.

CHAPTER ONE

Roman

I don't have anywhere else to go.

I don't want to need my ex-wife, as she has clearly demonstrated over the course of the four years we've been divorced that she doesn't need me, but Fate hasn't been kind lately and this is another one of her sick jokes.

The old beater I drove to camouflage my presence in Bridgeport creaks to a stop, and I park and kill the engine. I flick a glance into the rearview mirror, and Felicity's sleeping, her little face peaceful. She misses her mother, the way she squirms in my arms telling me I'm not enough, but Claire would do the same, always looking for something I wasn't giving her.

The street around the corner from Claire's penthouse is quiet, the excitement after the Fourth of July celebrations dissipating into a hot, sticky calm. Those tired of the heat are already looking forward to milder temperatures, and those who love the summer months try to deny that fall is only eight weeks away.

My fingers itch to light a cigarette, but I don't smoke around Felicity and I try to keep it away from her. There's a lot I should keep away from her, but that's a worry for a different day.

I climb out of the car, the door squealing on its hinges. I picked it up in a crappy town at a dealership that doesn't see a lot of customers. Paid in cash and prayed like hell it wouldn't fall apart until I reached Bridgeport. I don't have access to any money to fix it.

Trying to look casual and not call attention to myself, I open the back door and unlatch the carrier from the base allowing me to pull my daughter out of the backseat.

She doesn't waken with the jostling, but I'll need to feed her soon. You quickly learn the ways of an infant. When she's hungry, she doesn't let me fuck around. I grab the pink diaper bag sitting on the floor and sling it over my shoulder.

This wasn't what I had planned. Well, not entirely what I had planned. I love Felicity, I'd just wanted Claire to be her mother. Didn't work out that way.

I ask the bored concierge to ring her for me. He doesn't remember me, but I remember him. He held the same position when I lived with Claire in the penthouse, and he's just as smug and self-important.

"Miss Durand isn't here. You're welcome to wait," he says, not giving a shit what I do.

I wonder why she came back after she divorced Kavanaugh. All the penthouse would do is remind her of me.

Miss Durand. Not Mrs. Kavanaugh, or even Ms.

She went full-on backward like she could erase the last five years.

Felicity sighs.

That's not an option I have.

"Thanks. I will."

I wouldn't have to wait if I could text her I'm here, but I can't. I don't have a phone anymore. Too easily traceable, even a burner phone is a risk I don't want to take.

The waiting area is the same, though the furniture has been updated. I sit, unstrap Felicity, and settle her in my arms. She's already spent long enough in her carrier. I read a lot parenting magazines to prepare for Felicity's birth, and something stuck in my mind about flat-headed babies and how they should spend more time in a person's arms than a baby seat. A warning for parents who don't want to give their kids attention.

That's not my problem. I love Felicity more than my own life. I kiss her forehead and she snuggles into the crook of my arm, happy to be held.

I could be waiting all day, and I try to relax. I'm safe in Claire's building, and if I played my cards right, no one knows I'm back in Bridgeport.

My stomach is rumbling by the time she steps foot in the lobby, her heels snapping against the tile, her skirt stopping just above her knees. She never had to be blatant about her sexuality, she oozes it just by breathing. Her blouse hugs her breasts, and her hair is a little lighter than I remember it being. Her green eyes are the color of a forest, and I always teased her, comparing her to a woodland fairy. She'd laugh, but her cheeks would warm with this adorable blush.

I loved her so much, back when I thought my love would be enough.

"Claire," I say, or she'll walk right by me.

She freezes, and once she regains her composure, she turns toward me. "Roman," she says, her eyes on Felicity. "What are you doing here?"

"I wouldn't have come, but I need your help."

CHAPTER TWO

Claire

I haven't seen Roman since we stood outside my attorney's office, the afternoon sun lighting the parking lot, everything too bright, my senses screaming. It seemed surreal that I was still in love with a man I divorced. He took that first step away from me, and I wanted to beg him not to go.

He climbed into his car, gave me a faint smile, and drove off, and ever since then I've hated him for giving me what I wanted.

Sitting on a cream leather loveseat, he looks the same, maybe a little worse for wear, but he bears the evidence of those years in the attractive way a woman never could. His hair flops over his forehead, grey at the temples, and lines frame his eyes, but they aren't full of humor and happiness, not like on our wedding day. He couldn't stop staring and smiling at me, unable to believe we'd made it that far.

The sleeping baby is natural in his arms, the one thing he asked me for I didn't want to give him. Couldn't.

He's waiting for me to say something, and I unglue my tongue from the roof of my mouth. "Help with what?"

"Can we not talk here?" he asks, and just then the baby wiggles and opens her mouth to let out a weak cry. "I need to feed her."

I pause. "Okay."

With a grateful sigh, he stands. "Will you carry her?"

"What?"

"Take her. She's only fifteen pounds."

He gently places her in my arms, not giving me a chance to decline. I don't hold children. The closest I come is when Paige, Heath and Zoey Novak's youngest daughter, crawls into my lap. She's four, almost five, and she's nothing compared to this infant who opens her eyes to look owlishly at me, wondering where her milk is. Bottle. Where her bottle is. No one is breast-feeding around here.

Roman hooks his arm under an infant carrier's handle, letting it swing from the crook of his elbow, and hauls a heavy diaper bag's strap over his shoulder.

We walk toward the elevator.

"What's her name?" I don't want to know it, don't want to hold her, but it's rude not to ask, like she's not a human being who will grow into a person with thoughts and feelings of her own.

"Felicity."

"That's pretty. Did you name her?" Everything about this is going to hurt, and I need to give Roman a chance to say what he needs to say and get rid of them both. I can't look at this baby and see what I threw away divorcing Roman all because he wanted one of these with me, and I said no.

"Her mother did."

We step into the elevator, and we're the only two inside.

The doors slide shut and silence swallows us, not even music to buff the edges. I guess there are too many edges to buff.

Felicity fusses, wiggling like a worm in my arms, and I cast a panicked glance at Roman who isn't the least bit worried, leaning against the wall of the car, his eyes closed.

"Aren't you going to do something?"

He cracks his eyes open. "She's hungry. Not much I can do without water. Calm down, Claire. She's only a baby. She won't hurt you."

She won't hurt me? She already is, and I press my lips together.

The elevator bumps to a stop and the doors glide open. I haven't changed a goddamned thing since Roman and I lived here. I didn't want it, but he gave it to me in the settlement and all I did was move out. After Zeke and I divorced, I moved back in. I had nowhere else to go, and I was so lonely I felt I could die. The only things that have kept me together is Roman's presence and my brother, Jack's, support.

He pauses, his eyes sliding over everything, registering every detail that hasn't changed.

Emitting an ear-splitting wail, Felicity spurs him into action, and he darts from the lift to the kitchen. He knows exactly where everything is, and he's unloading the diaper bag at the island when Felicity and I reach him. He runs water from the tap into a pink bottle, measures formula with a tiny measuring spoon, and shakes it vigorously.

He nudges the nipple against the baby's lips and she roots for it desperately, never stopping until the entire nipple disappears into her mouth. It's awkward, me holding her while he feeds her, but we're close, and I breathe in the scent I've only been able to manufacture in my dreams—Roman's earthy cologne and the faint odor of cigarettes. He'd always had a penchant for a smoke, but after we married, he curbed it and it didn't seem like he missed it. I guess he did.

"Here, hold this, I need a second," he says, tilting the bottle to me.

Reluctantly, I steady the bottle. She sucks hungrily, her eyes on me as if daring me to try to stop her.

He shuffles into the living room, and if he's surprised the furniture is still the same, he doesn't give himself away. He sinks onto the couch and holds his head in his hands.

"Can you tell me what's going on?"

He draws in a breath. "I'm in some deep shit, Claire."

I came to that conclusion when he shoved a hungry infant into my arms. "I don't understand. What have you been doing for four years? Why are you here with a baby? I don't even know if she's yours."

His jaw is tense, and he visibly has to relax to say, "She's mine. Her mother's dead, and I'm wanted for her murder."

"Did you do it?" He looks dangerous enough to do it. Mean enough. Angry enough.

"Christ! No, I didn't do it," he bursts out furiously, shoving his hand through his hair.

I believe him. "Do you know who did?"

"No. If I did, do you think I'd be here?"

I look away. Of course, if he didn't need my help, he wouldn't be here.

Roman scowls. "What did you expect? You haven't reached out in four years, not even to text me happy birthday. It's obvious you want nothing to do with me, and I wouldn't be here if I didn't have to be."

Felicity empties the bottle, and I pull it from her mouth with a *pop*. Her tiny brows furrow in objection, but her eyes drift shut.

"You have to burp her. Rest her head on your shoulder. She's good at it, and you don't have to do anything."

"I don't know how to hold a baby," I snap.

Roman sighs. "Support her head and don't drop her. That's it."

"Easy for you to say." I set the bottle on an end table and adjust Felicity the best I can. Unbelievably, she snuggles into my body, my arm under her little butt.

"She misses her mother. You're the first woman who's held her in weeks."

In an ingrained motion, I smooth my hand up and down her back. "What have you been doing?"

"Hiding, mostly. Trying to stay off the radar. All those pharmacies, they have security cameras, and it's been harder than fuck to buy formula."

"What are you going to do?" I tuck my nose into the delicate curve of Felicity's neck. She smells like baby lotion, formula, and pee.

He leans into the couch, the one we made love on several times during our marriage. I can feel his body gliding over mine, he wanting more out of the act than intimacy and me always worried history would repeat itself.

"Find out who did it, if I can. The police won't work with me—they want me to come in. Like fuck I will. Brielle's parents want Felicity, and if they hold me for questioning, it's them or CPS. Neither is an option." He slides a pack of cigarettes from the inside of his suit jacket and taps one into his hand. He fiddles with it, his eyes never leaving my face.

I try to put this together. Roman's wanted for murder. His wife's? Were they married? He's spitting mad and exhausted, not in the mood to answer any more questions, but I'm working out my own shit and I ask, "How long will you need?"

Propelled by a fury I've never seen him display, even at his angriest with me, he flies to his feet and bursts out, "Fuck, I don't know. I'll be out of here as soon as I can. Jesus Christ. Can't you think about more than yourself for once? For one goddamned minute? I need a nap. Can you please hold her for an hour? I almost passed out driving here. I'm so fucking tired."

He strides down the hall to the master suite where he knows he'll find the king bed we used to share. He shuts the door with a quiet click, thinking about the baby and not wanting to wake her with a satisfying *slam!*

Felicity wiggles closer, burrowing her tiny head against my shoulder, wetting my blouse with drool. I don't know a thing about taking care of a baby. I don't want to hurt her out of ignorance, and I make a call.

Zoey says she and Heath will be here in a few minutes, and while I wait, I sing a lullaby that I picked up from only God knows where, imagining it's what my mother sang to me, but I don't remember.

CHAPTER THREE

Roman

I don't know what woke me up, the need for a nicotine fix, maybe, or the murmur of voices, or my body instinctively searching for Claire in a bed we made love in a million times. The faint scent of Chinese takeout? I'm surprised I could sleep, but deep down, for all Claire's protesting, I knew Felicity would be okay with her.

I roll over and ball a pillow under my head. I need another second to wake up before I face her. She looks the same on the outside, but she's turned so hard on the inside. Can't wait for a fucking second to kick us out of here. I'll need to think of an alternative place to lay low, but for now, Claire was as far as I got. Maybe I would have done better to call Jack. His fiancée would know how to take care of a baby and they wouldn't be so eager to get rid of me.

It was a mistake to seek out Claire because I wanted to see her. I accused her of being selfish, but I am, too. I should stick with what will be best for Felicity, and Claire isn't it.

Reluctantly, I roll out of bed. I won't solve Brielle's homicide hiding, and I'm curious who Claire invited over. I should have told her not to tell anyone I'm here, but no harm done if I have to move on. It's always better to know who's on your side . . . and who's not.

I stagger down the hall, rubbing sleep out of my eyes. I feel a little better, but the sunset glows through the sparkling windows in the living room and I panic. A set of French doors lets out onto a stone balcony that looks over Bridgeport, and it was my favorite spot when I lived here with Claire. I would sit outside for hours, sometimes alone, sometimes with her. We would make love, and I would feel like I had everything and nothing at all.

I slept for too long.

Claire meets my gaze, guilt shining in her eyes loud and clear. Did she call the cops? I wouldn't put it past her.

Instead, Zoey Novak hurries in from the kitchen. "Roman!"

She launches herself at me, and suddenly my arms are full of a beautiful, slender hippie. No one tells you that after a divorce you'll lose half your friends. Losing Zoey and Heath's friendship was a blow I hadn't counted on, and I hug her to me, burying my nose in her vanilla-scented hair.

"Claire called us," she says, peering up at me.

"Us?" I ask, my eyes roaming her body. She hasn't changed a bit. From her big blue eyes, to the freckles covering the bridge of her nose, to her long blonde hair, she looks the same as the last day I saw her.

"Hey," Heath greets me, walking in from the kitchen too, Felicity propped on his shoulder. He's comfortable with a baby in his arms. Well, he's been through it three times, so he should be an expert by now.

"Hey," I return, shaking his hand, my other arm still full of his wife. "Thanks for coming."

"Claire asked us for help," Zoey says, stepping away from me and brushing her hand over Felicity's back. "We've changed her diaper a few times since we got here. She had a little diaper rash going on, and we gave her some airtime. She looks better."

"Thanks."

Claire's standing on the other side of the living room, and she says, her arms crossed over her chest, "I didn't know what else to do. I hope you're not mad. I wouldn't have thought to change her diaper."

"It's fine, thank you. I guess I can't expect you to keep this a secret." I rub the grit out of my eyes and shuffle to her. I give into the need to touch, and I nuzzle a kiss to her temple.

She stiffens. "There's Chinese in the kitchen. I ordered you a carton of chicken and broccoli. I wasn't sure . . ."

Holding her chin in my hand in the familiar way I used to whenever I wanted her to kiss me, I say, "It's *fine*. As long as there's beer."

Claire tamps down a smile, and I relax. Maybe hiding here won't be as hellish as I thought.

"You can give me kisses for that," Heath says. "I brought the beer. It's in the fridge."

"I'll kiss your feet later," I say, stumbling into the kitchen. I haven't slept so soundly since Felicity's birth, and I'm muzzy with the dregs of my nap. Gratefully, I snag a bottle out of the industrial-sized fridge. An unopened carton of Chinese is sitting on the island next to a box of white rice and a bottle of soy sauce. Felicity looks at home in Heath's arms and I take advantage and dig in. "How long was I out?"

"Seven hours," Claire says, her eyes on the chopsticks we never used and how I now navigate them as easily as a fork.

I wince. "Sorry."

"It's okay. Gave us time with this cutie," Zoey says, tugging on Felicity's little foot. "Claire didn't know if all you have with you is all you had, so we bought a few things online that will be here in the morning. Crib and a changing table. Her sleepers are a little snug and we ordered her some more clothes in a size up. She's seven weeks old, about?"

I nod, a lump in my throat. I never should have doubted finding Claire was the best thing to do.

"More formula and diapers. We ordered the brands in your diaper bag."

"Thanks. That's a big help, really."

"It brings us back to the good old days," she says, her eyes crinkling at Heath.

"Yeah, but I don't miss the feedings every two hours. She went through two more bottles while you were out," Heath says, but he presses his lips to Felicity's head, his paternal embrace possessive.

"Growth spurt," I mumble through a mouthful of chicken.

Claire looks on, lost.

It's hard not to resent her. I wanted this with her. She was so adamant she didn't, she divorced me.

"Claire says you found a bit of trouble. It doesn't look like you want to get into it now, and I understand. It's late, and Zoey and I should be getting back anyway, but we'll rally the troops and figure this out, yeah?"

I'm too hungry to let Heath ruin my appetite. I have to look this straight on. I can't keep running. That's not a life for me, and it's not a life for Felicity. "Yeah. Thanks. I've been on the road for a couple of weeks now. It will help to have a solid place to hide." I glance at Claire, but all she does is stare back at me.

"You want Jack in on this? Rafferty Clark might have some resources up his sleeve."

"*Talk of the Town*, Rafferty Clark?" I ask, my eyebrows raised. Things really have changed if a gossip snoop is part of our group. Well, their group. It's not mine anymore.

"He's got a thing with Jack's ex. He's a good guy."

I grunt. I'll have to see that for myself. "Jack." I trust him. He was a good brother-in-law while he was one.

"Emma's ballsy, too." Heath's voice is full of admiration.

"Heard he's engaged."

"Trying for one of these," Heath says, transferring Felicity to Claire who scowls. She does not want to hold the baby again, but she has no choice. I'm still starving, and honestly, it's nice for Felicity to sleep in someone's arms and not in her infant carrier, even if Claire is reluctant.

"I need a day or two to get my shit together. I'm tired, and Felicity's strung out. If Claire can give me some time . . ."

When she hears this, her lips thin, but not from annoyance. No, I know my ex-wife. I know how her eyes blaze in irritation or frustration. This isn't that. This is fear. Afraid I'll bring some trouble to her door? She already had that when the Bridgeport Hotel went up in flames with her and all her friends inside it.

No, she's not scared of something like that.

It's more, and suddenly, I'm not in such a hurry to leave.

If she's not afraid of bodily injury, she's afraid for her heart, and that is very, *very* interesting to me.

CHAPTER FOUR

Claire

While Roman slept, I asked Zoey for a crash course. She didn't mention it, but I was the one who fed Felicity her two bottles and changed her diapers. All four times . . . she kept pooping the second we would put a fresh one on her. At one point, she was lying on the floor, airing out her little butt, and she smiled at me, grateful, I think, not to be in a car.

I can't imagine how hard traveling with a baby would be. No, not traveling, hiding.

Since the moment he told me Felicity was his, I've wanted to ask him, did he love her? Felicity's mother. It's stupid to hope he hadn't. No one has a baby with someone they don't love. Does he miss her? Is he mourning her? Maybe that's the few days he needs before Jack rushes in, throwing his money around. Mourning a woman he'll never see again.

I haven't mourned Zeke.

Maybe a little.

It's a strange feeling to have been married to someone who's not alive anymore, and it's a big coincidence that Roman and I used to be with people who are gone. Maybe he was married to her. Maybe once he clears his name, he'll move back to wherever it is he came from and let Felicity's grandparents be a part of her life. Children need people around them. It was amusing Emma dragged my brother everywhere in preparation for her to be a surrogate, but it was heartbreaking, too. Babies create family, whether we want them to or not, but it seems as if for now, Roman and Felicity are alone.

Roman's saying goodbye to Zoey and Heath, and I putter around the kitchen cleaning up after our meal, grateful for a moment alone.

"I really hate to ask this," Roman starts, walking into the room a few minutes later, "but can you listen for Felicity tonight? I'm so tired, Claire, and I'm afraid I'll sleep right through her cries."

We left Felicity sleeping on the couch. He explained how to position her so she's lying on her side against the cushions, and I promptly followed his directions. He slides onto a stool at the island and pokes at his Chinese, the carton almost empty.

"But her crib won't come until tomorrow." I grasp at any straw.

"She'll be fine in your bed. She's not rolling over yet, and she'll stay in the exact same spot you put her. Zoey show you how to fix her bottles?"

I nod. Roman would think I didn't want to help him if I pretended I don't know how to mix her bottles or change her diaper, and that's far from the truth. I'm not the insensitive shrew he seems to think I turned into, and even if I had some resentment toward him, I'd never take it out on a helpless infant.

There's a reason I didn't want children, though it was

nothing Roman tried to understand or anything I tried to explain.

"Felicity's a good sleeper. She'll wake you up once, maybe twice. Change her diaper after you feed her and she'll let you sleep."

He's exhausted and I would feel like an absolute bitch if I said no. "Fine."

"Thank you. Is there a particular guest room you want me to use? Why are you here, anyway?" he asks, holding another bottle of beer to his mouth.

"After I divorced Zeke, I didn't have anywhere else to go." I dump the empty cartons into the trash and shove the rest in the fridge. If Roman wakes up before me, he'll eat the leftovers for breakfast. At least, that's what he used to do.

He scoffs. "Claire, you're worth over five hundred million dollars. Don't give me that bullshit."

I'll never confess to the real reason I moved back in. "It was easier, okay?" I snap. "I was in love with him, and I was hurting."

Roman slides off his stool, setting the bottle onto the island with a clink that echoes through the entire kitchen. He advances and pushes me against the counter, his hard body aligning perfectly with mine. His eyes are narrowed, his muscles rigid with tension. His cold lips brush the shell of my ear and he says, "We might have a lot of things between us, but lies are not one of them. Don't you ever fucking lie to me again."

He glances quickly into the living room at his daughter, and he trots up the stairs to a den and three guest bedrooms. He doesn't have a bag, but the bathrooms are stocked with everything he'll need.

I shake with nerves and pour a glass of white wine. It seems wrong to drink around a baby, though Zoey doesn't have a problem drinking around her kids, sometimes sending one of her girls as a beer delivery if Heath's outside in their backyard.

"Well, Felicity, I sure fucked that up," I mumble, staring through the French doors at the city lights. "I should have known he'd never buy it."

I don't know what prompted me to try, either, except I need space. Roman's been here for eight hours, nine, and I already need space, a wall, no matter how flimsy. He was like that, when we were married. All of him, consuming all of me. I loved it, needed it, and for the four years we've been divorced, all I've done is struggle to figure out who I am, *what* I am, without him. So far, I haven't succeeded. The only thing I ever wanted since the night I met Roman Mansfield was to be his wife, and when I wasn't any longer, I was lost. So lost. Still am.

Zoey told me to fill the bottles with water beforehand and in the middle of the night when I'm half sleeping, all I'll need to do is add formula to the room-temperature water. "You don't want to burn her with microwaved formula," she cautioned, and she knew just how to scare the hell out of me. I don't want to hurt Felicity. I'd never recover.

I fill three with four ounces of water each, hoping she doesn't want to eat more than that and leave them on the counter with the canister of formula. I drain my wine glass and put it in the empty sink. The delivery is estimated for ten, but I don't need to set my alarm. I rarely sleep past seven.

"Your daddy has some misplaced trust," I say, sliding one hand under her head and another under her butt.

My bed has a divot right in the middle of the mattress where Roman napped, and I hold back a scowl. I don't mind he slept here, it's his scent I'll inhale all night that I can do without. It's not aftershave—he hasn't shaved in days, maybe weeks. No, it's remnants of my favorite cologne, sweat, and gritty cigarette smoke, and I love it.

Hard feelings aside, I hope we can get this figured out. His wife's, girlfriend's, whatever she was to him, death has pushed him to his breaking point, and I can't lie anymore. I'm glad he came to me. He and Felicity are safe in the penthouse. No one will be able to get to them.

I'm still wearing the clothes I wore earlier to run errands, and it's a relief to wiggle out of my skirt and bra. Felicity watches from her position in the middle of my bed, and I say, "Your time will come."

She smiles, thinking I'm kidding.

"I'm as serious as a heart attack, kiddo," I grumble. "Are you going to be okay? I need to wipe my makeup off and brush my teeth. I guess you need a diaper, too, and I'm glad Zoey thought to buy you new clothes. You can't even stretch your legs out."

She doesn't have a lot to offer in way of conversation, her eyes never leaving me as I walk around the bedroom, first to drop my dirty clothing into the dry-cleaning pile and then as I pull on a nightgown and robe.

I wash my face and brush my teeth, and I hurry into the living room, retrieve her diaper bag, and change her diaper. It's too early to fall asleep, and I lie with her. She stares at the lights streaking across the walls and reaches out her hand, trying to grab them.

Eventually, I drift off, and she wakes me once. We sit together in the rocking chair in my sitting room, looking over Bridgeport. There's something peaceful about rocking a baby in the middle of the night, nothing but the sound of her little sucks as she eats. She doesn't weigh much, and she fits into the crook of my arm like she's meant to be there. I wonder if this is how my mother felt when she had me. When a middle-of-the-night feeding was a chance to bond, not an annoyance.

She drains the bottle, and I set it onto the floor and prop her against my shoulder. Gliding back and forth, I doze, Felicity's formula-saturated breath fanning my skin. She falls into a deep sleep.

I can't get attached to this baby. Once Roman clears his name, he'll leave. He had a life for these past four years, and I know about hardly any of it. He could have other children, a house, staff. His law firm used to be the most sought after in Bridgeport. I don't know if he still represents clients.

He didn't come back here for me.

I have to remember that.

Content, I ease the rocker back and forth, cocooned in a calm I haven't felt in a long time. Hours pass and I rouse, sensing I'm not alone. The sun is rising, casting my sitting room in a delicate pink. Something touches my knee and I jerk, startled, blinking against the light.

"You scared the hell out of me," Roman whispers, his fingers grazing my skin.

Stifling a yawn, my heart pounding, I ask, "What? Why?"

"I went into your room to check on you, and you and Felicity weren't there."

"We're here." I try to move, and I wince. I shouldn't have fallen asleep in the rocking chair. Felicity's head is pressed uncomfortably against my collarbone and my neck has a crick in it.

Roman chuckles. "Go back to bed. It's too early to be awake."

I'm not going to argue with that. I don't want to wake Felicity, and gently, I stand from the rocker, a firm hand to her neck to keep her head from moving.

Roman's kneeling on the floor, his jeans undone and his unbuttoned dress shirt framing his bronzed chest. He stands, follows me into the bedroom, and waits for me to lay Felicity in the middle of the bed. I slide in next to her. Brushing my hair aside, he kisses my forehead, smooths his fingers over his daughter's, and shuffles barefoot out of the bedroom.

I fall asleep to the scent of coffee and don't wake until after ten.

Forcing my eyes open for a second time this morning, I don't see Felicity. I sit up in a panic until I realize Roman must have picked her up for her morning bottle and a fresh diaper.

The stale scent of leftover Chinese wafts into the bedroom, and I pad down the hallway and into the living room.

A large crib is sitting in the middle of the room near a matching changing table, a bouncy seat and infant swing positioned next to them, and boxes of diapers, formula, and clothes are scattered around the rest of the room.

On a new baby blanket, Felicity is lying on her tummy watching her daddy poke through a pile of baby sleepers and toys.

I slept through the delivery, exactly like I thought I wouldn't. Roman and Felicity are already shooting my schedule all to hell, but I can't be mad.

"Claire, this is too much," Roman says, looking up from the box. "Thank you."

I wave him off and retreat to the kitchen for a cup of coffee. "It was Zoey. I trusted her and it's better to have too much than not enough."

He follows me and scrubs a hand through his hair. "I have another favor to ask," he says, leaning against the counter.

I sip. "Hmmm?" I need the caffeine before I'm drawn into anything that requires a coherent reply.

"I need clothes, too." An embarrassed stain crawls up the back of his neck.

"Why are you asking me? What happened to your money?" It's not that I mind buying him what he needs, but he brought up my family's wealth and the divorce settlements from both himself and Zeke. He has his own family money, and his family has more than mine. He shouldn't need me to buy him anything.

"They froze my accounts hoping to force me out of hiding. I've been using cash on the road, but that's gone."

"Oh, well, it's fine," I say, my own blush warming my cheeks. "I didn't do anything with your charge accounts. Order what you want."

He frowns. "What do you mean you didn't do anything with my accounts?"

I'll have to admit this eventually, so I might as well get it over with. "Hugo Boss, Ralph Lauren. Tom Ford. Burberry. Your accounts. They're still open. Order what you want."

"Claire—"

"It was too much work to close them, okay?" I ask defensively, my voice rising in agitation, not wanting him to know the real reason why I didn't touch his charge accounts. It would have been another tie severed and I couldn't handle it.

He nods, scrutinizing me. He warned me to stop lying, but I don't see how I can tell him the truth. He's here because he had nowhere else to go that had the resources he needs. It has nothing to do with me and repairing our relationship. I ruined what we had, and there's no fixing it.

"Thanks. Can I borrow your laptop?"

"It's in my bedroom on the dresser."

"I'll find it after I take a shower. What's on tap for today?" he asks, adding more coffee to my mug.

There's a lot of crap I should do today. Zeke's attorney has been hounding me to stop by his office, claiming Zeke left me something in his will. I don't want whatever the hell it is, but his attorney won't accept any kind of response over the phone. I tried to have my attorney speak for me, but there's nothing I can do but go there in person and decline whatever it is.

I also want to speak to Jack about what our father did to our mother. The fire at the hotel the night of the fundraiser and what happened to Veronica put a lot of things on hold. Last night, Zoey said Gracie's been doing better with Veronica's help, and I was so happy to hear it. I know how hard it is to put the past behind you, and Gracie's too young for that.

There are also engagement parties to attend, my brother's and now Raff and Veronica's, an event Emma has been planning with glee because she knows how much Raff will hate going.

We've all been letting things calm down, but I haven't forgotten what Dad told us about kicking Mom out of his house . . . and out of our lives.

It's left me in limbo. I don't have a fiancé like Emma or Veronica or children to see to like Zoey and Heath.

I've been tempted to fly back to California, the sun and sand an excuse not to hang around like a fifth wheel, but Roman and Felicity changed those plans. I'm not sure if Emma would let me go, anyway. She's all about including me and would never let me miss another party.

"There are a few things I should be doing," I say, "but let's get Felicity settled in and you can order clothes first. What I have to do can wait, and in new clothes," I say, knowing Roman felt best in a crisp suit, "you'll feel like tackling what's next. I think Jack is champing at the bit to see you. He always did like you more than Zeke."

"That's not a surprise."

I quirk my lips and step away.

"Hey," he says, grabbing my arm. "I'm sorry he's gone. I can be glib and callous, but if you're really hurting, and that wasn't a lie, I'm sorry."

"Thanks," I say softly. "I'm not sure how I feel about it. We were divorced for longer than we were married."

"If you want to talk, I can honestly say I understand."

"Did you love her?" I ask, the words tumbling out of my mouth.

His eyes meet mine, hard, unforgiving.

"As much as you loved Zeke."

"Then not at all." I dodge around him, and I'm through the living room when I hear a sad, "Then not at all."

———

"Where should we put it?" Roman asks, his hand resting on the crib's railing. A pretty blonde oak, it's already put together and a mobile wrapped in plastic lays on the bare mattress, the light pink and blue of the butterflies glowing in the sun.

"Did you choose a bedroom upstairs?" Better for him to be up there than down the hall from me. I don't want to think of him sleeping so close.

When we lived here, he did a lot of work in the den. He used it as an office, which was fine with me. Though I attended a university, I've never had career aspirations and still don't. Raff's idea to stop hunting for husband number three and find something meaningful to do with my time cut me to the bone in a way I'm sure he never thought possible.

"Yeah. Kind of. I thought working through the murder investigation would be easier with a little privacy."

The quicker he can clear his name and find the real killer who murdered his . . . I still don't know if he was married to her or not . . . the sooner he can leave and start over.

"Put it in my room, then," I say reluctantly, knowing exactly what I'm signing up for by volunteering. "She shouldn't be alone. Security is good here, you know that, but you'd probably sleep better if she's not in a nursery by herself."

He blows out a sigh, and I know I did the right thing. "That's great, Claire. Thank you."

Felicity watches us roll the crib down the hallway and I start a load of laundry to wash the new sheets, bedding, and sleepers. Zoey even remembered to order infant detergent, and the clean scent fills my laundry room.

Roman lays his daughter down for a nap on the couch, and I gesture for him to meet me in the kitchen. I don't know what to order for dinner, and he hasn't showered, sidetracked putting Felicity's things away in my room. It's awkward being around him. He's a stranger but he shouldn't be, and it's my fault he is.

"You still haven't learned to cook," he teases, pouring a glass of wine and setting that and my laptop onto the island near me. "Help me order clothes. You always had such good taste."

I did enjoy dressing him, and I navigate to the websites he used to shop on. "All right. I'll help you if you cook."

"I will, but not tonight. No cooking until we get some food in here. You've got nothing. I'm good, but not that good."

We browse, and he leans over my shoulder, sipping on a beer Heath left behind.

My eyes on the screen, I ask, "Will you tell me what happened?"

Roman points to a navy blue suit jacket and without thinking, I choose his size and add it to the cart.

"I met Brielle outside a bar. I guess that was, I don't know, a couple years after we said our last goodbyes? I was still reeling. I thought our wedding rings meant forever, but all I got was eleven months. I had a rough time."

My fingers tremble over the touchpad, and Roman covers my hand with his.

"Shh. Her heel had broken off one of her shoes, and I hailed her a taxi. One thing led to another and we swapped numbers. She was so open, Claire. I don't say this to insult you or to start a fight, but when we were dating, you were so closed off. You never wanted to talk to me about how you were feeling. I always had to guess, and I always guessed wrong. Looking back, that should have been a sign you weren't ready to get married, and I shouldn't have asked. But I thought if I gave you time, as we got to know each other, you'd trust me. Brielle was different. She shared her hopes and dreams from our first date. We'd stay up late, talking. Nothing was off limits."

Listening to him, I can understand how he'd be enamored by something so simple. I made him fight for every inch, afraid of what he'd do with it. Afraid of what he'd do if I let him.

"We were with each other all the time. I met her family. She didn't come from money, something else that was different that I liked. She wouldn't know what to do in a place like this. She'd probably think it was a museum, afraid to touch anything."

I stare at my keyboard. The black plastic over a couple of the letters is chipping. I always took great care where I lived, memories stuck in the inanimate objects that make up a home. I didn't tell Emma the evening I gave her a tour of the house that Jack may have abandoned the nursery where he watched our mother ride away in a taxi, but the second I could, so had I. Zoey had wanted to order Felicity a white crib, and I told her no. When I was a baby, I had a white crib too, and couldn't stand to look at one in my house.

"She got pregnant," Roman continues, his hand resting over mine, "but I wasn't happy. I didn't want a baby with her, I'd wanted one with you. To have my dreams superimposed onto another woman . . . it was wrong, and it felt wrong. She grew bigger, and we talked baby names and where we would live and whether or not we should get married. When Felicity was born, I was almost happy, and I love that little girl more than I ever loved anybody, and that includes you. She's vulnerable and helpless, and I'm her father and she needs me. I will never give her up, and it's my job to keep her safe. But I didn't love her mother, and I was trying to figure out what to do. She disappeared after a girls' night with her friends. They searched for her for two days and found her body along the shores of Cavern Lake. Someone strangled her. I knew they'd blame me, and I ran. I told her I was thinking about breaking it off and sharing custody and she told her parents. They didn't waste any time telling the cops. I have the motive and the means, but I didn't do it. I was home alone with Felicity."

"Can you prove that?" I ask.

"No. I didn't order takeout or rent a movie online. I rocked Felicity all night, torn between staying with her mother to keep her, and leaving because when Brielle got pregnant, no matter how happy I was after she was born, I'd signed up for a life I didn't want."

"I'm sorry," I whisper.

"The only thing you have to be sorry for is saying yes when I asked you to marry me. It's my fault I asked in the first place. I was so in love with you, I ignored all the warnings."

"Can you finish ordering your clothes?" I slide my hand from under his.

"Where are you going?"

"I need some air. If you're hungry, my credit card information is stored in my laptop. Order whatever you want."

"Claire, I didn't tell you all that to make you feel bad. You asked, but you needed to know."

He's frowning, searching my face, concern in his hazel eyes.

"I know. For four years I've accepted the blame for what happened between us. It's too late now, and my apologies and explanations mean less than nothing. We'll help clear your name, find out who took Felicity's mother from her. And I'll understand when you move on, really move on, because there are things that have changed, but there are things that haven't. I can't give you what you want. I can't."

I pull on a cardigan and slip on my flats. Shaking, I ride the elevator to the lobby. The doorman opens the door for me, and I rush past him and onto the sidewalk. Tears blind me, but I don't stop until I find a bench under a tree planted between the cement squares of the boulevard.

I sit for a long time, Roman's words picking at my brain. *I love that little girl more than I ever loved anybody, and that includes you.*

He should never have loved me at all.

CHAPTER FIVE

Roman

I didn't mean to make her leave, but it's like Claire. She'd rather run than tell me what's going on inside that head of hers. She can't give me what I want. That's a no-brainer, but never an explanation, never any reason. Just cut and run.

I finish ordering my clothes and check out, amazed the balance due is zero. She didn't keep my accounts open because it was easier. I told her not to lie to me, but that didn't include the lies she's been telling herself. I can force her to admit she still loves me, but what good would it do? It would only hurt more when I left. I might still love her too, but I'm not going through again what I did four years ago. She decided she didn't want to be married to me, and that's the way it will stay.

I place an order for delivery, pasta from Claire's favorite Italian place, feed Felicity, and give her a bath. I gotta give Zoey credit. She thought of every fucking thing. Baby wash and a plastic tub that fits into the kitchen sink. Diaper rash cream, baby lotion, and more diapers than the pharmacy on the corner has in stock. Felicity loves the warm water, and she wriggles, the bubbles swirling around her.

The hours slide by, and I start to grow concerned. Claire knows what she's doing, but she didn't leave with her cell or her purse. The day gives way to night, and I worry. Someone killed Brielle, and I can't assume it was a random act of violence. Strangulation is a crime of passion, and it's why the cops cornered me so fast. They think Brielle's murderer knew her. I think so too, but that means he or she also knows me.

I let Felicity play until her skin prunes, and I dry and dress her in a new sleeper covered in caterpillars that I fortunately remembered to throw into the dryer earlier.

Maybe Jack knows where Claire went. I'm impatient and tired of waiting for her to come home on her own, and I call him using her phone. It's not password protected, but I'd like to think I still know her well enough to guess what she would use. Maybe.

"Claire, I'm sorry I haven't called. Are you okay?" he asks, not even saying hello.

I don't know what he's talking about, and I say, "Jack, this is Roman."

He pauses. "Heath told me you were in town."

"Yeah, and I, ah, I made Claire mad at me. She's been gone for a while. Do you happen to know where she is?"

"No. She's been keeping to herself a lot since some family stuff came out. I guess she hasn't told you about any of that?"

"Of course not, but to be fair, I've only been here since yesterday afternoon, and I've had a lot on my mind."

"For as small as babies are, they take up a lot of space," he says.

I can't disagree. "Yeah. Maybe too much."

"Claire will be okay. She's always needed room to herself.

With you and a baby there, she'll feel closed in. You have to respect that."

"That's one lesson I didn't learn very well, huh? I always needed to be around her all the time, know every little thing she was thinking."

"She's had a lot dumped on her. Dad dropped a bomb that I'm still dealing with, too. That and the fire, things have been fucked up. You're worried about her, but let her be."

I have no choice but to do what he says. "Yeah."

"Heath said you need some help. We can stop by tomorrow evening. Zoey was gushing to Emma about Felicity and now Emma can't wait to meet her."

"I'd like the same." I want to meet the woman who broke down Jack's defenses.

"Ask Claire to call me when she's home. I've been so wrapped up in my own shit, I haven't been the best brother lately."

"I will. Thanks."

"Good to hear from you, man," Jack says, sincere warmth in his voice. "Divorce fucks everything up. Missed you."

Jack fell in love and he got a huge dose of the touchy-feel-ies. "Right back at you."

I disconnect, but talking to Jack didn't calm my nerves. I won't breathe easier until I know Claire is safe.

I don't wait much longer. The elevator doors slide open half an hour later, and Claire steps into the living room. I'm feeding Felicity and standing in front of the balcony doors. I turn away from the view out there and take in the view in here. Her face is streaked with tears and her hair is a mess, but I only do what Jack advised, and say, "There's dinner in the kitchen if you're hungry and Jack asked if you'd give him a call."

She tries to smile and wipes her cheeks. "Thanks. Sorry I ran off."

"It's okay." I pause. I'll try not to be in her face every second, but she needs to know the score. "You should be careful. I might have brought a lot more than a baby to your door."

Her eyes widen. She hadn't considered that, but now that it's said, I'll learn from my mistakes and step back.

"Okay. Did you eat?"

"No, not yet. I gave Felicity a bath."

"Do you want to eat with me?"

Something flickers over her face, and I know exactly what it is. She's opening up, and she's afraid I'll give her a taste of her own medicine and shut her out. I'd never do that, for revenge or otherwise. I'm just grateful that in the four years we've been apart we both grew up. Maybe not much, but anything is a start. "I'd like that a lot."

We don't talk much while we eat, but that's nothing new. Instead, while I devour my lasagna, I devour her features. I never thought I would see her again, much less share a meal with her. Her hair is the color of melted caramel, a small sprinkle of freckles across her nose. I missed her dimple the most, licking at her soft skin, making her laugh. Sometimes when I talk about it, I sound like the eleven months we were together weren't happy, but they were. They were the happiest of my life, and it was such a blow when she told me she didn't want children but didn't explain why. It broke my heart, and she knew it did. I never asked why she wanted a divorce. I assumed so I couldn't pressure her to have kids. Too stunned to do anything but what she asked, I gave her everything laid out in the prenup and walked away.

Maybe I should have fought, but I don't think it would have helped. I would have driven her even farther away, and I wouldn't be sitting here now.

"You're still beautiful," I say, scraping my fork across my

plate. I prepare for her to rebuff me, but she scrubs her fingers through my beard.

"Thanks. And you need a shave."

"I suppose I do. Will you be all right if I go upstairs and do some digging online? Jack said he and Emma would visit tomorrow evening. Emma wants to see Felicity and Heath told Jack I need some help."

Felicity's dozing in the swing Zoey and Claire bought her, completely blissed out with the gentle movement. I could do what I want to do down here, but I want to search for news about Brielle alone. Sometimes Claire isn't the only one who needs space, and if I find out something terrible, I'd like to process it first before I share.

"Okay. I'm going to call Jack. He worries."

"He said something about family news. Is your dad okay?"

I always liked Ron Durand. Gruff and mostly unapproachable, he didn't bother me. We'd have intense conversations, and I always admired his wisdom. I never knew anything about Claire and Jack's mother, only that they grew up without her.

"Dad finally told us what happened with Mom. He came clean hoping Jack could shake off his commitment phobia and ask Emma to marry him."

Fury burns through me. "He did that for Jack, but he couldn't have done that for you?"

"I haven't talked to him about it, Roman. After I found out, I was barely hanging in there, and then the fire."

I give in and touch her cheek. "I've been such an ass. Were you hurt?"

"No, but you'll probably meet Veronica tomorrow night, she's got a story for you."

I drop my hand and fork up the last bite on my plate. "Veronica . . . Chapman? *Rise and Shine, Bridgeport!?* How are you friends with her?"

"She's engaged to Raff."

"How is Rafferty Clark in on this? Heath mentioned him last night."

"He's Emma's best friend."

"How did Jack meet Emma?" All of us together in the same room will be interesting.

"Emma was his PA for a few years, but Jack was dating Veronica—"

"What were *you* doing?"

"Marrying and divorcing Zeke."

"I missed a lot in four years."

Claire glances at Felicity. "You were plenty busy yourself."

"Yeah, I was. Do you want me to help you clean up?"

She waves a hand. "I got it. The charger cord for my laptop is in my bedroom. I think you're going to need it."

I kiss her cheek. "Thanks. You don't know what it means to me that I had somewhere safe I could go."

Resting her forehead on my shoulder, she says. "I'm glad you thought you could come here. I was never easy, Roman. I know that, but I won't pretend I've changed. I'm still the same person you said goodbye to in the parking lot. Don't think otherwise."

She unlatches Felicity from the swing and carries her down the hallway, already more comfortable with the infant than she was yesterday. She's wrong though. She has changed. The fact that she could admit our marriage was difficult is a huge change, and if she can see what was wrong, she can see what we would need for it to be right.

But I'm getting way ahead of myself. I need to clear my name. I won't be doing anything with anybody if I'm in prison for a murder I didn't commit. Felicity is safe, and Claire will do whatever it takes to protect her. I know that as sure as I know my own name.

I retrieve the charging cord from Claire's room and catch her playing with Felicity. She's dangling a set of toy keys above Felicity's head, but she isn't staring at the toy, she's got her eyes firmly fixed on Claire's face. I don't blame her there. Claire blushes, expecting me to tease her, but I would never be so cruel. I'm grateful she cares enough to give my daughter attention.

I sneak out again, grab a beer, and trot up the stairs. The rooms bring me back to the evenings and weekends I would work on cases, but I never thought I would go through my own divorce. I've represented some of the nastiest people, their divorces bringing out their very worst, and I was surprised and relieved Claire and I split up as easily as we did. No kids, I threw a wad of cash and this penthouse at her, and that was it.

Maybe I should have fought harder.

Maybe I should have fought, period.

I could have strung out our case, insisted on couples therapy. I don't know if it would have done any good. Maybe it would have made her hate me. Now that she knows about her mom, maybe it will help her see we don't have to bring our parents' flaws and mistakes into our relationships.

I bring my beer into the bathroom, and I shower and shave. I can let my guard down a little bit. Claire and Jack and Heath and Zoey are good people and it sounds like they're in with some good people, too.

I still don't have any clothes. Nothing will be delivered until tomorrow, and I dig through the closets and armoires, hoping for something clean to sleep in. I'm not surprised to find some of my old things. Claire didn't want to let go any more than I did. I find a pair of boxers that are a little snug in the waist but better than putting on the crusty briefs I've been wearing for the past couple of days and a pair of baggy sweats and a t-shirt. With food in my belly, my daughter safe and cared for, and a week's worth of grime scrubbed off my skin, I feel better than I have since the police called me in for questioning. I wouldn't have minded another beer, but using the intercom to ask Claire to bring me one is a little too close for me, and I don't want to waste time running down to the kitchen.

Sitting on the middle of the bed, I wake up Claire's laptop. The Burberry website is still open, the screen thanking me for my purchase. I close out of that and the Tom Ford website. Close out of *Talk of the Town* without scrolling—I have enough gossip in my life, and I don't need anymore—and I find Claire's email inbox still open. She was reading an email, and if I were any kind of gentleman I would close out of it, but the greeting catches my eye, and after that, I'm hooked:

Mrs. Kavanaugh,
It is much to my regret that this is one of several attempts at
trying to reach you. It is imperative that you arrange to see me at
my office. With his death, Ezekiel Kavanaugh left behind some-
thing of great importance, and you are the sole beneficiary. If you
do not see fit to respond, I'm afraid consequences will be such
that you will not have any recourse.
Thank you for your time,
Christopher St. James, Esq.

Zeke mentioned Claire in his will. I wonder if Claire knows what it is and doesn't want to claim it. They must have tried several different times, and in various ways, for them to resort to email. It has to be serious for them not to give up, and if Claire doesn't watch out, they'll subpoena her. Money? She would have gotten everything she could out of him when they divorced. A pet? Perhaps they shared a dog or a cat and he wanted her to have it back in the event of his death. Maybe she doesn't want Snowball but is too kind to admit all she would do is dump the animal at the pound.

No, that can't be it.

I barely knew Zeke Kavanaugh. He was a playboy and lived off his trust. Poor match for Claire who's always been floundering to find something meaningful in her life.

Approaching her and asking about it would admit to snooping, and I don't want to do that. I'm trying to build her trust, not break it down any more than it already is.

Pushing the email aside, I open an incognito window and search for Brielle McIntosh. Brielle gave Felicity my last name on her birth certificate. We should gotten married before Felicity was born, and it's something I might always be ashamed of. Not that my daughter's parents weren't married at the time of her birth, but my reluctance. I knew Brielle wasn't on birth control, but that never stopped me when I needed her. I was never so lonely than in the middle of the night thinking about Claire and how much I missed her.

Brielle didn't feel like Claire, or smell like her, but she was warm and kind, and I cared about her. Deep in the night, there would be nothing but darkness and pinpricks of light, and she'd weave her dreams, silver threads hanging from star to star. I would get caught up in it, the excitement of a future with a woman who wanted the same things. I think she loved me, and she was thrilled when she found out she was pregnant.

What would Claire do if I went downstairs and told her I wanted to make love? We never had a problem in bed. Needy, she was so needy, insatiable, looking for something that I tried with my whole heart to give her. Would she lay Felicity in her crib and draw her bedspread back? Would she guide my hand past her panties, let me feel how wet she is? Our time for children is gone. She's older and wouldn't want the physical discomfort of a pregnancy. Could I make love to her and not resent it? Sex doesn't always mean babies, but married to Claire, it was all I wanted.

There's nothing new in the search results. The investigation is ongoing, and the Bridgeport police set up a tip line asking for any information as to my whereabouts as a person of interest in the case. Going anywhere right now is a bad idea. I hope Jack and this Rafferty Clark can figure out how to poke around without my help. I wouldn't last a second on the street.

Succumbing to my want for another beer, I trot downstairs. The kitchen is clean and empty and there's not a sound in the entire penthouse. Maybe Claire went to bed, but I don't want to risk looking. She'd think I was checking up on her, and I wouldn't let her take care of Felicity at all if I didn't trust her. There's not much beer left in the fridge, and I grab another and look for something to snack on. Dinner wasn't that long ago, but my body is finally letting go of the adrenaline I've carried with me since Brielle's murder and no matter how much I've managed to sleep and how many meals I've eaten since Claire let me in, I'm still exhausted and punchy with hunger. Claire never was one for snacks, and I give up searching the bare cabinets and go back upstairs. For the first time in weeks, tension drains out of me and tears of loss leak from my eyes.

Brielle was compassionate and generous, and she would have been a good mother. She didn't deserve to die such a violent death. I'll figure out who killed her and see that he pays with his own life.

For tonight, I'm alone in a huge guest room upstairs in an elegant penthouse that I used to call home. The only things missing are Claire and my daughter, but I've learned a long time ago that if you ask for too much, you end up with nothing.

CHAPTER SIX

Claire

I like getting up with her. I'll never tell Roman, but I let her sleep with me again. I couldn't bear to have her across the room in her crib, even with the new fitted sheet and the adorable mobile hanging from the rail. I wanted her with me, wanted to listen to her little breaths as she slept, feel her wiggle as the first pangs of hunger hit her stomach and I could feed her before she cried.

Felicity is sneaking into my heart, and I have to stop it. I'll still take care of her, but I'm good at distancing myself and I have to do it now or else Roman will leave and tear my whole world apart.

The irony isn't lost on me, and the outcome is what I'll deserve.

He finds me in the living room, feeding Felicity her breakfast bottle. I'm better at changing her diaper, and she's already dressed in a new outfit for the day. He's mussed from sleep, rubbing his eyes. It would always turn me on, how sexy he looked first thing in the morning. We never could crawl out of bed until we had a long, slow bout of sex first. It would be almost like a dream, the slight haze of consciousness right before he pushed inside me, sucking a nipple into his mouth. I'd mew his name, encouraging him to take more. He'd consume me, his hand fisted in my hair, his words raking over my skin, always telling me how much he loved me, and I have never in my life felt more cherished.

"Good morning," he says, his voice gravelly. "I didn't mean to sleep so late."

"You've gone through a lot. Help yourself to coffee. Did you find anything last night?"

"No. Nothing except they set up an anonymous tip line asking for my whereabouts as a person of interest. I'm pretty much stuck here. I'm sorry."

"I'm sorry you're in this situation," I say, pulling the bottle's nipple out of Felicity's mouth. She's been draining four ounces at a time, but I don't know if I should give her more without asking Roman first.

"I'm sorry for Felicity. She'll grow up without her mother."

"Been there, done that," I say bitterly. "I spoke with Jack last night. He read me the riot act for disappearing on you. I'm not used to people—" Caring, is what I was about to say, but that's a lie and it would insult Roman. There was nothing he didn't do more than care. "—needing to know where I am. I'm sorry for running off."

"I don't want you to get hurt. There's a murderer out there. Maybe Brielle's attack was random, but until we know for sure, it's best to be careful."

"I know." I didn't know. I never lived the kind of life where things like that happened. Veronica kidnapped by a mobster. My ex caught in an arson fire. Now Roman's girlfriend is dead. Jack started dating Emma and everything went sideways. "Jack asked me to lunch. Do you mind if I go?" I won't if he feels trapped here, even if that's how I feel and need to get away.

"Not if you bring me back something. We didn't order groceries yesterday, and I will while you're gone."

"You better buy enough for a party." I wince. It won't feel like a party, but having everyone in the penthouse isn't usual for me. Heath and Zoey's brownstone has been the meeting place of late, but if Roman can't leave, then it's up to me to play hostess.

"How do you handle it?" he asks, holding out his arms to take Felicity from me.

"With lots of wine," I say, transferring her little body into his embrace.

"I better get more of that then, too."

I let Felicity wrap her hand around my finger, and I kiss her cheek goodbye. "That is a very good idea."

———

"There's my sister looking lovely and lively," Jack says, throwing his arms out as I walk across the rooftop to his table. The restaurant quickly became a favorite, and my brother's sitting next to a large planter filled with bright pink flowers. He stands, sweeps me up into his arms, and presses a hard kiss to my cheek.

"Jesus Christ," I say, laughing. "How much sex are you getting?"

"More than you, or is that not true?" he asks, holding out my chair and winking.

Emma has turned my brother into someone I don't know. He's so happy all the time, and I'm happy for him. He put them both through hell until he realized if he didn't stop he'd lose her. He was almost too late, and I say a prayer of thanks every day Emma loves him and never gave up on what they could have together.

I swat at him and sit. "I'm not getting any sex. You might not believe it, but I'm quite particular."

"Oh, I believe it, but Roman's been in your penthouse for what? Forty-eight hours? Plenty of time to catch up." He rounds the table and smooths his tie. He's already got a beer bottle next to his place setting. I don't mean to always be late, it just happens. My excuse today is that I hung out with Roman in the kitchen and helped him order groceries. I think he knew what I was doing, too, but it's so surreal to have him back. I wanted to meet Jack so we could talk alone, but leaving, if only for a couple of hours, turned out to be harder than I thought.

"It's not like that, and it won't be."

The server strides toward us, a notepad and pen in his hands and a tray tucked under his arm.

"Because he has a baby?" Jack asks.

I order a glass of wine, and Jack orders another beer. The server tries to hurry away, the tables filled to capacity, but we stop him and quickly choose open-faced chicken salad sandwiches from the substantial lunch menu.

"Not because he has a baby," I say, surprising myself. "I had a chance, and I blew it. There are no second chances at love."

He pulls from his beer and sets the bottle down. "I hope not. I used up at least twenty before Emma decided I wasn't worth it. Twenty-one time's the charm."

"She's in love."

Jack narrows his eyes at me.

"What? I'm not." I sound convincing because I'm not entirely sure I am. In love, I mean. Still in love. I used to love Roman with all my heart, but four years have come and gone. Four years of heartbreak, babies, divorce, and death. I don't know if I still love him and even if I knew, I don't know how it would work. Felicity has grandparents, and I have no idea where they live. The police are holding Brielle's body as evidence. Roman can't bury her yet, can't do anything until her murder is solved. That could take months. Maybe never. He can't start over like that, and he's never hinted that he'd want to start over with me. I tore our marriage apart. I was scared, and in that regard, nothing, absolutely nothing, has changed.

He holds my hand, rubs his thumb over my knuckles. "I'm on your side. I always have been and I always will be, but Roman is a good guy and he never hurt you. Our parents did the hurting, and you put that on him, like I put it on Emma."

I yank my hand away, nearly toppling my wineglass. "And you forgave Dad for all of it."

He sits back, turns his beer bottle on the table, his lips pursed, thinking. I didn't mean to sound so accusatory, but Dad stole our childhood and Jack was right there the minute he spilled his dirty little secret telling him it was okay.

"I understood, that's all."

I lean forward. "There's nothing to fucking understand. He thought Mom was having an affair and kicked her out. Didn't listen to her, didn't give her the benefit of the doubt. Just kicked her right the fuck out. How am I supposed to get past that?"

Jack's eyes blaze. "How about you have some fucking empathy? I thought Emma and Raff were more than friends, and jealousy clawed at me from the inside out. I was jealous, and I *hurt her*. And not forgiving Dad, yeah, that would make me the biggest fucking hypocrite alive. You ask Emma how badly I hurt her. I couldn't control it, and she had bruises for days. You never once, *never once*, thought about Roman making love to the mother of his baby? You never thought about how he gave her something he wanted to give you? You don't lose sleep over that? Because fucking Christ, if you don't, you're better than I am."

He looks away and presses a fist to his lips, his eyes shining with tears.

I sit back, trying to swallow. "You hurt Emma? Jack, for fuck's sake. Why would you do that if you love her?"

"I did that *because* I love her. I couldn't stand to think about another man's hands on her," he lowers his voice to a furious whisper, "his fucking cock inside her. I couldn't handle it, and I still can't. Raff and I will never be friends the way Heath and I are. He's always fucking touching her, and *I can't stand it.*"

I half rise from my seat. "You're out of your mind. Calm the *fuck* down." I'm shaken. I've never seen my brother lose control like that. "You'll lose her if you show even a hint of that to her."

"I know, I know." His voice comes out in an anguished whine. "We're doing couple's therapy. She knows what Dad did and what it did to me. She's working with me, and I can't ask her to give up her friendship. She'd never do it, and I'd be an asshole for wanting it."

"Raff wouldn't let you regardless. They've been friends since they were kids." This much I know from the stories Raff told me the night he helped me find information about Mom. "He doesn't love her like that. Deep down you know it, and I think Dad knew it about Mom, too. He was happy, and he was afraid it would all get shot to shit. Just like me. He ruined it for himself before something could ruin it for him, and that's going to be you if you don't get your shit together. Raff's in love with Veronica. *You know that.*"

"I know," he says unhappily. "I ignored how I felt about her for so long the lost time eats me up inside."

"You'll lose more if you're miserable. You're finally together. Enjoy it."

He sighs. "I'm trying. You can't be too hard on Dad, Claire. Emma said Mom is somewhat to blame—"

I bristle. "How can she say that?"

"Mom didn't tell him the truth. Emma was right, in a way. What was he going to do? Run tell the hospital's director? That would be like you calling the cops on Roman. Even if you hated him, you wouldn't do that because he's innocent, and Dad would never have done that to Mom. She should have trusted him and he could have helped her, you know he would have. Dad's always been big on women's rights and letting women decide. It's why he never gave you a hard time for not having kids or getting your tubes tied. He respected your choices. He would have for Mom, too, but she didn't say anything and she should have."

"He didn't give her a chance to explain. He blew up. He wasn't in any frame of mind to have a conversation after he saw that picture. He saw what he wanted to see, and you don't know if he would have believed her even if she had told him the truth. You didn't believe Emma, and if you're still questioning her friendship with Raff, you still don't. I'm not a hypocrite, either. I don't think about Roman with Brielle—I was with Zeke. Zeke and I were married, for Christ's sake. We had sex sometimes."

Jack glares. "Good for you. Veronica and I had sex, too. It's what couples do. It's not the sex, it's the feelings. Raff loves Emma—as a friend—but I can't separate the two in my head."

I sip my wine. This conversation went south fast, and we've barely scratched the surface of what I wanted to talk about. "Then try harder. Feelings aren't black and white. You still care about Veronica. What if Raff was pissed at you for that? You'd take umbrage because that's not how you feel. You can love her but not *love* her. If we're keeping score, Roman and I are tied. He gave Brielle a baby, I married Zeke. They cancel each other out."

"Do they? Felicity will be around for the rest of your lives. She'll always be a reminder Roman was with another woman."

"Yeah, she will be, and it's my fault he was. I can hate that little baby for my mistakes, or I can love her. Because of what I did, she exists."

Jack widens his eyes and leans back in his chair. "Wow, Claire. I'm impressed."

"What? It's my fault Roman and I aren't together—I'll own it. It's why we aren't together that I need to come to terms with. I want to find Mom."

"Why? She's a stranger. What good would it do?"

"Hearing her side of the story would be a good start."

"It's been forty years."

"Yeah, and it made me ruin the best eleven months of my life."

The waiter serves our lunches, and I pick at my sandwich.

"Do you know where she is?" Jack asks, moving his chicken salad around his plate with his fork.

"Still in the same town Dad said she moved to."

"What did you and Raff find out about her?"

"She's single. Never remarried. Doesn't have any more children. Only us."

Jack blows out a breath. "That's something, I guess. I wouldn't have wanted to meet them. You're the only sister I want."

"I love you, too, even if you can be a big dummy." I nudge his leg with my foot.

He chuckles wryly and sips his beer. "I'm sorry for yelling. Maybe you can't understand why Dad did what he did. Maybe we won't ever be able to understand why Mom didn't forgive him after he apologized. She could have tried, if only to keep us in her life, and she didn't. There are a lot of variables we don't know, that I'm not sure I want to know."

"It won't hurt more than it already does, and I'm going to talk to her with or without you. If she will. I don't know if she'll want to see me and that's something else I'll have to deal with if it happens, but first, Zeke's attorney is going to have an aneurism if I don't meet with him."

"What does he want with you?"

I lift a shoulder and sip the rest of my wine. I search for our server, meet his eyes, and lift my wineglass. He nods. "Zeke left me something in his will."

Jack frowns. "What?"

"I have no idea. His mother's china. His coin collection. Christ, was he proud of that thing. Could be anything. I've told him I don't want it, but he's legally obligated to tell me what it is."

"Zeke's been gone for a few weeks, now, Claire. Better take care of it."

"Yeah." I pause. "I'm sorry you're having trouble. Is there anything I can do?"

"No. It's all on me. I want to give Emma her happily ever after. She worked hard for it and has a lot of faith in me. I'm just paranoid. You deserve one, too, you know."

"Roman and I have both moved on."

"If that's really true, then actually do some moving. You've been stuck since you divorced Zeke. Find something to do. You have a degree, you've always like to write. I don't know why you don't. Pick Raff's brain and start something online for yourself."

"Now you sound like him. He told me the same thing."

"He's not all bad," Jack says grudgingly.

"Now there's some high praise. He'll have to be careful it doesn't all go to his head. First thing's first. Roman, Zeke's attorney, and Mom. Unfortunately, in that order. You're coming over tonight?"

"Yeah. Emma and I will be there. This is some fucked up

shit, though. I don't know how he thinks we're going to investigate something like that on our own."

"You helped Veronica."

"No, that was all Raff."

I push back a smile. "At least you can admit it."

"I've never had a problem giving credit where it's due. He might be the only one out of all of us who'll be able to poke his nose into this. At least it'll look like he has a legitimate excuse."

"I can't believe he's giving up *Talk of the Town*." We didn't resolve the subject of our mother, but my appetite is returning somewhat and I start to eat my meal instead of playing with it. Sitting outdoors on the rooftop is a nice change of pace, and I take a deep breath of air. The traffic's pollution doesn't reach us, and the sun warms my skin.

"It's a good trade. His talent is wasted running that e-zine. He'll be able to put his skills to better use as our mayor. I'm going to throw him a huge fundraiser. He'll create a lot of positive change."

"How can you talk about him like that in one breath, and in another condemn him for his friendship with your fiancée? You're so strange."

"I'm complicated."

I laugh. My brother is anything but complicated. "You just like to think you are."

Jack chuckles. "You're right. As long as Emma loves me, that's all I need. That's about as simple as I can get."

"That sounds more like you."

We spend the rest of our lunch chatting about babies. Sometimes it's uncomfortable, knowing Roman wanted children when they were never a consideration for me. He'd try to talk to me, and I'd shut him out. I didn't want to hear that he wanted children so desperately. I should have at least listened to what he had to say, though I'm not sure how you compromise. A couple either has children or they don't. Maybe he could have talked me into it, but is that any way to have a child? Being talked into it? If I had let him have his way, I could have easily grown resentful, but he could have known something I hadn't. I've grown attached to Felicity whether I like it or not, and she's not mine. Is that why I let myself? Because she's not mine? What if she were? Would I love her more . . . or less?

I don't know. I'll never know, and like Jack waiting too long to admit his feelings for Emma, that's something I'm going to have to live with.

CHAPTER SEVEN

Roman

I'm going crazy. Not because I'm cooped up but because after four years without Claire, being around her and not being able to touch her is driving me fucking *insane*. The scent of her hair, the way she moves. The night we met, I knew in that split second she was everything I wanted, and that hasn't changed.

I want her under me, around me, I want her so absorbed with me nothing else matters.

We used to have that, but I can't now. I have other responsibilities, but that doesn't stop me from wanting what I can't have.

Claire comes back from lunch with Jack quiet, reflective. They must had a heavy conversation, probably about the family stuff Jack alluded to but didn't share with me. Maybe Claire will, maybe she won't, but if I learned anything from our short-lived marriage, it's that I can't force her to talk to me. It does the complete opposite and leaves us both frustrated.

She walks into the kitchen still wearing the sundress she wore to meet Jack. Felicity's sleeping in her swing and I'm putting away the groceries away. Fifteen minutes after she left, my new clothes were delivered, and they're hanging in the guest room upstairs. It was a relief to have things that are *mine* again, and I immediately dressed in boxers that fit, khakis, and a dress shirt. If there hadn't been a murder charge hanging over my head, I would have been content.

Claire glances at Felicity and steps toward her like she wants to pick her up and thinks better of it, stopping before she moves another inch. "You look nice," she says, then pauses. "Why did you want kids with me so badly?"

I freeze, a box of spaghetti noodles in my hand, surprised she would bring up a topic that before I think she would have gladly run a marathon to avoid. Trying not to turn it into a big deal, I say calmly, "Sometimes I think you forget how old I am. I'm older than Jack, and I felt time was slipping away. You can blame a mid-life crisis, maybe, or the fact that our friends were doing what I wanted. I wanted to share that with you. Watch you grow with my baby inside you. Go to appointments, listen to the heartbeat in the exam room. Pick out names. Paint a nursery. I don't think it's odd to want what so many other couples do."

"We should have talked about it before we got married," she says, staring at a jar of tomato sauce. I guess one night we're having spaghetti for dinner.

"Yeah, we should have. It was my fault I assumed you'd want kids too, but Claire, it wasn't so important that I would have traded our marriage. You made that choice for me."

"I didn't want to keep hurting you."

I brush a piece of hair away from her cheek. Her green eyes bring me to my knees. They always have and they always will. "You hurt me way more asking for a divorce than you ever would have if we'd decided not to have kids. You don't get it, do you? *I loved you.* I still do." I lift her head with a finger under her chin. "I want to kiss you."

"Roman, no, I don't want you to." Her lips tremble.

I know when she lies to me, and I wait.

Finally, she capitulates. "Okay."

Maybe that's a lesson I should have learned long ago—if I wait long enough, I can convince her to do what I want.

I lower my head and brush her lips with mine. She feels how I remember, soft, warm, always holding something back, a deep part of herself I was desperate to touch.

In a move I never would have thought she'd do on her own, she steps into my arms and rests her hand against my cheek. Always reserved, always keeping herself in check, even in the most passionate of lovemaking sessions, she never let down her guard, but she does now, opening her mouth and letting me taste her, my tongue gliding over her silky skin.

She breaks it off and presses her forehead against my shoulder.

In regret? Maybe, but she doesn't step away.

"I missed you," I say, my hand to the back of her head, my arm around her waist.

We stand together in a kitchen that used to be ours, but is now only hers. I'm a ghost in my own home, memories of what we had my only proof the life I wanted happened at all.

She turns her head, brushes her lips over the skin under my jaw, and breaks my heart all over again.

"I missed you, too."

———

They arrive separately but all at once, and in a group this size with the food and booze, it's difficult not to feel like it's a party.

I sip on a drink to keep my temper from exploding. They're here to help, and I have to remember that.

Heath and Zoey brought their girls, and I tell Paige, "You were in your mommy's tummy the last time I saw you."

She grins, her eyes bright behind pink-framed glasses. "Me and Mommy played hide and seek. I fell asleep in Gracie's closet and she lost. She cried really hard."

I meet Zoey's gaze. "I bet that's exactly why she cried. Did she ask for a rematch?"

"No!" Zoey bursts out, and Heath laughs, his arms tight around her. "Don't put ideas like that into her head. Hide and seek is officially banned from our house."

Not to be outdone, Graciela says, "I almost died in a fire, but Veronica rescued me."

That must be the story Claire referred to. "I'm sure everyone is very relieved and glad you're okay. What about you, Hilary? What kind of trouble have you found?"

"None," she says grumpily and stalks off, her arms crossed over her chest.

I laugh, and Zoey says, "We couldn't handle it. Things need to calm down."

"That would be nice," I mumble, "but not in the cards for me yet."

Heath says, "We'll get it figured out. That's why we're here."

Jack and Emma arrive next. I haven't seen Jack in years, and he looks confident, happy. He grasps my hand and turns our handshake into a hug, slapping me soundly on the back. Emma's right behind, watching, an amused expression on her face. She's beautiful and looks good at Jack's side. "This is my fiancée, Emma," he says, finally releasing me. "We're getting married in November. I hope you'll be there. Emma, Roman

Mansfield. Claire's ex-husband and a good friend of mine. Where is my sister, anyway?"

"Nice to meet you," Emma says, holding out her hand.

I shake it and say, "She's in her bedroom feeding Felicity. We're not quite sure how she'll do with all the people around."

"The baby or Claire?" Jack asks.

I huff a laugh. "Point taken. Felicity, but maybe Claire too. I guess that's what wine is for."

"You know it," Jack says, grinning.

I may never get used to a lighter side of Jack Durand, but I can see how being engaged to Emma would change his disposition for the better. He's obviously in love with her, his eyes following her every movement. She looks curiously around the penthouse like she's never been here before. Maybe she hasn't. Zoey swoops in for a hug and they disappear from view, Jack close behind.

Rafferty Clark and Veronica Chapman are last to arrive, and the second Gracie hears Veronica's voice, she wastes no time gluing herself to the glamorous talk show host. She wraps her scrawny arms around Veronica's waist and stares adoringly into her face. Raff does the same, and it's clear he's head over heels.

"Mansfield," Raff says, already Raff in my mind because that's what Claire calls him.

"Make it Roman. There's no point in formalities when my head is on the chopping block."

"No fucking around. I like it. We'll get it sorted."

There's no one around to introduce us, and Raff says, "This is Veronica. I'm sure you've heard some shit about the fire and whatever. Nic, this is Claire's ex-husband, Roman Mansfield. He was a hotshot divorce attorney while he was married to Claire."

"It's nice to meet you. I hope I never need your number,"

Veronica says, holding out her hand, using what little space Gracie is giving her. She doesn't seem bothered by it, though. Used to it, maybe, but Gracie's attachment could spell trouble later on. I wonder if they're working that out. It would be something to ask Heath.

Raff turns Veronica's head and nuzzles her lips with his. "You will *never* need his number."

"I'll hold you to that," she says.

"Please do," Raff murmurs.

"Come on, sweetie, let's go find the others," Veronica says to Gracie, and they walk into the living room.

"That must have been some scary shit," I say, referring to Veronica trapped in the Bridgeport Hotel.

"You have no idea." He grimaces. "Maybe you do. Did you love her?"

"Not the way I love Claire, but yeah."

Raff stares at the floor, and I realize he's pushing back tears. "I'm sorry for your loss."

"Thanks. I just want to find out who did it, you know? It's not only about clearing my name. She deserves to rest in peace."

"I agree. It's not something your daughter should have to live with. You and Claire, then?" he asks.

Taking pity on the poor man, I lead him into the kitchen. He's been eyeing my drink since he stepped inside the penthouse. "I don't know. I had a baby with another woman. Some women don't want to raise children who aren't theirs."

"You'd know if Claire would be that way," he says, accepting the whiskey I pour into a glass. The others are standing in the middle of the living room, the girls exploring a place they haven't been before. Having the penthouse full of our friends would be nice if I were free to enjoy it.

"She didn't want to raise her own, so it's doubtful." And that hurts, it really does.

"Nic and I decided we wouldn't bother. I had a fucked up childhood, and she didn't have it any better than I did. A weight lifted, I think, for both of us."

"If only every couple were on the same page like that."

"I'm lucky," he says. Veronica looks over at us as if she knew we were talking about her, and he meets her eyes across the floor with an intense stare. He's got it bad.

"You are," I agree. There's no point in resenting him for it.

Claire carries Felicity into the room then, which is just as well. Jack and I could catch up all night and not run out of things to talk about, but I don't know Raff well enough to keep a conversation going and now isn't the time to bring up the murder investigation. I'm still on the fence as to whether or not he can help me, and the small talk is rubbing my nerves raw.

From the safety of Claire's arms, Felicity looks around with interest, but if she has my temperament, she'll run out of patience fast. For now, it's okay, but I'll keep an eye on her. If she needs quiet, it will be an excuse to take a break.

Zoey's not as enamored as Emma, having already met my daughter, but Emma looks right at home holding Felicity. Yeah, Jack's a lucky son of a bitch.

Relieved of baby duty for a moment, Claire greets Raff with a kiss to his cheek and a smile for me. "Are you doing okay?"

Risking pissing her off, I wrap my arm around her shoulders and cuddle her to me. "I am now."

Raff regards us with shrewd eyes. "Did Jack say something about dinner?"

"We ordered a shit-ton of gourmet pizza from a pizzeria a few blocks away. It should be here in about ten minutes."

"Good. Fill me up with more of this," he says, lifting his

empty glass, "and after we eat, we'll get to work. I want to know everything, from the second you and Claire said your see-you-laters."

"You make it sound so simple."

Raff smiles, and what he says turns the tide. I decide to trust him. "Someone killed Felicity's mother. All we have to do is figure out who."

"But no more favors," Veronica says. She wasn't too interested in Felicity, but she was peering over Emma's shoulder nonetheless.

Raff captures her against his chest. "I only pull out the big guns for you, dollface." He dips her and covers her mouth with his.

Everyone groans and snickers. They must get like that a lot.

He lets her come up for air, and she says, "You better keep it that way."

———

The pizzas are good, and sipping more whiskey, I'm loose and looking forward to talking. Zoey and Claire set the girls up with a movie in the den, and I lay Felicity in her crib to give her a little peace and quiet before all the noise overstimulates her. The monitor Zoey also advised Claire to purchase (bless her) sits on an end table, allowing us to watch Felicity kick and reach for the the mobile circling above her head.

We sit in the living room, some of us drinking, some not. Raff holds a notebook and a pen he pulled out of Veronica's purse.

"Start from the beginning," he says, and he listens to me recount the story I told Claire, about how I met Brielle outside a bar, how one thing led to another and how all of a sudden she was pregnant and I didn't know what I wanted.

"Were you living together? You were here, in Bridgeport?"

I sigh. "After Claire and I divorced, I wanted to get away for a bit, and I spent the first year with my parents in Florida, getting my head on straight. I closed my firm and took a breather. Spent a lot of time on the water trying to figure out where it went wrong. When I came back, I had to find a place to live, and basically put one foot in front of the other. It was a year later—"

"So, two years after you and Claire divorced?" Raff interrupts. "Sorry, getting a timeline down."

"Yeah, Brielle and I met about two years later. I'm not sure what she was doing outside the pub. I was playing trivia with some of the guys who worked with a different firm in my building, catching up on industry gossip, but she never said why she was in that part of the city."

"You were here then, but she didn't move in with you?" Raff asks, scrawling in a messy script I'm not sure he'll be able to read later.

"No. I spent a lot of time at her place. She lived in a little apartment in north Bridgeport."

"What did she do for work?"

"She managed a twenty-four hour diner not far from her building. She made okay money. Enough she paid her bills and had some left over. After she got pregnant, I told her to quit. I didn't want her working all the time—she'd fill in for a waitress if someone called in sick—and I said I would pay for everything."

Raff doesn't look up from the notebook. "And she agreed?"

"Not right away," I say, not wanting Brielle to sound like a gold digger. "She worked until she started showing."

"What about her parents? Where do they live? Here?"

"In a mobile home park in the same neighborhood as Brielle's apartment complex."

"Did you meet them?"

"I met her whole family. Parents, aunts, uncles, cousins. They expected us to get married. It's all her mom could talk about."

Raff scribbles, mumbling to himself, and I try not to be embarrassed. I didn't do anything wrong. I'm not with a group that would care Brielle didn't come from money, and getting sucked into an investigation like this can happen to anyone. But I feel to blame, like it's my fault Brielle's dead and I'm wanted for questioning.

"Did she have any friends? Have you spoken with any of them since they found her body? Who found her body, do you know?"

"A guy playing Frisbee on the beach with his dog. Her body washed up on shore." My voice cracks, and I want more than a glass of whiskey. I want quiet and a cigarette, but those are the last things I need.

Claire squeezes my hand. It helps she knows how I feel. We might have admitted we weren't in love with our exes, but we wouldn't wish them dead. Especially with how violently they died.

"Friends?" Raff asks, glancing quickly at me.

"She didn't hang around many people, not after we started seeing each other. You know how that is—"

"Not with this group," Raff mutters, and Emma nudges him. His pen slides across the paper, leaving a thick line, and he scowls good-naturedly at her.

"—when you're getting to know someone. You don't make time and people drop off. She stayed in touch with a few of her friends, but she didn't usually go anywhere without me. I encouraged her to go out the night she disappeared. She didn't come home, and I talked to her family the next morning. I thought maybe she had too much to drink, didn't want me to see her like that, and was sleeping it off somewhere. Her mom and dad told me they hadn't seen her, and that was when I started worrying. I reported her missing that afternoon."

"You waited to call it in?" Raff asks.

I'm defensive. "I went to bed with Felicity. The next morning I called her family. It's what anyone would do."

"No blame, just looking at it from a cop's perspective. They want to talk to you, and that will be a natural question. Did Brielle say when she would be home? Text you? Call you from the bar? They went to a bar?"

"I think so. She said they were going to, but they could have ended up anywhere. She didn't text or call."

"Do you know her friends' names? I'll need to speak with them. You haven't spoken to the police *at all?* Do you know how much information they have?"

"I talked to an officer who stopped by Brielle's apartment. It was only after her body washed up on the beach that they wanted to question me more formally. Sometimes I would visit her at the diner, and I met a couple of the people she worked with. I don't know if she considered them friends or not."

Raff rubs his forehead and continues to write. His leg starts jiggling, and I get nervous.

"When did the guy with the dog find her body?"

"Two weeks ago."

Raff lifts his head, his eyes wide. "You've been hiding for two weeks? Christ."

"I didn't want to risk them taking Felicity. I can't lose her to CPS. Her parents will want custody, and they aren't going to get it." I would die if I lost my daughter. "I made a run for it and until I took a chance and came here, I was crisscrossing the state. I didn't know what else to do."

"You lawyer up, for one thing," he says, and not a little bit sarcastically. As an attorney, I should have known the first thing to do is find representation, but all I could think of was keeping Felicity safe.

"I think I just did."

"Barely, but I'll do my best. It's no surprise the cops will think you're guilty. Do you have an alibi?"

"No. I was home alone with Felicity."

Raff scowls. "This keeps getting better and better. Don't leave this penthouse. Don't let anyone in who doesn't have a warrant, not even a harmless social worker. Once I start asking questions, I'm going to pull a lot of rocks out of the dirt exposing all sorts of bugs. Spiders bite, be careful. With this much time gone by, someone thinks they got away with it, and they're gonna be really pissed when I start poking around."

I blow out a breath, his competency dropping my nervousness down a notch. "Thank you."

"Don't thank me yet. I need a list of her family and friends. Claire, do you have a computer and a printer? I want to do a little digging while all this is fresh in my head."

"Yeah, there's one upstairs. I have colored ink, but no photo paper."

"That's okay. If I need something better I'll do it at my office. Give me your cell number," Raff says to me, pulling out his.

"I don't have one. I didn't want anyone tracking me."

"You can't be without a means of communication. I'll get you one. It'll be registered under *Talk of the Town*, and no one will be able to trace it to you. The only people who get that number is us," he says, circling his hand around the living room.

"That's great, thanks."

I recite the names of Brielle's parents, their addresses I know without having to look them up, Brielle's apartment address, and the diner's name and her coworkers. Raff's pen whips across the paper. The information seems woefully inadequate, but he's nodding, pleased. "Nic and I have a thing tomorrow with the mayor and his wife, a quick lunch. I'll start digging after that. I'll request a copy of the police report and her autopsy report. Claire, show me where your computer is." He kisses Veronica hard on the cheek and hefts himself from the couch.

"The girls should be almost done with their movie," Claire says, walking with him out of the room.

"What are they watching?"

"*Frozen,*" Claire says, and they step out of sight.

Raff laughs. "Again? We need to show them there are better movies to watch . . ."

It isn't long after that Jack and Emma leave. Jack traps me in another hug, thumping my back. "Anything you need, ask. We'll get you out of this. If Raff hits a dead end, we'll hire a private investigator. The son of a bitch is out there. We'll find him."

The only thing I can do is pray that's true. I could be hiding for weeks, months, before we puzzle out who killed Brielle, and if we don't, I could be running for the rest of my life. The more time that goes by, the more desperate the cops will be to pin her murder on someone. Anyone.

Zoey and Heath herd their kids out the door, and Gracie's near crying, trying to hide it and blinking back tears. Veronica talks to her for a moment alone in the kitchen, and Gracie meets her parents dry-eyed but still sad. Yeah, there's definitely an attachment issue going on there.

Raff and Veronica are last to leave, and the proficient way he gathered facts about Brielle's case fills me with confidence. Questioning Brielle's family in guise of doing a story for *Talk of the Town* is a brilliant cover and will allow him to come and go as he pleases. I hope he can get more out of the people he questions than the cops have.

The penthouse is quiet and I try to relax, pushing back the need to sit outside on the balcony and smoke. The support is welcome—and needed—but friends overall can be stifling, their intentions good but borderline oppressive.

Claire fixes Felicity a bottle, mixing the formula and water. She's already used to doing it, adding the powder without sprinkling it onto the counter.

I sag against the kitchen counter. "I'm sorry, Claire."

"For what?" She too, looks relieved everyone is gone, tension draining from her rigid shoulders.

"Dumping this on you."

"It's okay. Go up to bed. I'll listen for Felicity again tonight."

I want to ask to stay with her in the master suite. Her confession was unexpected, and now I know she feels things for me I never thought she would again—or ever did, for that matter. She divorced me so easily, broke my heart without a blink of her lovely eyes. I swallow back the request. "Thanks."

"I have some errands to do in the morning," she says to my back.

Kavanaugh's lawyer, no doubt, and maybe something to do with what she and Jack discussed at lunch earlier today. I can't expect to keep her here, and I'll miss her like crazy and worry about her until she's safe and sound in the penthouse again.

"Be careful. I'll snoop around online while you're gone. I won't be able to help as much as I'd like, but I don't want Raff to have to do all the heavy lifting."

"Okay. Goodnight, Roman."

"Night."

She steps toward the hallway that leads to her bedroom.

"Claire."

She turns and meets my eyes.

There is so much I want to say to her. So much in the last

four years that I need to say, but they're trapped in my chest, my tight throat obstructing the need to purge. I love her. I missed her. I want her back, but nothing has changed since the day in the parking lot where we said our final goodbyes. Why we divorced is still between us, and we've added more. She's already said she can't give me what I want from her, and the evidence of that is in my penthouse across the city, printed papers sitting in my filing cabinet. A dissolution of a marriage, but not of feelings, and certainly not of my heart.

"Don't." Her voice is thin and sad, but she means what she says.

I scoff. "Don't worry. I won't. Ever again." Furiously, I push away from the counter and trot up the stairs, my footfalls heavy in my anger.

A shower doesn't do anything to dispel my fury, and I flop onto the bed wrapped in a towel.

Staring at the ceiling, I count to fifty. I shouldn't give her the power to make me this angry. She's not giving me anything more than what she did during our marriage, and that's not what I'm here for. We're not getting back together.

I don't care how gently she holds Felicity or if I catch her humming "You Are My Sunshine." Claire has issues that have nothing to do with me. Maybe Jack can get past them enough to ask Emma to marry him, but Claire won't. Possibly can't. Felicity's mother was murdered, and that is something my little girl will have to live with all her life. I don't know what happened to Claire's mom, or if I ever will, but she obviously hasn't dealt with it. The best I can do is see to it that Felicity doesn't grow as cold as Claire.

Her laptop is still on the bed, and I can't forget I need to do my part in the investigation. I dress in new pajamas and resist going downstairs. I want to go outside and light up, and I need to stop that. I also don't want to bump into my ex-wife. With my temper, all I'd do is push her up against the wall and have my way with her, which would be worse than a nicotine fix. I don't need another addiction.

I brush my teeth instead, and still simmering, I start typing out my own notes—everything from the beginning, no matter how small. Anything could help.

The sooner Felicity and I can get out of here, the better. Build a house with a yard and forget I was ever married to a woman with a diamond for a heart.

CHAPTER EIGHT

Claire

I know I hurt him, but when haven't I? He should be used to it by now. I am.

Felicity wakes me twice, and I stumble around the kitchen putting her bottles together while she cries into my shoulder. I didn't prepare them ahead of time, too eager to get away from Roman, and he must make them as he needs them—he didn't measure water ahead of time for me, either.

My alarm chimes and I groan, but I turn it off quickly and Felicity sleeps through it. She slept with me again last night, easier, I told myself, cuddling her after a bottle rather than hoping she'd fall asleep by herself in her crib. I'm setting him up for some bad habits to break, but that will be Roman's job and I won't be sorry when he moves out.

I need to shower and dress for my appointment, and I don't have much time. If Emma went to work today, she'll already be at Variant, and I call the number I have in my phone that used to reach her desk if I needed to talk to Jack.

"Jack Durand's office, how may I help you?"

The voice is unfamiliar, and stymied, I take a deep breath and ask, "I need to speak to Emma Cox."

"Please hold," the voice says pleasantly. If that's Jack's new PA, she sounds like she'll be okay. I don't care for people who fluster easily.

"Emma Cox's office, how may I help you?"

I'm out of touch not to know Emma has her own office. "I'd like to speak with Miss Cox please, this is Claire Durand."

"One moment. I'll see if she's available."

It's very possible she's in a meeting. I should have texted her instead of going through all this hassle.

"Claire, what's up?" Emma asks, cutting off the holding music.

"You have your own office now?"

"Kind of? Not really. I have a desk and a computer and a phone, obviously. Mostly I work with Jack and Ron in Ron's office. They're teaching me a lot. I might need to go back to school."

"You won't have time for that if you're pregnant."

"You're right, but eventually. I would learn faster if I understood half of what they're talking about. Are you and Roman okay? How's Felicity?"

"She's, ah, sleeping in my bed." I blush.

"Is Roman there, too?" she asks, tongue-in-cheek. "He's very good-looking."

"*Pfft.* Don't let Jack hear you say that. You have enough problems."

She pauses, and I feel like shit for mentioning Raff. "He's doing okay. We've started therapy, and Jack dumps on her from the second we sit down until her timer goes off. She's always a little shell-shocked when we leave. One day I'd like to ask her how much time she needs to decompress after one of our sessions. I don't mean to make light of it. It's the unknown that bothers him. No one knows what will happen, what could happen. He's nervous all the time."

I frown in concern. "I didn't get that from him last night, though he did seem a little on edge when I had lunch with him yesterday."

"He keeps it buried, which isn't good, either. Therapy helps. Anyway, why did you call? Not to talk about Jack."

"No. Are you busy this morning? Can you go somewhere with me?"

"There's a meeting Ron wanted me to sit in on, but that's not a big deal. Sure. What time?"

"Aren't you going to ask me where we're going?"

"If you need me to be there, I'll be there. It doesn't matter where."

"You really are too good to be true, aren't you? No wonder Jack is always worried about losing you."

"I care about my family. I don't think that's unusual."

Stupid tears fill my eyes. "I'll pick you up in an hour and a half."

"I'll be waiting downstairs."

"Thanks."

I disconnect the call and rub at my cheeks. Felicity's waking up and watching me from her place in the middle of my bed, blinking her big blue eyes.

Could it really be that simple? Care for family and let them care about you in return? What would these four years have held if I hadn't run? If Roman hadn't let me? We'd be alone, and there wouldn't be Felicity. Roman might have gotten something out of his relationship, but I didn't get anything out of my marriage with Zeke except feelings of not belonging I already battled on a daily basis. It was a relief to divorce him. We never should have married.

Now he left me something, and I'm probably lucky it wasn't an STD.

Christ.

I'm glad Emma will be with me. I don't want to go to Zeke's attorney's office alone.

I scoop up Felicity, change her, and dressed in my nightgown, carry her into the kitchen. Roman has always been an early riser, and now that he's on a mission, he'll spend all day doing what he can to help Raff.

I step into the kitchen, and Felicity smiles at her father. Roman's sitting at the island, sipping on a mug of coffee, and taking in his daughter's outfit, his eyes light up. I dressed Felicity in a pink, lacy romper Zoey picked out, and she looks adorable. I'm not stupid. He wanted kids, and if I wouldn't have left him, he wouldn't have had this. That's not something I want the blame for. Then we would have gotten divorced for a different reason.

Resentment can turn to hate, and I'd rather we parted as friends than have Roman hate me.

"Good morning," I say, transferring Felicity into his arms. "She hasn't had a bottle yet, but I need to shower." He settles her protectively against his chest in the way he once held me, and I step away.

"Claire, please don't be like this."

"I'm not like anything. You want things, Roman. Be happy with what you have." I brush my lips against Felicity's cheek and turn toward the bedroom.

He grabs my shoulder, and his thumb grazes the curve of my neck. "I'll never be happy unless I have it all."

Is that a threat? No, Roman's never threatened me. It's a promise he won't leave me alone until . . . until what?

Sparks fly around my heart. Fear, hope. "What do you want me to do?"

He wraps his hand in my hair and drags me against his chest, Felicity and me, anchored to him. He kisses me and mumbles against my lips, *"Give it to me."*

———

Emma's waiting on the sidewalk dressed in a taupe sheath lined with cream pinstripes, a cream belt secured around her waist, and a matching purse hanging from her arm. Her hair is twisted into a bun, but little tendrils escape in the breeze. Speaking to a woman I recognize from the executive floor, Emma brushes them out of her eyes. She spots the truck as we glide to a stop at the empty curb, the No Parking signs in front of the stone steps keeping cars from clogging the street. She smiles, says something in goodbye, and the woman drifts away.

My driver opens the back door for her, and I scoot over.

"Hey, Brian," Emma says.

"Miss Cox," he replies, nodding briskly and shutting the door.

"Hi, Claire. Are we doing lunch after this? I told Jack I wouldn't be in until after one."

I hadn't considered it, but depending on how much time Mr. St. James needs from me, we would be finished around the lunch hour. "Did you tell him what we're doing?" I ask.

She laughs. "How could I? *I* don't know what we're doing. He knows I'm with you, though. I hope that's okay."

"Yeah." I pause. "Did you ever tell him what I said to you at the house? About how you shouldn't get too invested?"

"No. There's no reason for him to know."

"Why? It wasn't true, and it wasn't very nice." I still feel guilty I said it.

"It might not have been, but you didn't want me to get hurt. A lot of things changed between you saying that and when he proposed. You should speak with your father, Claire. He wants to see you, but he doesn't know how to ask."

"I'm not ready for that."

"Okay."

She stares out the window, the sun lighting her face. I wish I could find that peace, that serenity. It comes from more than knowing my brother loves her, it comes from the security in knowing who she is, that she has family and friends who care about her. She's found her place in life, and I wish like hell I could find mine.

"I'll tell him what I said."

She squeezes my hand. "If you feel you have to, but it's completely up to you. I'll never tell him . . . it's not for me to share."

I sigh, and a weight drops off. I was afraid she would say something and I would have to scramble for an explanation. Now, if I decide to tell him, I can figure out what I need to say. He'll be angry, and he should be, but I was only doing what I thought was best. "Thanks."

Brian drifts to a stop in front of a building not far from Variant. I don't want to go up there, don't want to hear what Zeke's attorney has to say. I wish he wouldn't have left me anything. I don't want anything. His family has more money than practically anyone in the world and they didn't miss the millions he dumped into my account, but I didn't need that, either.

"What is this place?"

"I suppose saying hell would be too glib," I say, following Emma out of the car and onto the sidewalk.

"Is this a doctor's office? Are you sick?"

"No. Zeke left me something in his will, and I need to claim it."

"Oh. I'm sorry."

"Yeah, me too."

Emma and I walk through security and toward a bank of elevators located at the rear of the enormous lobby. With clients like Zeke, Mr. St. John must have quite the view.

I would always love visiting Roman at his office, so stern and sexy in his suits, barking orders. He hasn't worked since our divorce. Another thing I stole from him.

We wait in the crowded elevator.

"Do you have an appointment?" Emma asks.

"Yes. It really shouldn't take too long."

She nods, unconcerned.

A businessman standing in the corner of the lift eyes her appreciatively, but his glance lands on her rock and he looks away.

I push back a smile.

That's one thing I haven't cared about since Roman ambushed me in the lobby of my building. Trolling for a husband.

Now the idea makes me sick.

The elevator stops on our floor, and we step out with a handful of people. A receptionist asks my name. I supply it and tell her I have an appointment.

"He's expecting you," she says, and a legal assistant joins us and ushers us down a quiet hallway.

"Mrs. Kavanaugh," Mr. St. John says, standing from his massive desk as we enter his office.

I grimace. For lack of anything better, I changed my name back to Durand when I filed my divorce papers. I wanted to be Claire Mansfield for the rest of my life, but that didn't work out so well.

"Mr. St. John," I say, holding out my hand. "I can't think of anything so important that you needed to threaten me."

"Miss Cox," Mr. St. John greets Emma.

"Good morning, it's nice to meet you," she says, shaking his hand.

"Sit down, please. I wouldn't say I threatened, but things are urgent at this point. Mr. Kavanaugh didn't mention he named you a beneficiary in his will?" he asks, settling behind his desk.

"No. We've been divorced for over a year now. There shouldn't have been a reason why he needed to leave me anything."

Mr. St. John removes his glasses and rubs his eyes. "Things are complicated. What do you know of his parents?"

I curl my lip in distaste. All his mother and father care about is their standing in London society, an invitation to Meghan Markle and Prince Harry's wedding a coup of a lifetime. "Not much, and what I do know I wish I didn't."

He huffs a laugh. "That seems to be par for the course when it comes to Mr. and Mrs. Kavanaugh. Let's just say, they are not a consideration if you choose not to accept this responsibility."

"If you're trying to make me feel better, you're not."

"I'm trying to lay some groundwork so you understand the implications if you choose not to do this."

"Choose not to do what?"

"Mr. Kavanaugh had a child—"

"Zeke had children with one of his ex-wives. I never met them."

Mr. St. John chews the inside of his cheek. "Did you know he was dating Lacey Lawton, the woman who was with him the night of the fire?"

"No. The last time I saw Zeke in person after our divorce went through was at Cloud 9's opening. I bumped into him and immediately left. Though our divorce was amicable, I avoided him when I could."

"So you know nothing about her."

"No. How does this concern me?" I'm growing irritated. I don't know where Mr. St. John is going with this. Zeke's death shouldn't involve me at all.

Emma rubs my arm, and I try to shake off my annoyance.

"Mr. Kavanaugh met Miss Lawton at the Bridgeport Country Club. She was a bartender there. After playing a round of golf, he and his friends stopped for a drink in the bar. They started seeing each other."

I scowl. "It sounds exactly like him."

"Digging into her background, I found she doesn't have much family. An elderly grandmother and a brother who is in and out of prison for this and that. She never knew her father and her mother passed away some time ago."

I gnash my teeth. I don't care about her family. I've never met her and don't know what she looks like. She could have been with Zeke at Cloud 9, and I never would have known.

"Mrs. Kavanaugh, they had a daughter."

"Then I am extremely sorry for their deaths. Is there anything else, Mr. St. John? I have commitments—"

"Mr. Kavanaugh left guardianship to you."

Emma gasps and covers her mouth.

I laugh. "I almost thought you said Zeke left me a child in his will."

"I did."

"But, but . . ." I can't get anything out.

"Her name is Daisy—from what Mr. Kavanaugh told me, Miss Lawton was a *Great Gatsby* fan."

"What? Mr. St. John, I think you're mistaken."

"Claire—"

I blink.

"—she's ten months old."

At this, I spring to my feet. *"Ten months."*

"Is that bad?" Emma asks, clearly not understanding the timeline of my marriage and subsequent divorce.

"Zeke and I were married for seven months and have been divorced for a little over a year, Emma. Women are pregnant for nine months. Daisy," I say, furiously staring at Zeke's partner in crime, "is ten months old. Lacey was pregnant almost the whole time we were married. In fact, I would bet all my money he was seeing her before we even met."

"Oh," she says faintly, scrambling to do the math.

I whip my gaze to Mr. St. John. "Did he stop seeing her at all?"

He shrugs. "I don't know, Mrs. Kavanaugh—"

"Miss Durand."

A corner of his mouth pulls down. "Miss Durand. Even if I did know, I wouldn't be able to tell you. Client/attorney confidentiality continues after death."

"I think, in this case, I have a right to know."

"Daisy was born late on a Monday night. He came to the office the next day and requested the revisions. That's all the information I have. I'm sorry."

"Where has she been since Zeke's death?" Emma asks.

"Because of the situation, his estate is still going through probate. A nanny hired by Mr. Kavanaugh and Miss Lawton has been caring for Daisy in their penthouse. Miss Lawton moved in with him after the divorce."

"You mean after I cleared the way," I say bitterly. "It's no wonder why he didn't fight me on it. Why did he marry me if he had her?"

"I don't know, Mrs.—"

I glower.

"Miss Durand. Those questions are out of my scope. All I know is when Daisy was born, he immediately named you sole guardian in the event of his untimely death. He may truly have wanted you to raise his daughter."

"Because the alternatives are so much worse," I grumble, dropping into my seat again. "Fuck. What will happen to her if I don't accept guardianship?"

"Mr. Kavanaugh's parents know of her existence, of course. I don't know what their response would be if I reached out regarding Daisy's care. I wouldn't gather anything positive. I could get in touch with Miss Lawton's grandmother. There's a healthy stipend that accompanies the guardianship. His ex-wife may not be opposed to Daisy growing up with her half-siblings . . . if she were paid."

"His kids are in their teens. They wouldn't have anything in common."

"You could raise her with—" Emma starts.

Knowing exactly what she's going to say, I cut her off. "You're out of your mind." I press a finger to my lips. No one is supposed to know where Roman is.

Mr. St. John curiously lifts an eyebrow.

She winces. "My mistake."

"Who's paying for Daisy's nanny?" I ask.

"His estate."

"Who has been in contact with her?"

"Only my office, Miss Durand."

This is ridiculous. "Then you don't know if she's being cared for properly."

"A social worker has briefly been in touch, as a minor is involved, and it appears Daisy's happy, if not a little lost at sea. I'm sure even at her age she's wondering where her parents are. They were quite present in her life, if his prompt changing of his will is anything to go by. Needless to say, I have contacted you on multiple occasions since the fire. I realize you were attending an event that night and may have needed time, but some things cannot wait."

"Where do the rest of his assets go?"

"They revert back to his parents, besides the stipend that will run out when Daisy turns eighteen, of course."

"Did he leave her a trust?"

"Yes. She'll have access in increments starting the day the stipend ends."

"At least he was responsible about that."

Mr. St. John pulls a piece of paper out of a file and slides it across his desk with a pen. "Sign here."

I rear back in horror. "What for?"

"You are claiming guardianship, are you not?"

"No!"

"Claire!" Emma exclaims, appropriately appalled.

"Emma! I can't take care of a baby!"

"You can't leave her with a nanny. Who will raise her if Claire declines?" Emma asks, standing in agitation, her fingers twisted tightly in front of her.

Mr. St. John tilts his head. "As I said, I can reach out to Mr. Kavanaugh's parents. Miss Lawton's grandmother may take her for the money alone as it appears she's been down on her luck most of her life. Mr. Kavanaugh's ex-wife may find it in her heart and open her purse as well. There are options, but please know, Mr. Kavanaugh wanted you to do this, Miss Durand. You were his only choice."

"If you don't want her, Jack and I will take her," Emma says.

I know she's trying to help, but it doesn't. I wouldn't claim Zeke's baby only to turn her over to my brother and sister-in-law. If I assume responsibility of her, then I'll follow through. It's not like I wouldn't have the resources—

"She needs love, Claire." Emma knows me well, and she frowns.

There's the rub, isn't it? Little Daisy will need love, and I don't have it in my heart to love anybody. I'm too afraid that love will get thrown back into my face and break my heart.

"And you'd love her from the second you saw her, wouldn't you?" I ask bitterly.

"Yeah, I would, because she's a baby, and none of this is her fault."

"When do you need to know?" I ask Mr. St. John. I already let so much time go by, and he reluctantly leans back into his chair, thinking through my question.

"Miss Cox is correct, Miss Durand. Daisy's basic needs are met, but ultimately what she's going to need is to be loved. If you feel you can't do that, then you need to let me know as quickly as possible."

"I need to discuss this with a few members of my family. I'll contact you tomorrow. Do you have a picture of her?"

Mr. St. John slides a photo from the file sitting on his desk and passes it to me. Emma stares over my arm at a little girl with bright carrot-orange hair and the bluest eyes I've ever seen. She's sitting on the floor grinning, pearly white teeth poking out from her bottom gums.

"Oh, she's adorable," Emma whispers.

I toss the photo onto the desk. "It was a mistake bringing you along."

Emma's grin is as bright as Daisy's. "I think you did exactly the right thing."

"You would think so. Come on."

Zeke's attorney stands from behind his desk and walks with us to his office door. "I'll look forward to hearing from you. If you need anything, the estate can provide it. The nanny, a nurse to help settle her in—"

"No!" Emma and I both say at the same time. Roman and Felicity are there and no one can be in the penthouse.

"I mean," Emma says, her voice calmer, "it would be no trouble helping Claire get Daisy situated. Thank you," she holds out her hand. He shakes it briskly, and she yanks me out the door.

I let her drag me down the corridor and into the elevator. I can't lose my cool—the elevator is packed with people going to lunch. Emma leans into me, excitement vibrating off her. She's got babies on the brain, and it *was* a mistake asking her to come along. I thought this meeting would be about one of his grandmother's rings, or his mother's china set he offered to me but I didn't want. I didn't pay close enough attention to know he had a baby. Christ.

Emma's patient enough to wait until we're on the sidewalk, Brian and the truck waiting for us. She opens her mouth and I hold up a finger cutting her off before she says even one damned word. I pull out my phone. I don't clean out my contacts, and I bring up Jill Kavanaugh's cell phone number. I lean against the car, the hot afternoon sun doing its best to thaw my bones.

"Claire," she answers in distaste. She must not have cleared out her contacts either. "It's a fine time to offer your condolences. Three weeks after the fact. Can you imagine? Teddy, it's Claire," she says to her husband in the background. I didn't mind Zeke's father. When he's drunk, he has a wry sense of humor and is observant enough to put it to good use. "You didn't attend the funeral."

"I wasn't aware it was expected."

She sniffs. "At the very least, you could lay flowers on his grave. It would be more than what you did for him when you were married."

I have no intention of visiting Zeke's grave. "Did you know about Daisy, Jill?" I ask, formalities out the window.

She pauses. "Don't you dare ask me to take in that little gutter rat."

"I-I'm sorry? *What* did you just call her?"

"You heard very clearly what I called her. She's nothing but white trash dressed up in a pretty bow. You know nothing about her mother, do you? Her family," Jill spits. "Trash."

"You're talking about your granddaughter." My eyes meet Emma's, and hers are full of tears. She can hear every word Jill says.

"No, I'm not. You take her in, if that's what you feel you need to do, but don't bring Teddy and me into it. We won't have anything to do with her. We spoke to Mr. St. John when we were in Bridgeport for my precious Zeke's funeral. We paid for Lacey's, too, as her family couldn't even see fit to claim her body—what there was of it."

"And you left Daisy in Zeke's penthouse with her nanny."

"Her nanny, an orphanage, whatever it is you Americans do."

I roll my eyes at Emma. *Whatever it is you Americans do.* She's as American as we are, she chooses to live in London.

"And don't think for a moment we'll approve that stipend. We'll fight you on it, Claire. You have plenty of money. Zeke already paid you in the divorce settlement. The trust we can't do anything about, but it's insulting."

"Then you want nothing to do with her. Holidays, her birthday. Nothing."

"Is this why you called? I was dressing for a party."

"I'm sorry to have bothered you. Have a nice evening."

Jill hangs up without a goodbye.

"Holy shit," I mumble. "I don't remember her being like that while Zeke and I were married."

"You must have met her daughter-in-law requirements," Emma says.

"Lacey sure as hell didn't. No wonder he married me. He was using me as a cover to spend time with the woman he really wanted to be with." I lean against the car, press the heels of my hands into my eyes. "Fuck."

Emma nods at Brian and he opens the door for us. "Let's go get a drink and regroup."

"Aren't you pregnant yet?"

"I wish people would stop asking me that. It will be another few weeks until we know. We're trying to enjoy the process. Things keep popping up." She settles into the seat and latches her seatbelt.

"You're telling me."

"You never wanted to be a mother, did you?"

"No. I never thought I'd be a good one."

Brian melds into traffic. I don't know where we're going.

"Talk to Ron. If you decide to accept guardianship of Daisy, you may appreciate the support."

"I don't want her, Emma."

"Are *you* saying that? Or is that what you imagined your own mother said about you? You have to separate the past from your future or history will repeat itself. Jack almost lost me before he learned that lesson. Please don't do anything you'll regret."

It's already too late for that.

Roman

Felicity sleeps, and I dig for hours, creating my own timeline from the second I met Brielle to the day that guy and his dog found her body on the beach. There's no way I can risk calling any of her family and asking them what they know or what they've told the homicide detective, and in the two weeks since her death, the news reports have dwindled to almost nothing, the repeated refrain, "There are no new leads at this time."

The only thing I know for sure after spending my morning scrolling through articles is that Brielle's death has nothing to do with me. I don't know what I'm going to do if Raff can't find her killer. I can't run my entire life. I'll have to lawyer up and pray they don't have any evidence pointing in my direction. Running wasn't wise, but I was desperate and did the only thing I could to keep the authorities from taking Felicity away from me. I'd do it again.

The fact I wasn't involved in Brielle's life is a fist in my face.

Admitting to Raff I didn't know her friends' names, barely knew the people she worked with. We never went out with anyone—her friends or mine. It's not that I didn't think she wouldn't mix well, but after the divorce, I thought it was a nice change to slow down. Brielle's apartment was cozy and I was content to spend time with her there, especially, like I told Claire, when we would talk all night. I found shade in my relationship with her after getting burned by the scorching relationship I'd had with my wife. She too, seemed content to keep me to herself, and I'd had no complaints.

But after a year of dating her, and then during the nine months of her pregnancy, it sounds odd and suspicious that our lives weren't more entwined.

I know why that is now—I'm still in love with Claire.

Brielle might have been in love with me, but I didn't love her back, and because of that, as with any crime of passion, I'm suspect number one.

A little after one the elevator doors slide open, and Claire's heels click across the tile. She drops her purse to the floor, her keys onto a decorative table, and kicks off her shoes. I quickly carry Felicity downstairs, and she's already in her room, lying on the bed, staring into space.

I lay Felicity in her crib and turn the mobile on.

Claire won't want my company. Whenever she was in a sour mood, she never did. I asked her why she always wanted to be alone, and in a moment of honesty that surprised me, she said she didn't want to learn to need me.

It broke my heart. All I ever wanted from her was to be needed.

Took me a while to understand Claire didn't want to need anyone. I wasn't special.

I'm still not.

I crawl onto the bed and curl my body around hers, spooning. Her hair is scented like strawberries, and her skin is saturated with a fragrance that will only ever belong to Claire. Sliding my arm under her pillow, I wrap my other arm around her stomach. My lips brush the shell of her ear, and I say, "Do you remember the night we met?"

She stiffens but doesn't say anything. It's the only answer I need to keep going.

"It was at that masquerade ball the mayor threw for breast cancer awareness. Remember? October, the summer finally giving way to fall. You walked by me in a slinky green dress and a black lace mask. I didn't know who the fuck you were, but all it took was one look, and I knew I needed you for the rest of my life." That night will be forever seared into my memory. How many nights after our divorce did I relive that evening? The electricity? The need? One touch of her hand, and I was lost.

"You followed me outside," she whispers.

"I did. Were you leading me out there? I like to think you were. To get me alone. I pulled you to me, like this," I say, yanking the hem of her blouse from her skirt's waistband and splaying my hand over her skin.

She shivers.

"We danced for hours, and I never knew your name."

The cool air, the music floating from inside the hotel's ballroom. The stars overhead, and only her, nobody else.

"I had to stop and rest," I continue, and she knows what comes next. "I sat on a bench in the shadows, the fountain hiding us from the guests who also came out for air. You sat on my lap and brushed your lips over mine. I wasn't sure what you wanted, and I asked—"

"'What are you doing?'" she says, filling in the story. "'Kissing you,' I said. 'Don't you want me to?'"

"I said, 'Yes, but I didn't come out here for this.'" My heart is hammering, remembering that night so clearly. "I wanted to give you an out in case you changed your mind, but you straddled my lap and gave me the sweetest kiss. I still remember how you slanted your lips over mine, teasing me with your tongue. I got so hard, and I knew you could feel it. Finally, I couldn't take it anymore and I said, "'Let me have you.'"

She did, undoing my belt and my pants. All she had to do was move a little scrap of lace away to give me access, and slowly, so slowly, she took me inside her. No talk of babies, or condoms, or STDs. Simply slid herself over me, her dress hiding what we were doing.

She came with a tiny gasp from the back of her throat, and I climaxed with her, my cock buried to the hilt.

I fell in love with her that night. Completely. Irrevocably.

And I didn't even know her name.

She came down from her high, and I untied her mask, revealing her face. The only other time I have ever felt like that was when the nurse laid Felicity in my arms after she was born. Claire smiled at me that night, her arms wrapped around my neck, my cock still inside her, eager for another go. I was completely shattered.

I move my hand from her stomach and glide my fingers up her leg. I find the apex of her thighs and move the tiny bit of lace away. She's hot and wet, and gently, I nudge her folds apart. "Let me have you, Claire."

I'm prepared for her to tell me no. From the moment I stepped foot inside what used to be our home, I've asked for more than she can give me. More than what she wants to give me. Sex always meant something to us, a way for us to get closer, a way for us to share without words because Jesus Christ, getting Claire to talk to me was impossible. If she hadn't shown me with her body what she couldn't say with words, I never would have believed she loved me as much as I loved her.

She rolls onto her back and I wait for her to swear at me,

tell me to fuck off, but she widens her legs and drags my head down to devour my lips with hers. I slide a finger into her and mimic the motion of my tongue inside her mouth. She whines and lifts her hips.

Still so passionate, still so needy.

I gave her everything and it still wasn't enough.

I lean forward, my finger rubbing the inside of her, searching for the one spot that would always make her fall to pieces. Her lips are already swollen, her skin flushed. "This will change things between us. You know it will. Sex has never been simply sex, and if you can't handle it, you shouldn't let me do this."

Her green eyes are glassy with so much confusion. I ignored that once, hoping she would figure things out, but she didn't and I won't ignore it again. I can understand if she has doubts. I haven't been here but for a couple of days and we didn't talk about this. We spoke of Felicity and Brielle's murder, clothing and groceries, but not why we divorced, not her reasons, and certainly not the fact that she still loves me even if she won't admit it, to me or to herself.

"Please," she whispers.

"Please what?" I *will* get her to talk to me. I'm playing for keeps and I learn from my mistakes.

"Make love to me." She starts unbuttoning my shirt.

"Is that what it will be for you? Because it's what it will be for me."

Her hands still, and I stroke her with my finger, her muscles rippling, clenching at me, needing more.

Tears drip from her eyes, down her temples, and into her hair.

I'll force her to say it.

"Yes."

I brush my lips across her cheek. "I love you so much,

Claire. I wanted to stop, Christ, how I wanted to stop. But I can't. I'll never stop loving you. Tell me you love me, too."

"I do, I really do." Her voice is half a sob.

Gently, I pull my finger from her and undo the first button of her blouse. "I'll always have Felicity. This will eventually blow over, and maybe she'll spend some time with Brielle's family, but she'll always be mine. If you say you love me, you're saying you'll love her too." I don't know where her hang up with children came from or why. If her aversion is to her own children or children in general, but I can't put off this talk because I want to fuck her. When I asked her to marry me, I thought I had the rest of our lives to understand and resolve her conflicts, but I don't have that time now. My heart is on the line . . . and Felicity's future.

She looks toward the crib. The mobile's tinny music stopped, and Felicity's breathing fills the room. I can't see my daughter, the pink bumper obstructing my view, but I don't need to. I know she's there—her heart fills mine.

"I don't know if I can do that," she says.

I'm grateful she can tell me now, be honest enough to tell me. I'm not angry, only resigned. I thought maybe these past few years apart would have made her see nothing is more important than us being together, but there's something still standing in her, *our,* way, and I don't know if we'll ever overcome it.

I move my hand from her blouse, my finger still sticky. "Thank you for telling me the truth for once."

She lies in the position I found her in, tears wetting her pillow. It's so difficult not to comfort her, but there's nothing I can do. Whatever's hurting her, she'll have to face alone.

Felicity is soundly sleeping, and I pick her up. She doesn't stir. "I'll keep Felicity at night from now on. I'm sorry she's such an inconvenience."

Only silence follows me from the room.

————

I set up as much of Felicity's things in my bedroom as I can. I can't move her crib, and though the bathrooms are huge, they won't take the place of a kitchen. I can mix her bottles up here at night, but in the morning, I'll have to use the sink to wash them.

It would be nice if Claire found somewhere else to stay, but I can't kick her out of her own house. I would leave if I could, but even butting heads with Claire, I feel safe here and don't want to find somewhere else to hide.

Around dinner time, I hear the elevator doors open and close and I can't help but feel relieved. I carry Felicity downstairs. I'm starving. When I brought up Felicity's things, I was only thinking about her. I didn't want to bump into Claire, and I've gone without something to eat all day. It's no way to live, but better than taking my chances on the street or going back to my own penthouse. The police are probably watching it, hoping they'll catch me. They may be watching Claire's building too, and it's all the more imperative I stay put.

I reheat some of the gourmet pizza, the spicy scent churning my stomach in nauseous hunger.

The elevator doors slide open, and I suck in a breath preparing to apologize. Raff steps into the kitchen wearing a dress shirt open at the throat and an unbuttoned vest, a bulging manila envelope in his hand. The words die on my lips.

"Sorry for the no-announce. The concierge let me up. I have a little news and I figured I could clue you in and drop this off at the same time." He sets the envelope onto the island. "Hey, kid," he says to Felicity who's happily swinging back and forth. She grins at him.

He chuckles and slides onto a stool. "Got more of that?" he asks, jutting his chin at the microwave and the scent of chicken, bacon, and ranch.

"Yeah, sure."

"Beer too, if you have it."

"Yeah. Coming up."

I grab a beer out of the fridge for him first, and he downs most of it in two swallows.

"Rough day?" I ask, surprised. Raff doesn't seem like the type for anything to crawl under his skin. Except for maybe Veronica.

"You ever wanted to get into politics?" He spins the cap to his beer bottle and watches it twirl on the countertop.

"Not particularly." The microwave dings, and I serve him first, ripping off a paper towel in lieu of a napkin and sliding a fork across the island.

"It's not so much that I didn't want to, you know, it's that it wouldn't have been something I'd do on my own," he says around a mouthful of onions and cheese.

"Is that the favor Veronica was talking about? Running for mayor?"

He shakes his head. "The shit you'll do for a woman, huh?" he says, but there's no venom in his voice. Amusement, perhaps. Bemusement. Befuddlement. But there's a lot of joy on his face, too. I'm talking to a man who found what he was looking for. Should all of us be so lucky.

Shoving another couple of pizza slices into the microwave, I say, "Sometimes you can't budge."

"Sometimes you can't," he agrees, and he steps away from the island only long enough to pull another beer out of the fridge.

"For what it's worth, you seem like you'll be a good mayor." I uncap a beer with the hem of my shirt. Claire's rejection is hot in the back of my heart, and it goes down nice and smooth.

"It's the same kind of shit, only a different pile. It'll help Nic will be with me. She's the one who'll get me into office. You're probably not following anything but your own fucked up mess, but the story got out she was going to marry that Barker slime to help her dad. We can't walk down the fucking street without someone wanting her autograph." He sounds proud of her. "Dragging my heels about the 'zine, though. I don't want to let it go. Luckily, there's a lot of time before I have to make a decision either way, but it's tough to say goodbye to all that hard work. You miss your job?"

I stand opposite him with my own dinner and jerk a shoulder, wash some pizza down with a gulp of beer. "Divorce, you know? I don't know what I was thinking."

Raff quirks the corner of his mouth. "Job security is my guess. My brother's a defense attorney. The sleazier the crime, the prouder he is."

"He likes the legwork. The verbal sparring in the courtroom, the word play and mind games. The drinks and the slaps on the back."

"Hell, yeah. He turns into a goddamned Oscar nominee."

"Nah, I can do without that. I'd rather find pride in the personal, not the professional. I'm not looking to reopen my firm. I don't need to. Maybe find a part-time job, blog about divorce law, maybe, help abuse victims who can't afford attorney fees. I've always liked to write, it was one of the very few things Claire and I had in common. Maybe a book. I mean, a guy needs a reason for the wheels to turn, but other things creep up on you—" I tilt my head toward my daughter— "and other crap has a way of taking a backseat. I need to get some shit straightened out and get the hell out of here."

Raff forks up another huge bite of pizza. "You and Claire not getting along?"

"She's got this thing with kids. She can't get past it. I can't get past it. I'm not choosing Claire over my daughter, and I shouldn't have to."

Felicity watches us curiously, and it sends my stomach into knots that Claire could be so callous toward a little baby. Maybe, deep down, she's not the person I thought she was. Maybe I fell in love with someone who truly doesn't exist.

"Yeah, that's some fucked up garbage. The way Ron threw their mother out on her ass for cheating? It's no wonder Claire's confused and Jack's in therapy. My parents are rough, but Christ."

"I'm sorry, what?" This is the first I've heard about Claire and Jack's mother.

Raff grimaces. "I said a bad thing, didn't I? You didn't know."

"No, I didn't, but it would be fucking terrific if someone told me something."

He shoves his empty plate away. "Look. Some of what I know is from Emma, some from Claire, and I would never betray a trust. I threatened Jack a long time ago and told him if he couldn't deal with his childhood trauma and he hurt Emma, I would kick his ass. Em's a lot more patient than I am, and I would have used him as a punching bag long before this. She convinced me to give Jack a little leeway, but there's only so long you can cry about your childhood. Suck it up. I did."

"That didn't tell me a goddamned thing."

"I'm not getting into specifics. If Claire wants you to know, she'll fill in the blanks. Ron kicked Elizabeth out when Jack and Claire were small. Jack was four, that would have made Claire—"

"A baby."

"Yeah. He thought she was cheating. Long story short, she wasn't. He asked her to take him back, and she said no. He was a fucking asshole, and you have to respect her for that. Ron retaliated, cut her off from the money and her kids. She's been on her own and hasn't seen them since. Ron *just* came clean. Jack struggles, and some of that's my fault because I'm an asshole too and I like to poke at him. I've been friends with Emma since we were kids. He dislikes it, but tough shit."

"So . . ." I'm trying to piece all this together. "It's Ron's fault Claire's mother left them."

"Yes and no. I mean, to give Ron credit, he did admit he was wrong. You need a lot of guts to do that, but she said fuck off and he got mad. Wouldn't you, if you were down on your hands and knees groveling, and she kicked dirt in your face? When you have kids, it's not all about you anymore. I think Jack and Claire put Elizabeth on a pedestal and she doesn't belong there."

"This is starting to make sense. Claire's mother didn't want her family back, and now Claire has attachment issues." That's too simple of a description as to what happened, but Claire's mother walked, and it sounds like maybe she didn't have to.

"That about sums it up. I suppose at this point, the whys don't matter, but I've already said too much, and you'll have to ask her for the details. I'm sorry. I probably shouldn't have opened my mouth. I report gossip, but not where my friends are concerned. I care about Claire, and she's been struggling for most of her life."

I open another beer. "The whys don't matter. Seeing Claire again, I want things, but I can't force her to be where she doesn't want to be. In my life. Part of my family. She's determined to be alone, and maybe I would have fought her on it if it had been only me, but I have Felicity now. I have to cut my losses. The last thing Felicity needs is a mother figure who doesn't want to be one."

"Maybe that's best. She's lonely, fishing for husband number three. I told her not to, but what do you do if you don't want to be alone? You look for someone to be miserable with."

"I should let her," I say thickly, my heart shredded at the thought of having to sit through her marrying another bastard. I couldn't stand it. I really couldn't.

"If you can," he says carefully. "I went through my own thing when Jack and Nic were dating. It's tough thinking about the woman you love giving herself to someone else. I can be fucking annoyed with Jack—he throws a lot of shit at Emma for being friends with me— but I did the same thing and almost lost Veronica. Jealousy is not good. Anyway, I didn't come by for that. Here." He pushes at the manila envelope, and I tip it. A cell phone and charging cord slide out. "I put all of our numbers in it, and I forwarded yours to everyone. You've probably been digging online, but don't use Claire's internet connection anymore. Use the cell's hotspot and no one can trace your movements on the web."

"Thanks." I wake it up and open the contacts. Everyone is there, even Ron's cell phone number, work number, and his house landline.

"I talked to Brielle's mom and dad earlier this afternoon. They're grieving, as you can imagine, and they want to see Felicity. They asked if I knew where you were, and I said no. Let's keep it that way for the time being. I didn't get any nasty vibes from them, but at this point, I wouldn't trust anyone. I got a list of Brielle's friends from her mother, the women Brielle went out with the night she disappeared. I'm going to talk to them tomorrow, see if they saw anything or if Brielle even met up with them. I got a copy of the autopsy report. The ME places her time of death between midnight and four the night she disappeared, and her body washed up on shore close to forty-eight hours later. The water rinsed away what little evidence there could have been, but, no matter where she was killed, someone transported her to Cavern Lake. Which means she was sitting or lying in a vehicle for close to six hours. Maybe she left some hair or fibers behind."

I wince. It sounds like I'm watching an episode of *CSI* or *Law and Order*. "Was she . . ." I don't even want to think it, but anything is possible.

"Maybe. They found semen in her vagina, but she was still healing from a vaginal delivery, so it's difficult to say if it was consensual. You dated her for a couple of years. Do you know what she could have been into? Drugs? Was she hooking on the side? Anything?"

"From the second we met, we were together unless she was at work at the diner. Could she have been lying to me? Yeah, but I had no reason to think she would. I wasn't working, I was still—"

"Too busy being in love with Claire. I got that. Okay. I'll talk to her friends, her coworkers. There were a couple more family members I think you said she saw on a regular basis. Some cousins and aunts and uncles. I'll get to all of them, eventually. I want to be aggressive, but I have to pretend this isn't a big deal. People won't talk to me if I'm not my usual charming self."

He's trying to lighten the mood, and I appreciate it, but we're talking about my daughter's mother's murder. All I want is to be cleared so I can mourn and move on. Maybe that's with Claire, maybe it's not, and her petty issues aren't high on my list of concerns. "I appreciate it, really. Her friends' names are more than what I had."

A corner of his mouth lifts. "I'm in my element. If you need anything, use the cell. Remember the hotspot. I'm going to go home and pop open another beer. Thanks for the company. Nic's having a girls' night out. Helluva thing. Now I'll be pacing the floors until she's home."

"Is she with Emma? Can you ask her if Claire's with them? I asked her not to go anywhere without letting me know, but we had a fight and she left without saying anything."

"Ah, yeah. Let me text her." He tugs his phone out of his pants pocket, opens his messages app, and shoots off a quick text.

He's skimming an answer seconds later, and maybe I wouldn't like it either if my fiancée was so quick to text another man her whereabouts.

He shows me his phone.

Hey, baby girl—

"Baby girl?" I ask, my eyebrows raised. "I think if I were Jack, I'd have problems too."

"Force of habit. I've called her that for thirteen years. I'm going to need more time to stop than a couple of months. I try, really."

"Ah-huh." I lower my gaze back to the phone.

Hey, baby girl, is Claire with you?

No. I asked if she wanted to come along, but she got some news today and she was upset. I think she's at Ron's house.

"Must be some shitty news for her to spend time with her dad after what you told me," I say, handing the phone back to him.

His thumbs fly across the screen. Checking in on his own fiancée, I bet. He reads Emma's response and tucks his phone into his pocket.

"Yeah, well, if you guys are fighting, she probably didn't want to stay here."

"You wouldn't be able to set me up with a different place to lay low, would you?" I ask on a lark. The only places I can think of to go are my penthouse or a hotel, but a hotel wouldn't give me much privacy, not with housekeeping nosing around every morning, and I can't pay for it with my accounts frozen.

"Actually, if you mean that, yeah. Nic's apartment is empty. Of people, I mean. She moved in with me, and Emma's apartment is empty, too. Emma's mom lives in Bridgeport, and my aunt wouldn't mind rocking Felicity, so if you and Claire are spitting at each other, we can get something figured out. Let her know, though, right? Don't leave without running it by her."

"Yeah. Having a different place to go takes some weight off. I don't want to be in her face if she doesn't want me here. Well, not me. Felicity."

Raff walks across the kitchen and drops to his haunches in front of Felicity's swing. She regards him coolly, but finds him to her liking and smiles, reaching her little hand out. He lets her wrap her fingers around one of his. "What's it like?"

"Scarier than fuck."

He chuckles and pulls his finger free. "That's all the proof I need not to have any of my own. I better get going. Emma will tell Nic I was asking about her, and she'll be home soon. I'll let you know what I find out talking to Brielle's friends. Maybe I'll get more out of them than the police did. Not many people like talking to the cops—especially if they have something to hide."

"Thanks. I appreciate all you're doing."

He pauses by the elevator. "If you love Claire, I mean, really, truly, can't-live-without-her love her, wait. She's like Jack, and she's going to have to figure out a few things. If you leave her while she does, she'll come out the other side and you won't be there. Goodnight."

"Be careful."

"I will."

The elevator carries him down to the lobby, and I clean up the kitchen.

I don't know how long I should wait for something like this. If you want to get technical, I've given her over five years to get her shit together and she'd rather run than face the truth. That she's lovable, that she has something to give. I don't care if her mother left her. That has nothing to do with her, but she won't believe it.

Since Claire probably won't be home tonight, I give Felicity a bath in the kitchen. Once she's dressed in a sleeper and her tummy is full, I turn on a movie upstairs in the den. I stay up, waiting for a text, something that will tell me Claire's okay, but I don't get anything.

It's a big fat metaphor for our entire relationship.

The longer I wait, the more fucked I am.

CHAPTER TEN

Claire

Shaking, I remember to pick up my keys and phone on the way out of the foyer, and barefoot, I step into the elevator.

My blouse is untucked, Roman's touch leaving behind a searing pain. I can still feel his finger inside me, the desperation of needing him to fill the emptiness. When we were married, it was the only way I could show him how I felt, the only way I could keep him with me. Words, he wanted me to say the words, but I never could. Not even during our wedding ceremony. My lips moved, but I couldn't give the words voice, life, meaning. Instead, I cried. The minister told Roman he could kiss me, and he wiped my tears away thinking I was sentimental. He didn't know I was already saying goodbye.

I stand on the sidewalk, confused, not knowing where I should go.

People walk past and gawk at me, concerned, maybe, seeing my tears. The sun is too bright and I squint against the light.

It's after six, and I order a car.

I open my own door and climb inside the cool interior that smells slightly of citrus. The driver meets my eyes in the rearview and parts his lips to ask if I'm all right, but I turn away and stare out the window.

My hand is wrapped painfully around my keys, their teeth biting into my skin. I'm quiet, huddled against the door, and he navigates the route I've taken only a handful of times since I've been old enough to stay away. I hate our house, more than Jack, I think. The driver pulls up along the curb and lets me out, and I stand on the sidewalk, little rocks digging into the soles of my feet, wishing I never had to see this place again.

One of Jack's trucks is parked in the driveway and rage rips through me.

I let myself in through the laundry room, flashes of Emma and my brother standing in the hallway blurring my vision. My bare feet slap against the wood.

Jack and our dad are talking quietly in the library, sipping whiskey, and to get their attention, I throw my phone against the wall. It bounces off wallpaper that hasn't been changed in decades and skids across the floor.

"Claire." Jack stands. "What's wrong?"

"You forgive him so easily," I choke. "You forgive him so easily for destroying our lives."

"Claire," my dad says, rising from the couch. "I know you hate me—"

I laugh, a hand to my throat. "Hate you? I don't hate you. I despise you. Do you know what you did to me, kicking Mom out? Do you know what it did to me, to our family? To the family I'll never have? All I ever wanted was to have a husband who loved me, children I could kiss goodnight. You took that from me," I cry, tears blinding me, my father's face an ashen streak. "You made me believe Mom didn't love me enough to stay. I don't know what I am. I don't know how to be. I don't know how to be a wife or a mother. I don't know how to be a daughter. I never had a chance to be one."

Jack steps closer, his hand out. "Claire. I love you—"

"No, you don't, or you wouldn't be here, on his side. Always on his side because of Emma. I told her, you know."

He pales. "You told her what?"

"The night we had dinner here and we went upstairs. I told her not to get involved with you. I told her all you would do is hurt her. She didn't listen, and I hope to God you hurt her as much as you've hurt me. You son of a bitch." My breath catches in my lungs and I stagger backward, forty-one years of pain and a belief I was nothing worth loving clogging my throat.

"You didn't," he whispers. His fingers loosen and he drops the glass. Whiskey splatters onto his pants, but his eyes never leave mine.

"I did, and now she'll always wait for the day you rip her to shreds. You deserve all you get."

"That's enough," my father says, resting a hand on Jack's shoulder.

"It's never going to be enough. It will never be enough until you can give me back the years you've stolen. Until you can give me the husband I haven't been able to love, the children I haven't been able to watch grow up. I hate you both."

I back away, brushing past Irene who came to see what all the yelling is for. I stumble down the hallway, out the back door, and onto the patio where my father, the mighty Ronald Durand, confessed all his sins.

I stub my toe against the patio table, and hobbling in pain, I land hard on top of the steps that let down to the grass I didn't play in as a child. I cry into my knees, keening so terribly I don't know if I'll ever stop. I didn't mean to say those nasty things to my brother. Seeing him sitting with our father as if nothing happened, as if these forty-one years never happened, I felt so betrayed. Out of anyone, I thought Jack would be on my side.

The sun sinks and I sit, my heart full of such misery I can't stop crying.

The patio door opens and closes, and Jack sits behind me the way he used to when we were children and we would play Legos together, his legs flanking mine. He wraps his arms around me, and I cry harder, my tears wetting his thigh instead of falling into my lap. He presses his lips to my hair and rubs my back.

"It's okay," he says, comforting me in the same tone he would speak in if the nanny was upset with us for being children. "I'll always love you. It will always be us against the world."

I have no idea how much time goes by until I'm so exhausted I can't cry another tear. I'm embarrassed and ashamed. I don't want to lift my head and look at him.

"I'm sorry," I whisper, my throat raw, my wet cheek resting against his knee.

"You have a right to say those things," he says, still rubbing my back in the same slow circles I remember. He would try to coax me back to sleep before I woke the nanny, his scrawny arm poked through the slats of my crib.

"No, I don't. I'm happy for you, but you won't believe that now."

"This isn't about me. It's about you and what you need to put this away. Claire, it's been so long, and I'm so tired. I'm tired of running from something I don't need to run from, I'm tired of hating Dad for his mistakes. I'm tired of hating Emma for something she hasn't even done. Aren't you tired, sweetheart?"

"Yeah, I am."

"Tell me what this is about. Why are you here without your shoes?"

"Roman said he loves me." Something that should make me so happy brings me so much pain instead.

"You hate him for that, don't you? So much." His lips move against my head, my hair catching in his whiskers. "And it's worse now. He brought you a baby."

"I can't be her mother."

"Not the way you are, you can't."

I stiffen and jerk away. "Thanks a lot. You're saying that to pay me back, aren't you?"

He yanks me against his chest, and his tie clip grazes my cheek. "You should know me better than that. Have I ever said anything nasty to you? Have I ever lied? You can't be her mother if you hate her for belonging to Roman. You can't be her mother if you hate her for not being yours."

"I wanted to give him that family, but I didn't know how."

"And he didn't stay to show you. Claire, I don't know how to help you. I'm still dealing with it myself. All I know is I chose to forgive Dad. I can't let that bitterness eat at me. It's poison, and eventually, it will kill you. Emma and I will never have something real, something we can build on, if I can't put this away. I miss Mom, what I could have had as her son, what we could have had as a family. I really do, but that time is gone. You know the truth now . . . it's up to you what you do with it."

"I don't know if I can forgive Dad for what he did. I can understand he thought she was cheating, I get it. I can understand he would be angry she didn't want him back, but why did he have to do what he did? Why did he have to cut us off from her?"

"He was weak and he was ashamed. Haven't you ever been? Weren't you weak when you asked Roman for a divorce? Weren't you ashamed when he asked you why and you had nothing to tell him, nothing to say except your own excuses? Isn't it why you have a difficult time dealing with him now? You destroyed your marriage and broke Roman's heart because you were weak. You're not so different from Dad."

"Dad made me that way." I'm not going to empathize with a man who's to blame for my issues in the first place.

"Maybe he did." He pauses. "When I was dealing with my own shit, Heath told me something and it stuck in my head. We never worked out our childhood trauma, not in the healthy way adults should. It didn't matter we didn't know everything—we never faced what happened. We never thought to until it was too late. It was only something we lived with, and we chose to let it control us."

"I'm not going to sit here and let you defend him. We grew up without a mother because of him."

He sighs. "Yeah, we did. And you can hate him all you want, but it's done. We let it ruin our lives so far, but now what? Now that we know? Will you let it ruin the next forty years? You're right, you know. If I did that, all I would do is hurt Emma, hurt, and possibly destroy, the family I'm creating with her. I chose to forgive Dad and put it away. Emma's proud of me for that, and not only is she proud of me, but she appreciates the hard work it took for me to get to that place. I did it because I love her. I've got nothing without her. The choice was simple, Claire."

"It's not simple for me." I wish it were. Then I wouldn't be here, barefoot, my makeup streaked from tears, my relationships in shambles. I would still be married to Roman. We'd have children and a solid relationship built on love and trust.

With a finger under my chin, Jack turns my head, asking me to look at him. He's changed so much since he let his guard down and let Emma love him. There's something softer about him, more human. "I love you. I promised when we were little that I would always be there for you, and I hope I have been. Tell me what you need so I can help you put this away."

"I want to find Mom." He doesn't want to, but all this talk of putting it behind us? Forgiveness? How can he say those things and expect to be able to without the full story? Without being able to talk to her? What I want to know, above all else, is if she ever loved us at all.

"Okay. When do you want to go?"

I don't have much time. Once Raff clears Roman's name, he'll leave and take Felicity with him. Then there's Daisy. I can't not claim her, even if it's only to let Emma and Jack raise her. I was married to her daddy and it's my responsibility to see that she's loved. By someone.

"In the morning."

"I'll go with you, but on one condition."

I never could ask Jack for anything without expecting a compromise. "What?"

"Talk to Dad tonight. There's no point in finding Mom if you can't deal with Dad. He's the cause of it, but nothing Mom will say will change what's between you now."

I sit and hold my head in my hands. I'm not ready to talk to Dad, to forgive him.

"Do you want to keep Roman?" Jack asks over the silence.

"I don't deserve him." Not after the way I hurt him. I'm not talking about the divorce, either. I'm talking about today, two hours ago. I let him believe I could never love Felicity, that I could never love him as long as he was her father.

"I thought that about Emma, too, and I was right. I didn't, but I worked on myself until I did. Work for it, if that's what you want, and if you don't, after Raff figures out who killed Felicity's mother, let him go. For good. Let him move on, and then you do the same. For good. Open yourself up to a relation-ship you can invest in, with a man you can truly love."

The thought of living without Roman scares me. The thought of being with another man churns my stomach. I don't want anyone else. I don't want him to go after Raff finds Brielle's killer. I don't want him to take Felicity away. Roman and Felicity will only be two more things my father will steal from me if I let him.

"I'm sorry I said that to Emma," I say, my voice cracking. I never wanted to hurt Jack. He's never done anything but be there for me every time I needed him.

He laughs, and it really is proof of how far he's come. "At the time you said it, it was true. I can't argue with that. I look back at that stupid surrogacy thing, and it's amazing no one had me committed. I was out of my mind with fear and jealousy. All I wanted was her and I was too much of a coward to admit it. Be brave, Claire. I'll help you however I can."

"Thanks. Dad, huh? I don't know what to say."

"You don't have to say anything, just listen. He's only human, and he's hurting. Listen to your heart, and do what it tells you to do. Find peace. I've come to realize that peace and happiness, it's all a journey, not a destination."

"Christ," I say to hear him laugh again. He's my brother, my pillar of strength, my shield from the world.

He kisses my cheek. "Let's go inside. Then I want you to come home with me. I don't want you to be alone tonight, and maybe you and Roman need a little space until you work this out."

"Thank you. I didn't mean to hurt you."

"Yeah, you did," he says, standing and tugging on my hand, "but you don't need to be angry anymore."

I follow him into the house, and I try to do what Jack says—leave the resentment, anger, and unhappiness outside. Despite what Dad did to Mom, for Jack and me, there were some good times in this house. I don't want to throw our entire childhood away because Mom was missing.

Dad's waiting in the library, staring out the window watching the day turn to night. He looks his age, and Jack didn't say so, but I know he was thinking about putting this aside and enjoying the last few years we have while Dad's still here.

"I'm sorry, Claire," he says, but I don't let him say anything else. I step into his arms and for a long time, he cries into my hair, letting go of his guilt in my forgiveness.

———

Irene serves us dessert and wine, and we talk late into the night. Not only about what Dad did, but other things. Happier things. Childhood memories that aren't tarnished by Mom's absence. As the years went by, Dad convinced himself he'd been a poor father, but we reminisce about the stupid stuff Jack and I did and the way Dad would respond, and we remind him he was better at it than he thought he was. Maybe I needed that reminder, too.

Jack yawns near one in the morning. He's missing Emma, the urgency to go home to her vibrating from him, but I appreciate the time he gave me tonight. I needed it, and like he always said, he was there for me.

At the door, Dad hands us a thick file full of information about Mom. He's been tracking her since she told him to go to hell after he kicked her out, wanting to help her if she ever needed it. He's given her money through the years, contests she's "won," bank accounting "mistakes." He wanted her financially secure, trying to right his wrongs in the only way he knew how. I scan the list of ways he concocted to slip her some cash, and I smile. She must think she's the luckiest woman in the world. She probably did think that at one point, when Dad said he loved her.

"She still lives in that little house," he says, Jack jiggling his keys, eager to go home to his fiancée. "If you talk to her, it's probably best you don't mention all this." He nods at the file in my hand. "I doubt she'd appreciate what I was trying to do."

"Money can't buy the truth," I murmur.

"No, it can't. And even if it could, it wouldn't matter if you don't want to hear it. Thank you for talking with me, for listening. It means a lot to me." Dad opens the door, reluctant to see us go. We reconnected tonight, a corner turned, and it will be up to me not to look back.

I kiss his cheek, my lips lingering over his leathery skin. He's always worn the same aftershave, and I inhale, letting the scent comfort me. "To me, too. We'll have to have a family dinner again sometime soon," I tease.

Dad chuckles, maybe for the first time in years. "Emma's been good for our family, but it should have started with Roman. You'll never know how sorry I am for that."

"I think I do, but I need to take ownership of some of those mistakes. I married him, and I was my own person. The choices I made were mine, and they still are. It doesn't mean I don't have a lot to work through. It doesn't mean that Roman and I can repair what I ruined, but accepting responsibility is the first step in fixing a relationship I want to keep. If it's not already too late."

"I think you can do whatever you set out to do."

"I hope so. Goodnight, Daddy."

"Goodnight, Claire. I've never been as proud of you as I am at this moment."

I step outside, and Jack and our father shake hands.

Jack opens his truck door for me, and we're quiet on the

way into the city. I'm tired, more drained than I ever remember being, and that's saying a lot with as shitty as my life has been.

Barefoot, I walk through the parking garage under Jack's building. We ride in the elevator to his penthouse, and he leans tiredly against the wall. I expected Emma to be sleeping, but she's waiting for us, and the second I step into the foyer, I'm trapped in her arms.

There is so much I want to say to her, so much I'm grateful for. Jack hurt her, and if she wouldn't have been so compassionate and so quick to forgive him, I would still hate my father for everything he ever did to us.

She pulls away, her eyes misty. "Will you text Roman to let him know you're okay? You left without saying anything, and he's worried. Raff dropped a cell off at your place earlier and he was asking about you. Raff texted you his number."

My phone survived my hissy fit, but I didn't think to check for messages. "Yeah, I will. Thank you."

"You're welcome. Raff said Roman was a little down. Maybe he could use some company."

I'm beginning to get to know my soon-to-be sister-in-law. There's nothing Emma likes better than when we're all together—and I bet having Felicity there is an extra bonus.

"You want to have another party."

She smiles impishly. "Maybe a get together. A small one. Though, Haisley and Mia would love to meet Felicity . . . and Roman, of course."

I resist rolling my eyes. What exasperates me about Emma, I love her for, too.

"We can talk about that tomorrow," Jack says. "It's late. See you in the morning."

"Goodnight, you two."

My brother tucks Emma under his arm, and they walk

down the hallway toward the bedroom. It does my heart good to know that relationships can survive even the worst odds.

I open my messages and save the number Raff sent me. I send Roman a text saying that I'm staying at my brother's tonight, that I have an important errand in the morning, and if he's still willing to talk to me, I have a lot I need to say.

I wait for a moment, hoping for a response, but unlike Emma, Roman's sleeping.

In the kitchen, I find a bottle of wine and sit at the island with a glass.

Emma pokes her head around the corner, and I gesture her over.

We sit in silence as we sip, sisters connected in pain and heartache, sisters formed in friendship, and family forged from love.

CHAPTER ELEVEN

Roman

She sent it after two o'clock in the morning. I try not to be pissed off she texted me *after* she went to Jack and Emma's. That she clued me in she was staying there and that she had plans this morning only because Emma asked her to. *And* that's only because Raff told Emma I was wondering if Claire was all right. Maybe it's none of my business, but I don't like not knowing where she is. There's a killer out there.

When Claire and I were married, we kept to ourselves, and this group thing, these *friends,* are going to take some getting used to. Not that I would resent Raff. Christ, is he doing me a favor, and I know it. I could never investigate on my own. I'd be stuck in jail, maybe out on bail if I were lucky, or if the evidence was flimsy, of my own recognizance, but I know damn straight if I hadn't run, they would have tried to charge me with Brielle's murder.

Then it would have been my attorney's job to get me out of this mess, and I might have lost Felicity. Permanently.

I do a little straightening up and run the dishwasher, vacuum, and dump the trash. Claire must have canceled her housekeeping. I've been here for four days and no one has come to clean the bathrooms. I do that too, since I know even if we were getting along better, me hiding here is an inconvenience, and I don't think Claire has ever scrubbed a toilet.

I don't mean to make her sound spoiled. Like me, she grew up with money. Why do something if someone else is paid to do it for you?

Raff must come from money too, or he made his own fortune with *Talk of the Town*. It's not cheap to run for a government office. He and Veronica won't be able to work while he campaigns. Gotta pay bills somehow.

I use Claire's laptop (I remember the hotspot—don't need to cause her anymore trouble using her ISP) and unabashedly check her email. Kavanaugh's attorney hasn't emailed her today. She came home upset yesterday, maybe that's where she went. Didn't like the country house he decided to leave her in a fit of sentimentality. Too bad.

Raff didn't give me much to go on yesterday, but investigations are slow and it might be he won't find out anything without a lot of luck. I search for more news, but nothing pops. I don't have any police connections, no one I can call on the down-low. Even with the phone Raff gave me, I shouldn't contact anyone unless I'm serious about lawyering up, but I don't want to do that yet. If I do, I'll need to find someplace safe for Felicity, and this isn't it.

My parents will be worried and wondering what's going on, and I should ask Claire to call them from Variant's offices and tell them Felicity and I are okay and that I'm handling this the best I can.

Fuck.

I wish I could do more. I wish my head were in the game and I could stop worrying about Claire. Not worrying about her well-being. I mean, us. I want there to be an us. I really do. I didn't come here for that, but Christ, the second I saw her walk into the lobby, it's all I've wanted. Lying with her yesterday, touching her. It brought back every second, every painful second I've spent living without her, and I don't want to do that anymore.

Four years gone the moment our eyes met. I could believe they hadn't passed at all if Felicity wasn't here.

I don't have social media, and I log into Brielle's instead. I'm lucky her parents haven't shut down her accounts, but maybe they don't know her passwords anymore, if they ever did. She changed them after Felicity was born to Felicity's name and the date we met. Not the most secure, but a change from the SupernaturalFan28 she used before. It's interesting no one has brought up our age difference. She was twenty years younger than I am. Another motive, I suppose. Easy for anyone to say I got tired of her, couldn't buy her off, got angry when she wouldn't go away. Not that it's true. I wasn't sure what I wanted with her, but she was adult enough she would have accepted it. She acted older than she was, having to pay her own way because her parents are low-income, but she never lost her joy.

I might be preoccupied with getting myself out of this shit-storm, but I'll miss her.

So many people have posted on her wall, telling her good-bye, asking what happened to her, to Felicity. Asking about me and where I am. I should have looked here for a list of her friends. I'll give Raff access to her accounts, too, if he stops by later.

Christ, she posted hundreds of pictures of Felicity and me.

I click through them, fascinated. Me sleeping, me shaving in her steamy little bathroom after a shower, a towel wrapped around my waist. I would have told her not to do it if I'd known, but I hadn't realized how important I was to her. I should have. From the second we met outside the bar, I spent all my time with Brielle, but my heart was always with Claire.

I should have left her before she got pregnant.

I keep scrolling, and all the pictures her mother took of her in the hospital the day Felicity was born are here. There are several of the three of us, Felicity lying on Brielle's chest immediately after the doctor delivered her, covered in blood and goo, Brielle's eyes filled with tears. She's not looking at the baby though, she's looking at me, at my reaction—if I loved our daughter. If Felicity's birth would turn us into a family.

My answer would have broken her heart.

That I never wanted a family with anyone but Claire.

Raff finds me hours later, tearing up looking at picture after picture.

"Here, it looks like you could use this," he says, setting a bottle wrapped in a brown paper bag and a beige file, white printer paper peeking out from the edges, onto the island.

I push the paper bag down and reveal a bottle top-shelf whiskey. "You're not wrong."

"What are you doing?"

I slide off my barstool and grab two lowball glasses from the cabinet. Claire didn't touch the wine glasses, champagne flutes, or the cocktail glasses we received for wedding gifts. The two I set on the island were presents from a work associate, our names and date etched into the glass.

"Going through Brielle's social media accounts. I was hoping to give you a hand. Feeling pretty useless right about now."

He pours. "Did you find anything? Did she post any pictures or selfies from that night?"

"I didn't get that far. I was sidetracked by all the pictures she put up of me and Felicity."

"Did she ever make a big deal about your money? Did she know who you were when you met?"

"She had no idea who I was, but I never expected her to. I'm not a mini-celebrity like you and Veronica. The heel had popped off her shoe, and she'd twisted her ankle. I was just leaving the bar to go home, and I caught her leaning against the building. I offered to wave down a taxi, and I helped her into the backseat. I think she was relieved she didn't have to go home by herself."

Thrumming his fingers against the marble, he asks, "Did you sleep with her that night?"

I let myself go back to the taxi ride, how lonely I was, missing Claire. Brielle's embarrassed laugh, her ankle swelling. Joking about cheap shoes.

"No. I carried her up to her apartment. She lived on the fourth floor and her building doesn't have an elevator. She didn't have any ice and we made do with a bag of frozen peas. I teased her that she would have peas in her freezer, and she said she liked eating them with butter and salt." I glance at him. "I don't know why I remember that. I saw that she was comfortable on her couch, and I admit, I lingered. I needed it, you know? Her laugh. The sparkle in her eyes. That she would have vegetables in her freezer. I don't know why that charmed me, but it did. I asked her for her number, and I think she was more surprised than I was when I called the next day and asked her out."

"She sounds sweet. Did she ask to move into your place? Did she ask you to pay her bills?"

I sip, appreciate the smooth flavor, and then say, "No. I

liked being at her apartment. The whole thing could fit into the living room, but she turned it into something cozy. Fairy lights and plants. She painted the walls even though it was against her lease. She liked pink, the soft kind, like roses. I didn't have to be anybody when I was there. I was only a guy she met outside a bar."

"So, as time went on and you got to know each other, she didn't ask you for anything. Not to get her parents out of debt, not to buy her a car, pay off her credit cards, nothing."

"No, not at all. She wasn't that type of person. Why?"

"I'm getting a baseline for your relationship. A Cinderella story always has a couple of ugly stepsisters in it."

"I didn't consider our relationship like that."

"Did she get pregnant on purpose?"

I shrug uneasily. "Maybe? I can't say yes because the first time we had sex, she was clear she wasn't on birth control. She said she was single and didn't need it. I wore condoms until I started sleeping at her apartment on a regular basis, and in the middle of the night, it happens."

"Did you ever have sex while either of you were drunk? In the middle of the night, was she awake?"

I scowl. "Why am I feeling like a rapist right now? Everything we did was consensual."

He drills holes into me with his stare. "You're sure."

"Yeah, I am. Why? You talked to some of Brielle's friends today, didn't you? What did they say?" My heart starts to beat a nervous staccato against my ribs. If any of Brielle's friends accused me of raping her, I would have no way to defend myself and it would give the cops more motive to pin me for her murder.

"Before I answer that, let me ask you this. You're going through her social media. Is there a vibe she put out there?

Anything that might indicate she didn't want to see you? That she was thinking of dumping you?"

"No. The opposite, in fact. I'm embarrassed how many photos she posted of me, of us. I'm glad I don't have any of my own accounts. She couldn't tag me."

Raff pours more into our glasses, and Christ, do I need it. "You said you talked to her about splitting up. Did that upset her? You said she told her parents and they fed it to the cops."

"Of course she was upset. There's not a lot of security if you're seeing someone who doesn't know what they want. I didn't know for sure, and I shouldn't have told her I was thinking about ending it. It was unfair to her. After Felicity's birth, I was confused. I wanted what I had with Bri with Claire, and I knew I was never going to get that but I didn't want to settle."

"Did you bring up Claire at all?"

"No, but if Bri did any kind of online search after we met, she would have known Claire and I were divorced. Even before our marriage, she was a well-known socialite, and it made a lot of headlines. Can you tell me where you're going with this?"

Raff pulls out a few sheets of paper, handwritten notes scribbled along thick blocks of text. "I spoke with a Louise 'Call me Lulu' Parker, cute little thing, resembled a raccoon—"

I frown in confusion.

"A lot of this going on," he says, circling a hand around his eyes. "You never met her?"

"No. The name sounds familiar, but it could be because I've been scrolling through Brielle's social media all day." I skim my finger down the list I made earlier. "Here. Yeah. She commented on every post."

"Lulu had a lot of nice things to say about you. A little jealousy there as Brielle landed a pretty big fish, and a lot of bitterness because mainly, after you and Brielle started dating, she missed her friend. Down on her luck, beauty school dropout, but not a surprise considering she doesn't have a very light hand with the eyeliner. Struggling to figure out how to cross the tracks. She thought you were Brielle's ticket out of there."

"She didn't have nice things to say about me, she had nice things to say about my wallet."

"No, not entirely. Said you were good looking, nice to Brielle. Brielle wasn't lying to her friends since Lulu didn't have first-hand evidence of how nice you are, but she said she told the cops all nice things."

I blow out a breath. "That's something then. Where did you talk to her?"

"At a fast-food joint a few blocks north of Brielle's complex. I went by the building. Her apartment's not a crime scene and it's not cordoned off. I can get into her place if there's anything you left there."

"Nothing incriminating if that's what you mean."

"Maybe. Anyway, I felt sorry for her and slipped her some cash and my business card in exchange for talking to me."

"Why?"

"I'm not entirely sure. There was something about her that reminded me of me. Not everyone has an Emma. Not sure where I would be right now if Emma hadn't saw the need in me for friends. Not here talking to you, and not with Nic. I owe her a lot, and I thought maybe I could do the same. But the ball's in Lulu's court now, let's see how badly she wants to cross those tracks."

"What would you do for her?" I'm touched he thought to do anything for her at all.

"Put her through school. I think she has a brain, just not for makeup. Anyway," he says, waving it off, "next I spoke with Anastasia 'I'm looking for my Christian Grey' Peterson—"

My mouth twitches. "That's her name?"

"Not the Christian Grey part, but she did mention it and after checking out my suit, asked me to hook her up. She was named after a great-grandmother or some such. I thought with an attitude like that she would have been a little meaner, but honestly, Brielle had good friends. Anastasia missed Brielle and didn't like you for the simple fact you stole her away, and it was worse when Brielle got pregnant. I have a feeling that these women had a good friendship going, lots of emotional support, and you upended that. She did say something interesting though, let me find it."

"Are you going to?" I ask.

He shuffles through the paper. "What?" he asks, pulling out a piece from the bottom of the stack.

"Hook her up."

"With whom?"

"There's gotta be somebody."

He shoots me a look. "I'll play employment agency, but you can do the matchmaker stuff if you're that worried about Ana's prospects."

"Maybe there's someone in your office."

"I'm sure there is. Okay, she said, and this is a direct quote, 'He took up all her time. When she wasn't working, she was with him, and you know what she said? She wished she could have had some time to herself, and that they were always having sex. She told me she got tired of it.'"

I straighten, offended and concerned. "That's why you were asking me all the sex questions. Raff, I swear, I never coerced her into it. She was always a willing participant."

"Was she willing because she thought she had to be?"

"No!" Agitated, I slide off the stool and check on Felicity who fell asleep in the bouncy seat near the couch. "No. We didn't have that kind of relationship."

"What kind?"

"The kind where I was buying her things or giving her money and I wanted sex in exchange. We were equals."

"She might not have felt like you were. Your relationship was unbalanced by the very nature of it."

"Fuck you. Where is all this going?" I'm all for Raff helping me, but I will not stand here and let him call me an unfeeling asshole who used my baby's mother for sex.

Raff doesn't care I told him to fuck off, simply lifts another paper out of the file. "Don't forget I'm on your side. I'm putting this together and I'm going to try some wrong pieces before I find the right ones. I thought Lulu and Ana had a case of the ditched-friend syndrome, but then I spoke with Courtney Armstrong—"

"No cute names for her?" I ask sarcastically.

"I sense you're not in the mood for it," he says, following me into the living room.

"You're right, I'm not."

"Your loss. So, I talked to Courtney, and the four of them seemed tight. She wasn't as bitter as the other two. Courtney's trying a little harder to do better for herself, working a day job and taking classes online at night. Brielle met you and dropped off the grid, but Courtney didn't have time to notice. She did say, and this is another direct quote, 'Bri was never materialistic, you know? Never cared much for money or looks—Pres was proof of that—and when she started hanging out with Roman, it made him real upset.'"

"Who the fuck is that?"

"That's what I asked her. Lulu and Ana mentioned him, but casual, and I thought he was a part of their friend group, like if I mention Zoey in passing. Courtney implied they were more to each other, and I asked her if they were dating. She said yes, absolutely, but they stopped when she met you. Why did she start dating you if she already had a boyfriend?"

"Come on. You're asking me? Maybe they weren't exclusive. I never asked Brielle for more than what she wanted to give me. I practically had to force her to go out the night she disappeared—" I choke. If she would have stayed home, she'd still be alive. Felicity would still have her mother.

"Don't do that. I know what you're thinking, and don't do it."

"I can't help it."

"Yes, you can. It's not your fault."

I'll always blame myself. If she'd stayed home like she'd wanted, there wouldn't have been a chance for some sick fuck to grab her off the street. All she wanted was an evening home with us, and I wanted her to go out because I wasn't sure if that was the kind of life I wanted to live. I sink onto the couch, close my eyes, and wish desperately for a smoke. As if my brain wasn't fucked up enough, glimpses of the last time Claire and I made love here flash behind my eyelids.

Raff sits on the armrest. "I get it. I do. There's not a day that goes by I don't ask myself, what if we'd never gone to that fundraiser? Nic almost died. Fuck, we even talked about skipping it, but that kind of bullshit is more work than play. I don't know what I would have done if going to something like that would have gotten her killed. I understand, but you're missing the point."

I tense, preparing for a "life isn't fair speech," or, I don't know, a "things happen for a reason" litany.

I don't know him well, but I should have known Raff wouldn't be so trite.

"This Pres guy, Preston Nelson, sounds like he could fit the bill as a jilted lover. We might have just found our killer."

CHAPTER TWELVE

"Thank you for coming with me. I know you don't want to," I say.

Jack's driving down a two-lane highway toward a little town called Lilyvale. I've never been there, never needed to go there, but it sounds pretty, someplace my mother would have ended up.

I tell myself to be quiet. I have no idea where my mother would have ended up. She'll be nothing but a stranger. She could have driven into Bridgeport countless times for shopping or lunch with friends or old colleagues, and I never would have known if I'd seen her two inches away from me. The photo Dad showed us the night he confessed what he'd done proved I'm her daughter, our features identical, but that doesn't mean I'd know her on a crowded sidewalk, know her likes and dislikes. Just because I'm a chocoholic like Jack doesn't mean it's something I inherited from her.

"It's not that I don't want to. It's that I'm not sure if what she can say will do any good. I haven't thought about it long enough to decide if I want a relationship with her, and we have no fucking clue if she wants one with us. Maybe all the intel Dad collected over the years is incomplete. She could have moved on, Claire, and you need to be prepared for that."

"Moved on how? It would be easy to find out if she remarried and had more kids. We know she didn't do that."

He cuts me a look and stomps on the gas to pass a tractor going the speed limit. "That's not what I mean. She could have moved on mentally. Emotionally. Spiritually. However people move on. In their hearts. What good would it have done to hang on to us? Dad fixed it so she couldn't see us anymore."

"Yeah, that worked until we were both eighteen. Neither of us wanted to find her either, so maybe this, uncertainty, isn't only on our side. She could think we hate her, too."

"I did."

I did, too, but not as passionately as Jack. Maybe hate isn't even the right word. What is it called when someone lets you down so devastatingly you never recover? That's what it was. She let me down. Letting Dad kick her out, choosing her colleagues over us. I was her *daughter* and she didn't fight. But maybe I let her down, too. When I was old enough to push back, I never did.

I've always been weak, and the people I love paid the price.

Daisy's paying, right now, as I sit in Jack's truck. I should have gone for her weeks ago, and she's with a nanny who probably doesn't give one fuck about her. She's paid to change diapers and feed her, not to love. The same way I was brought up.

Jack reaches for my hand and twists our fingers together.

"Did you talk to Emma about what I said?" I ask reluctantly. I don't want to cause problems between them. Emma is so good for my brother. If I ruined it, I'd never forgive myself.

"I did. I was still awake when she was done drinking with you. I asked her why she didn't tell me herself, and she said she didn't need you to tell her what she already knew. You didn't cause any damage, Claire. That was all me."

"I'm sorry." It's all I can think of to say.

"You know what you can do to make it up to me?"

"What?" I ask hopefully. If I can make amends for being a crappy sister, I will do it, gladly.

"After we speak to Mom and hear her side, put it away and remarry Roman. You know it's what he wants. Put all this away, admit you love Felicity, and start building the life you wanted when you married him the first time."

"I don't know if I can."

Jack slams on the brakes, fishtailing into the middle of the road, and stunned, I brace myself with my foot against the dash. The truck skids to a stop. I'm glad no one is behind us on this stretch of road or they would have rear-ended us. He drifts to the gravel shoulder and shifts into Park. "Then what the fuck are we doing?"

"What do you mean?"

"I mean, what the fuck are we doing if this isn't going to help put this behind you once and for all?"

I grab at anything. "You and Emma—"

"Fuck that, Claire. I don't need this. I'm here for you, and if you're telling me this visit is for nothing before we even meet her, then I'm not doing it."

I scramble out of the truck, lean against the front fender, double over, and struggle to breathe. Remarry Roman. That's what I've been working toward, isn't it? Trying to find some semblance of peace that would allow me to tell him our divorce was a mistake? I need him, as much as the air I'm sucking into my lungs now, scented with soil and sun, the rolling plains, the earthy aroma of their crops dancing in the summer breeze. I need him, and I would never let myself have him because I convinced myself I was unlovable. I convinced myself that I had to leave him before he discovered it for himself and abandoned me like Mom did.

Jack stands next to me and wraps his arm around my shoulders. He's always been there for me, and I've never doubted he loves me. "You can be a good mother, even if you didn't have one. You can love Felicity with all your heart, and that will be enough."

"One day she'll leave me," I whisper into the horizon.

"Yeah, she will. That's what kids do. They grow up, and then, like us and Dad, they'll bring grandchildren back to you. It's a cycle, and you can be a part of it or not."

"Do you think Roman wants that with me?"

"He came to you for help, knowing you wanted the divorce, knowing you didn't want kids. He had other options—me, Heath and Zoey, but he chose you. Why did he do that?"

"Because he loves me." The words begin to mean something. He loves me, and he never stopped.

"I'd give you a cigar, but I already did that once and you threw up all over. Come on. I don't want to be gone all day."

I wrap my arms around his neck and hang on. He has every right to be pissed at me, to hate me, but he doesn't. "I love you, Jack."

He lifts me up off my feet and kisses my cheek. "You're a pain in the ass, but I love you, too."

We climb back into the truck, and any confidence I found on the side of the road dissipates with every passing mile. I want to meet my mother. I want to, and despite what Jack said,

I need to. He might have been able to move on with Emma without putting this behind us, but I can't. I have a feeling Emma wanted him to do this, too, and Roman will appreciate knowing I did everything I could to prevent something like what I did to him four years ago from ever happening again.

It's time I stop running.

The GPS in Jack's truck directs us straight to Mom's house. It sits on a quiet street, sandwiched between two other houses that look identical to hers. Someone mowed her grass, and flowers border the sides. A wooden rocking chair sits on a white porch, and a cat sleeps in the seat.

"Mom has a cat," I say, dumbfounded. We've never been pet people.

"You have to stop thinking you know this woman," he says, killing the engine. "You don't know a thing about her."

"I want to."

"It's not the same. What you find out, you might not like. Come on."

"What? Now?"

He turns to me, exasperated. "I didn't drive two hours to stare at her house. Do you need to pee? Should I have found a coffee place first?"

"No. I—"

"Yeah, you'll never have enough time. Come on."

"Jack."

"Come on, or I'll ring her doorbell alone, and you can explain why you stayed in the truck."

I open the truck's door, my fingers trembling, and crossing the street with Jack, my stomach is tangled into a nervous knot. "Maybe she's not home."

"The car in her driveway says that's not likely."

I follow him up the short walk to her porch. It's a tiny

house, but well-kept, the paint fresh. She's proud of the home she's created for herself, and I admire her for it. Everything Dad stole from her, she replaced with other things that would give her joy.

Jack rings the doorbell, and I clutch at his hand. No matter what happens, we'll always have each other.

I didn't search for her online, and the older woman who answers the door, her faded, ash blonde hair and her green eyes that are so like mine, surprises me. I was expecting the woman in the picture, but despite the differences, her hairstyle is the same, a bun at the back of her head.

She stares at us through the storm door glass, her eyes darting back and forth between us.

I don't know what to say. Mom sounds too familiar. Elizabeth? She's not a stranger, but she is. Mrs. Durand? I don't know if she kept Dad's last name, and I don't know what her maiden name is. Heat stains my cheeks. For as many times as I've said I missed her and wanted her in my life, I took absolutely no interest in hers.

Several uncomfortable moments pass and Jack takes control. "Mom."

She pushes the door open. Her lips tremble and her eyes fill with tears. "Jack. Claire."

He grins weakly, not sure how to interpret our mother's reaction. "Surprise."

She laughs and pulls us to her, but instead of her comforting us as I imagined she did when we were children, she cries against Jack's chest. I rub her back, telling her everything is going to be all right.

———

Things aren't all right, and they haven't been since Dad kicked her out of our house. She invites us into hers, and tentatively, I step into the living room. Beige carpeting covers the floor, and mint green paint colors the walls. There are several framed pictures of us, Jack and me, and I look around the room in awe.

"I never forgot about you," she said, echoing the words in my head. "Can I make some coffee?"

"That would be great, thank you," Jack says, his eyes glued to a picture of himself posed in his high school graduation gown, proudly holding his diploma.

She disappears down a hallway, and the sound of running water carries to us. Jack gives me the side-eye, checking in. I lift a corner of my mouth. She didn't send us away, and that had been a big fear of mine.

Ten minutes later, she returns carrying a tray. Jack relieves her of it and sets it on a white coffee table, the middle made of glass. "Thank you," she says, wiping her hands on her pants. "I'm nervous. I didn't think I'd ever see you again."

"Dad did his best, didn't he?" Jack says, sinking onto the couch and helping himself to coffee.

"Is he always so direct?" she asks me, and I could try to joke or pass it off, but her question only reminds me of how much she's missed.

"Yeah, he is."

"Your father was like that, too. It was nice. I never had to guess what he was thinking, communication was easier, but if he didn't like what he was hearing, he stopped listening. How did you know where I live?" She sits next to Jack, and she searches his face, trying to find the little boy she left behind in the man who came to find her.

"Dad told us. We've had trouble . . ." Jack fades off.

"You're wondering what to call me. Mom is okay, because

that's who I am, but if that doesn't feel right, you can call me Elizabeth. We can't pretend we're family."

"No one calls you Bess?" he asks.

"No. That was what your father called me. I would prefer you didn't use it."

"Okay. We've had some trouble, Mom," Jack says, deciding for both of us what to call her. I'm glad he took the decision out of my hands. I'm not sure what I would have chosen. "And he told us how to find you hoping it would help."

"You've had trouble with what?"

Jack presses his lips together. It's too soon to get into something so heavy.

"You kept up with us?" I ask instead, and Jack throws me a grateful look. "When Dad kicked you out, we thought you left us behind."

"I did everything I could without him knowing. I went to your high school graduations. They were large enough I wasn't seen in the crowd. I was there when Jack graduated with his MBA. I sat in the stands when you graduated with your journalism degree, Claire, and ever since I've been waiting to see your byline in the paper," she says, holding her hand out to me, encouraging me to sit in the chair next to her. "What happened?"

"I could never get my shit together."

"Is that why you've come to find me now? Jack, I saw your engagement announcement, a little late, don't you think? And Claire, two divorces and no children. Not every woman needs to have children to live a full life, but I hope it has nothing to do with what happened between your father and me."

"Everything Jack and I have done, or not done, is because of you and Dad, Mom." Jack said it, so I say it, but it feels foreign. Anything I would have chosen to call her would. "Why did you let him kick you out?"

"Your father was, and still is, a very formidable man. He accused me of cheating. He had proof, what looked to be proof, no matter the story behind the photo he shoved in front of my face. He told you about all that?" she asks.

"Yeah, he did, and we saw the photo, too. He said he apologized but you didn't accept it." Jack's voice is gruff with emotion.

"I regret that now," she says, holding my hand and wrapping hers around Jack's. "I really do. I didn't know how far your father would push it. Revenge. If I had known he was going to cut me off so completely, I would have swallowed my pride. Jealousy and guilt turned him into a stranger—certainly not the man I married. I didn't want to leave you behind and I didn't want to give up, but your father wasn't anyone I could legally confront on my own. You must know that, how powerful the Durands are. How powerful you are with your billions of dollars. It's intimidating to someone like me. My family wasn't poor, but he played on a level I couldn't win. And I didn't try." She pulls her hand from my grasp, pours coffee from a lidded carafe into a mug, and using great care, adds cream.

"Why didn't you tell him what you were really doing? He loved you. He would have helped," Jack says.

"You have to understand the atmosphere in Bridgeport around that time and in the state in general. The fear. Whenever abortion rights are threatened, there is so much pain and anger. Demonstrations turn violent, domestic abuse skyrockets. We were helping women who had nowhere to go after getting hurt. And they were getting hurt because they had nowhere to go. You grew up privileged, with choices. The women my friends and I were treating so they wouldn't go to prison for seeking illegal and unsafe abortions . . . you will never understand that kind of desperation. We didn't tell anyone not only to keep ourselves safe, but to keep our patients safe. Your dad thought he deserved to know. He didn't. He didn't trust me, and that's not my fault."

"Trust isn't easy for us," Jack murmurs.

"Trust is earned, and I thought I had when your father asked me to marry him. No one should marry someone they don't trust. If Ron had doubts, he should have come to me. He knew the kind of nurse I was. He knew what was going on. He chose to believe what he wanted to believe instead of putting together the facts. I should have accepted his apology, if only to be there to watch you kids grow up, but I didn't want to be married to a man who would believe lies instead of the woman he claimed to love."

He covers his face with his hands. "It's easier."

Mom turns on the couch and pulls his hands away, forcing him to meet her gaze. "No, Jack, it's not."

Tears drip from his eyes. He almost lost Emma believing what he told himself instead of listening to her, and I did lose Roman for the exact same reason. It was easier to believe the bad than accept we deserve the good.

"Why didn't you reach out when we were older? You said you attended our university graduations," I say, leaning over and fixing my own cup of coffee to give my hands something to do.

"I didn't know what your father told you, what lies he poisoned you with. The more time that went by, the more I believed you didn't want to hear from me, and I let it go. It was difficult to come to that conclusion, but safer for me, I think. I couldn't lose you twice."

"He still loves you, you know." Jack wipes his eyes with a napkin off the tray.

"You have a lot to learn if you think that's love, and I feel sorry for your fiancée. Do you love her?"

"With everything I have."

"Then you treat her like you do. Your father said he loved me and at the same time kicked me out. Which do you think my heart believed?"

I told Roman I divorced him because I didn't want to keep hurting him. He didn't believe me any more than Mom believed Dad. He showed me he loved me, and all I did was call him a liar. "That's why I'm divorced," I say, standing from the chair and leaning against a large picture window that looks out over her front lawn. "I left before they could kick me out."

"And that's our fault, mine and your father's. Not everyone who marries gets a divorce, and not every divorce is for nothing. People *do* grow apart, and sometimes there's nothing you can do about it. But preventing yourself from finding happiness because of the risk of that happening . . . if we all did that, no one would be happy, and what a sad world that would be. Claire, I never stopped loving you and your brother. I wasn't there for you as a mother, and you've chosen, I think, not to have your own children?"

I nod. I could untie my tubes, but with Felicity and Daisy, I don't know how beneficial that would be. I'd rather put all my energy into raising them to be the best women they can be than worry if I'm healthy enough at my age to carry a healthy pregnancy, too.

"Then you will never know how sorry I am. How sorry I am for both of you that your father's and my choices shaped what you thought family is instead of what it could be. If your father would have had a little more trust and if I would have had a little more backbone, I think things could have turned out very differently for all of us."

"Do you blame us for waiting to hear your side of the story?" Jack asks.

"Am I sad so much time has gone by? Yes. But I think the time for blame is over. I am extremely grateful that you're here." She gently tugs at the napkin in Jack's hand and wipes her eyes. "You two grew up into such fine adults. I'm sorry I wasn't a part of that."

"You were more a part of it than you'll ever know," Jack says.

"You meant that as a compliment, I think, but it's hard to take it as one. Claire, come sit and tell me what you've been doing with yourself. I want to hear everything."

I sit, and Mom links our fingers.

We spend the rest of the morning catching up, Jack having a lot more to say than me. He talks about Variant and Emma. The wedding. Trying to get pregnant. I sit silently, forty-one years of my life fitting into a few sentences.

"Will you come to the wedding?" Jack ask, our conversation winding down. Discreetly, I wake up my phone inside my purse and check how long we've been here. I need to contact Mr. St. John, but I have to speak with Roman first. If I want to keep my promise to Zeke's attorney, I don't have much time. I don't think Roman would object to me, us, raising Daisy, but we have so much to work through before I can mention it. I hurt him, and he might not be willing to give me as many chances as Emma gave Jack. Not after our already tumultuous history.

"I'd like to meet her first. Would that be okay?" Mom asks, tension pulling around her eyes. Our relationship will be a tightrope until we know each other better.

"I think she would love it. She's half the reason I'm here. The other half is Claire. I don't think I'd be here on my own."

"You're supporting the two most important women in your life, and I'm proud of you for that. Bring her by sometime. I'll give you and Claire my phone number. I don't know how comfortable I am going into Bridgeport. Not because of your father, but my eyesight isn't what it used to be, and that's a long drive." She pauses. "Claire, you're so quiet. Is something wrong?"

"No. I have a lot to say and don't know how to say it." I'd rather talk to her in private about the things I hold secret in my heart. Jack and I are close, but even he doesn't know all the hopes and dreams I have of what it would mean to me to be Felicity's mother as Roman's wife. There are some things I want to talk to Mom about that as a man, I don't think Jack would understand.

"There's time. We won't fit forty years into a morning's worth of conversation. Both of you are welcome to visit anytime. Anytime. Can you stay for lunch?"

Jack looks at me. It's my choice. "Actually, Mom, there are a few things I have to do this afternoon. We weren't sure how this would go, and there are appointments I can't postpone."

"I understand. Promise me this isn't the first and last time I'll see you."

I wedge myself next to her and lean my head against her shoulder. I'm too big and too old to fit into her lap, but it reminds me of how I held and fed Felicity in the middle of the night. I want to keep doing that.

Felicity isn't mine, but I don't feel like I belong to Mom, either. It isn't the blood that runs through our veins that connects us, it's love. And maybe that love has only been in existence for a short amount of time, but it's there, and it's true, and that's what matters.

Mom brushes her hand over my hair, and Jack sinks lower into the cushions. We sit like that for a while, speaking more in those silent minutes than we did with any of the words that were spoken aloud.

———

We say our goodbyes and promise to stay in touch, but I hesitate by the door. Mom doesn't want me to go, either, and she stands uncertainly on the porch. Jack lopes down the sidewalk, always excited to see Emma.

"I do have kids, but they're not mine." I want to tell her the whole story, but I don't have time. We still have two hours on the road, and Jack's eager to leave.

"If you say they are, then they are," Mom says. "It doesn't have to be complicated. Love doesn't have to be complicated. We twist it out of fear. I want to meet them. I want to be a grandma, in whatever way you see fit to include me."

"I want that, too." I rest my forehead against hers. We're the same height, our body type the same. My hair would be like hers if I let it grow, and our hands are identical in shape as hers grasp mine. She's my mother, and it doesn't have to be complicated if I don't want it to be. "I love you."

"I love you, too. My little baby. I missed you."

"I missed you too. I'll call soon."

"Drive carefully." She waves to Jack, and he lifts a hand, waiting for me by the truck.

"Bye."

Mom doesn't say anything, too choked up with tears, and I hurry away. I don't want to cry. If I start, I'll never stop.

"What do you think?" Jack asks, pointing the truck toward Bridgeport.

"She looked old, didn't she?"

"She's only a little younger than Dad, but we can't think we found them only to lose them again. We wasted a lot of time, but we can stop now."

"Are you going back to visit her?"

"I told her I would. She wants to meet Emma, and it meant a lot to Emma that I did this with you. Dad was to blame for most of what happened, but I think Emma was right, too. Mom should have said something, even if it was only a half-truth. That she was volunteering, or working an extra shift here and there. Mom talked like the only thing she could give Dad was nothing, but nothing is pretty difficult to accept."

"Sometimes the truth is difficult to accept, too," I say, scooting over and resting my head against Jack's shoulder.

"Yeah, but Claire, something is always going to be better than nothing, don't you think? Dad thought he had proof she was cheating. He showed her the photo. All she would have needed to say was she saved that man's daughter. Dad loved her, whether she thinks he did or not. He would have listened."

"The way you listened to Emma when she kept telling you she and Raff are only friends, or the way I listened to Roman when he told me the cost of our marriage wasn't worth me not wanting children? We can't pretend to know what was really between them. We don't know, and after forty years what they say will be diluted by time and their own view of how things ended. We need to stop using them as an example or as an excuse. Emma loves you, and you going off like you did at lunch the other day—you can't do that anymore. Mom and Dad both played a part in their marriage crumbling. It wasn't all her and it wasn't all him, but if you don't put Raff and Emma's friendship in a lockbox and throw it into Cavern Lake, it will be all you."

A quiet mile goes by, and he says, "You're right, and all Roman ever did was love you. You never stayed to work it out and if you don't figure out your own heart, Roman will walk away, and it will be all on you, too," Jack says, flexing his hand against the steering wheel. There's nothing but farmland, but it's soothing, the open space. I should get out of the city more.

I sigh. "Yeah, it's all on me. I have a lot of apologizing to do."

"An apology doesn't mean anything if the actions aren't

behind it. I'll put Raff and Emma's friendship away, once and for all, but it's not that they're friends, it's that I had a belief he was better for her than me. When I act on it instead of talking with her, I take away her choices. She wants to be with me, and she has for a long time. I need to let her. Therapy has been really eye-opening, Claire. Mom and Dad did more to me than only how it looks on the outside. If Roman wants to be with you, you don't have any right to tell him he doesn't. He knows his own mind."

"I didn't want to keep hurting him," I whisper.

"You thought Mom left you behind, and you took that personally. Why wouldn't you? We were children, but it didn't have anything to do with us. She still loved you from the second he kicked her out. She proved that to you today. Roman never stopped loving you either, and it hurt him to live without you. Mom and Dad fucked us up, and now that we've met Mom, now that we know their truth on both sides, we can put that in the lockbox too, and throw it into the lake."

We drive into the Bridgeport city limits, skyscrapers cutting through the sky. This is our home, this city with all its energy. This city with all its possibilities. For the first time in a long while, I'm excited. We'll clear Roman's name, rebuild our life together, and raise our children.

"So," my brother says, casting a side-long glance at me. "Did you find out what Zeke left you?"

I blink in surprise. I thought Emma would have told him. She's careful not to blur the line of our friendship and her relationship with Jack, and I'm grateful she knows when to keep to herself or if she should interfere. Raff and Veronica had trouble after the police rescued her from Blaise Barker and his family, and she believed things about Raff that weren't true. They wouldn't be together now if Emma hadn't urged Veronica to give him a chance to explain.

Emma's a wise one, and I'm thankful we're sisters.

"Yeah, actually. I did."

"Do you want it?"

I lean back into my seat and picture the smiling red-headed little girl. When the photo was taken, I bet no one knew what kind of future would be in store for her.

"With all my heart."

CHAPTER THIRTEEN

Roman

"Are you going to question him?" I ask, tamping down the hope that's zipping along my skin. This could be it. This could be the big break I've been waiting for. "And why haven't the cops?"

"Courtney said she didn't say anything because good ol' Pres has done a little time. B & E, grand theft auto. He's on probation now, for selling weed. You were a few steps up for Brielle. It's no wonder her parents were thrilled when she met you."

"He doesn't sound like the type Bri would fall for."

Raff chuckles. "I'd like to see you choose who to fall in love with. You wouldn't be here, would you?"

"I guess not." Claire was my first and only choice because of our past, because of the future I still want with her.

"Some women like bad boys, and I'll question him later tonight. He fixes cars out of his mother's garage during the day and after he closes up shop, hangs out at a bar not far from the fast food place where I met Lulu. First, I want to try to reconstruct the night Brielle went out with her friends. Her autopsy puts her death between midnight and four, but the drive to Cavern Lake is a little under six hours. I want to know if she was killed here, if she went with him willingly and they fought on the road and he killed her on the shoulder of the highway, or if they made it to Cavern Lake."

"What does it matter? Who cares where she was killed?"

"If she got into a car and rode with whoever killed her all the way to Cavern Lake, she knew him and was comfortable spending that much time with him in an enclosed space—say, for instance, Preston. If he killed her here and then drove her body out there to dump it, that means it could be anybody. A stranger dragging her into a vehicle from the street."

I shake my head. "That doesn't jibe with how she was killed. Strangulation is personal, a crime of passion. She knew him, and he was pissed at her for something. It's why the cops want me for it so badly."

"Okay, not a stranger, but maybe a guy at one of the bars she went to was hitting on her and she blew him off. Maybe he's had his eye on her for a while—a customer at the diner who never forgot her. Men have such fragile egos these days."

"She didn't text me or check in all night. I don't think she planned to be out long. She only went to make me happy, and I only encouraged her so if I broke it off with her, she'd still have her friends."

"Big of you," Raff says, backtracking into the kitchen.

"No point in lying. I love Felicity, but her birth made everything real. I didn't want to marry a woman I didn't love. I was comfortable with Bri. She made me laugh, and I could be myself around her. But I never felt like someone punched me in the gut whenever I looked at her, not the way seeing Claire makes me feel. She steps into the room, and there is nothing else. Nobody else. For four years, I felt like I was starving to death."

I lift my daughter out of the baby chair to feed her while we go over Brielle's last few hours on this earth. I wish I could be more valiant about it, heroic. That I was helping him solve her murder only to see the maniac pay for the crime, not for me to clear my name. No one likes looking like an asshole, and no one likes feeling like one, either.

"I understand. If I had wanted to settle, I could have married Emma and lived half a life. We both deserved better, and since we held out, we found it. Only you can decide how long you can survive on scraps."

I follow him into the kitchen and hold Felicity out to him. I'm comfortable with her and take it for granted everyone else is too. I place her in his arms, and he wants to object, stiffening, but it's easier to mix a bottle if I'm not holding her. I fill a bottle with lukewarm tap water and add formula. Zoey and Claire ordered so many cans Felicity will transition to solid food before we run out. "I don't plan on surviving on scraps. Claire doesn't have a problem with me, she has a problem with babies and Felicity. I have to convince her to talk to me, decide if we can work past it. It's the same shit she divorced me for, but the main reason I'm here isn't because I love her and she's the only one who can help me. She's letting me be here, and whether or not she admits it, that's a real big clue she wants to try again."

"Maybe she doesn't want you to go to prison for a crime you didn't commit."

"She believes I'm innocent. I told her I didn't do it, and she believed me without an ounce of doubt."

"She doesn't have to be in love with you to believe that. I don't believe you're guilty, either, and I'm not in love with you."

"Funny. Just for that, you can feed her." I push the bottle at him, and reluctantly he takes it from me and nudges the clear plastic nipple between her lips. She watches him with huge blue eyes. I'm waiting for them to turn deep brown like her mother's. Brielle was beautiful, but it wasn't her looks that shined. She was happy and I wanted that happiness to rub off on me. It never did.

I wake up Claire's laptop. Brielle's profile didn't sign me out, and I scroll to the top of her feed. "What are we looking for here?"

"You'll have to dig around in my notes. Lulu, Ana, and Courtney all had the same story, so I'm going to trust my instincts and believe they told me the truth. The first bar they met at was a little hole in the wall called Last Call. Why didn't you give her money? They could have partied somewhere classier, gone downtown in a limo and had a real girls' night out."

"I did. I asked her to quit her job, but she said she wasn't comfortable with that unless she had access to some money. I opened a checking account and dumped a hundred grand in it. We were always together, and I bought her everything she and Felicity needed, but she said she wanted to get her hair cut and buy some new clothes. The pregnancy messed with her figure, and nothing she had fit right anymore. She didn't have much in savings, and I understood. I didn't argue with her at all."

"Was she only a signer or was the account in her name, too?"

"The account was in her name too. We went to the bank together and Bri gave them her social security number. She was excited. She said the account would give her credit score a boost."

"You trusted her not to clean it out. She could go into the bank, withdraw all of it. She had that kind of access."

"Yes, but if she had needed that kind of money, I would

have given it to her. All she had to do was ask—she didn't need to steal it."

"Have you looked at the balance since she disappeared?"

"I haven't had a reason to, and no one knew about it besides us. I never told anyone, and I doubt she would have. The cops stopped by her apartment and asked me a few questions after I reported her missing, but I didn't mention it to them, either. I didn't think it was important. You talked to her family, did they say something?"

"No, but I think her parents, her mom, especially, were looking at the bigger picture. She wouldn't have cared about a hundred grand. Your family's worth billions."

I wince. "The stock market hit us a little bit over the past few years. My parents don't have as much as they used to."

Raff *tsks*. "You should talk to Heath. He's like Midas."

"Yeah. I got other things on my mind at the moment."

"Like logging into your account. Look and see where she used her debit card that night. It will help put their evening together. What do I do now?" he asks, pulling the nipple out of Felicity's mouth. The bottle's empty. I may need to start mixing her more.

"Prop her on her shoulder. She'll burp a little and fall asleep. The nurses at the hospital said the formula is a good match for her tummy. She never spits up."

"That sounds lucky," he says, setting the empty bottle next to his file and gently positioning her against his chest.

"It is. You sure you don't want one of those?"

He scowls. "Why? I've got yours, and pretty soon, I'll have Emma's. The earth has only so many resources, you know."

Chuckling, I search for the bank and click on the sign-in link. At the appointment, we set up online banking, and I log in using the username and password Bri created. I have my own personal account, but it's frozen along with my savings and all my money market accounts. I'm surprised they didn't find this one when they ran a check of all my assets, but maybe they left it alone and they're monitoring it, hoping to draw me out.

"Will you be happy with that?" I ask, clicking on Account Home.

Raff answers, something slick, I think, about liking to do other things at night than feed babies, but I stare at the balance and it's lost in my shock. "There's thirty cents in here."

He looks over my shoulder. "When did she drain it?"

I click on Account Activity, and my stomach churns. "She withdrew ninety-five thousand dollars the night she disappeared. That explains why it's not frozen with my other accounts. It's empty."

"She found a branch that was open after business hours?" he asks, reaching over my shoulder and using the touchpad to scroll through the account activity.

"There's one in a grocery store near her apartment. They close when the store does."

"Convenient."

"Yeah. It's one of the reasons why we chose it."

"Okay, according to the withdrawal time, she hit it up right before it closed at nine. I'm surprised they had enough cash on hand to fulfill her request. I'll go talk to them. She may have needed to call ahead and tell them what she planned to do."

"She might not have withdrawn cash. Maybe she requested a money order or cashier's check."

"If that's the case, then we're looking for someone who cashed it. They may or may not be the same person who killed her. Lulu, Ana, and Courtney said they met up with her, so start from the beginning. What time did she leave your apartment?"

"About six. She was dawdling. She didn't want to go. In retrospect, I suppose it seemed like I was pushing her out the door, but after Felicity's birth, she didn't go anywhere. I didn't want her to feel cooped up, and after five weeks of us being together in her little apartment, I needed the space too."

"Think back now, really think. Was she dawdling because she didn't want to go, or was she dawdling because she was scared?"

I watched her do her hair and makeup that night. She hadn't lost all the baby weight, but she'd ordered a few things online and her breasts filled out the new dress she wore. She caught me eyeing her and wanted to have sex, but I was concerned I'd hurt her and told her we should wait for her six-week checkup. Heat crawls up my neck. "I think she didn't want to go. She was all over me, asking me to take her to bed."

"She didn't seem nervous about leaving Felicity?"

"No. I drove Bri and Felicity home from the hospital, and we were together every second after that. Bri slept a lot, and I did more than my share of changing and feeding Felicity. Bri knew I would take good care of her and that we would be fine. She said she'd be back in a couple of hours. I told her to have a good time and kissed her goodbye."

"Did she drive herself?"

"Yeah."

"Where's her car?"

"I . . . don't know. I reported her missing and lost track of it. It completely slipped my mind when her body was found."

"I'll call the city's impound lot. But back to Brielle. She wasn't scared to leave, so chances are someone intercepted her that night. Someone who knew she had money."

"Preston sounds like a good bet."

"If she was in love with him, maybe she withdrew it to help him. Did she use the card at Last Call?"

I scroll, but I don't need to go very far. There aren't a lot of transactions to search through. "Yeah. For eighty-two dollars."

"Is that the only charge there?"

"Yeah."

"She probably opened a tab and paid the whole thing when they left. The next place the girls said they went to is a sports bar called The Dugout. She like baseball?"

I shrug. "She never watched a game while we were together."

"Did she use her debit card?"

"Yeah. They might have gotten something to eat. The charge there was for a hundred and fifty."

"Does it say what time that was?"

"Eight-fifteen."

"Can I put her down somewhere?" Raff asks, rubbing Felicity's back.

"Are you sure you don't want to keep her?" He looks very comfortable with a baby in his arms. Very comfortable.

"If I wanted one of my own, I would have one. We're good. We don't want to do something we might regret later. They're a big commitment and Nic and I have enough irons in the fire."

"You can lay her on the couch. She's not rolling over yet. Will she miss *Rise and Shine, Bridgeport!?*"

"She says she won't," Raff says, settling Felicity on the couch and holding his hands over her little body as if she were going to spring up and land on the floor. "But she doesn't have to quit until I officially start campaigning. That won't be for a few months yet, and right now she can still host the show and do the things we need to do. The mayor's wife is prepping her, introducing her to the women's groups and whatnot. I think she enjoys being a part of something bigger than herself."

"That's what any of us want, isn't it? To feel a part of something big, something meaningful? It's why a lot of people have children."

"I suppose, but I fell in love with Nic and all I want is her."

He clears his throat. "Anyway, I needed my hands free. I don't remember the last place Lulu said they went. There's about half an hour between Brielle paying at The Dugout and when she went to the bank and withdrew that money. Look through her social media account, see if you can find any pictures. The debit charges are good, but if a creeper picked her up, her banking history won't tell us that."

"Right. You fell hard," I say, clicking the tab to Brielle's social media window.

"No other way to go."

There are several posts on her wall, prayers, friends saying they miss her. Some thoughts directed at me, nice ones, hoping Felicity and I are okay, some nasty ones wanting to know what I did to her. I could easily have gone out with Brielle and her friends that night or turned the evening into our first date night after the birth of our daughter and let her parents babysit Felicity. I scroll past all that and try not to let it get to me.

Finally, I find the night two and a half weeks ago. She posted some selfies of herself, one with a pout and a caption that says, "Missing my babies! Love you, Felicity and Roman!" and lots of blowing heart emojis and the one that's crying.

Raff studies the screen over my shoulder, a hand braced against the counter's edge. "She's pretty. I can see why you'd go home with her."

"It wasn't only her looks, it was her personality. She always had a glow, you know, but if something made her happy, she sparkled, and I needed that so badly."

"Claire's never been happy, you know that. Same as her brother. Emma's helping Jack find what he needs, but it's a process and she's been hurt. A selfie isn't going to tell us much. There's nothing in the background, and I can't tell where she is. Keep going."

"She was never happy," I agree, scrolling. "I was a stupid jackass and thought I could change it."

"There's one of the four of them," Raff says pointing, identifying each woman in turn. "Lulu, Ana, and Courtney. They asked a server to take it. The timestamp says they're at Last Call, but we need something where we can see other people. Do they get up and dance? You did, more than you know."

I did make Claire happy, but it wasn't enough. I chew over that as I click through the pictures. At one point, they do dance on a small dance floor near a couple of pool tables, a few men ignoring them to actually play. Brielle is laughing with Lulu and Ana. Courtney must have taken the photo—she's missing from the group. No one is hanging out near the dance floor who doesn't look like they belong there.

"That's it for Last Call," I say, clicking out of the thread.

"They spent more time at The Dugout. They had a meal there."

I open the next set of pictures. Lots of selfies of Brielle with her friends singly and pictures of her friends that she's not in because she's holding the phone. Despite me having to encourage her to go, she looks like she's having fun, and my guilt fades. She'd needed to reconnect; I did a good thing.

Raff motions for me to keep going.

Another person joins them at their table, and I abruptly stop. A man is sitting so close to Brielle she's practically in his lap. His shirt is streaked with grease, and tats cover every inch of skin on his arms. She's snuggling into his side, and he's kissing the top of her head.

"That must be Preston," I murmur. "He's completely in love with her."

"And she with him. I'm surprised Courtney posted this picture. I doubt Brielle knew," Raff says.

"If she was in love with someone, why was she dating me?

Why did she let herself get pregnant? He couldn't have liked she gave me a baby."

"You have to ask? I bet that night he pocketed ninety-five thousand reasons."

"She wasn't like that."

"That doesn't mean he's not. Maybe he thought she owed him for dumping him."

"It doesn't look like she did," I say, clicking through to another picture of Preston, his hand possessively cupping Brielle's breast through the thin material of her sundress. She's leaning into his touch. I wouldn't have asked her out if I'd known she had a boyfriend, but she didn't say a fucking word.

"You said you were with her all the time. How did she find time to keep her relationship with him going on the side?"

"She kept her job until she was about six months along. The first year we were together, she was at the diner fifty hours a week. I stayed at my penthouse when she worked her shifts."

Raff straightens and trickles a couple fingers of whiskey into his glass.

Instead of succumbing to a smoke break on the balcony, I nudge mine over and he does the same. I sip gratefully.

"Then it's only been the past five months or so she hasn't seen him much. You couldn't have been with her every minute."

"Well, no. No couple can be. She went grocery shopping, visited her family, brought her car for an oil change—"

"I bet Preston does a helluva job."

"Fuck you. The point is, she had time here and there. Despite what Ana said, we weren't always screwing, especially toward the end of her pregnancy. She was uncomfortable. I liked being with her. I'm not going to apologize for that."

Raff drains his glass. "Is Felicity yours?"

I don't need to think about my answer. "I don't care who her father is. She's mine."

He raises his eyebrows. "Preston might care. His family might care. Now that you know what Claire and Jack are dealing with, Felicity might care."

Pissed, I finish off my glass too. "Fuck. How did this get complicated?"

"It's always complicated when a woman is fucking two men at once. Is there anything else in the pictures?"

There are a lot more of Brielle with Preston, and from the position he's sitting in one, I think his hand is up her skirt. "I wonder if her not wanting to go was an act. I swear to God, though, if I would have said I didn't mind if she stayed home, she would have."

"She was torn between the love of her life and your money. Not so hard."

"You don't know her like I did."

"She was swapping spit with a grease monkey and popping out a kid who may or may not be yours. You didn't know her at all."

I bury my face in my hands. He's not wrong. Looking at Brielle in these photos is like looking at a stranger.

"You need to lay low," he continues, gathering up the papers lying scattered on the island. "All these photos do is give you more motive. The cops must have seen them—her profile is set to public. I'm going to talk to Preston tonight. I think I know where that half an hour went between The Dugout and when she withdrew that money."

I slide off the barstool and follow him to the elevator. "I don't know how to thank you for all you're doing. You know, since I met her outside the bar, I really thought she was in love with me."

"Did you want her to be?" he asks.

The doors slide open.

"I needed something."

"We all do. But we have to be careful where we look for it . . . and where we find it. I'll let you know as soon as I can what I dig up. Preston knows something. And I'll look for her car. Have you called her cell? We're assuming it went into the water with her, but it could be around somewhere. You paid for her cell service right? Did you combine your plans?"

"Yeah, it was easier to pay one bill."

"Then you have access to her phone records. Look up her last few texts and phone calls. Maybe something will pop."

"I will. Thanks."

"Keep your chin up. You didn't do it, and we'll find out who did." He steps into the elevator. The doors hide him from view and it carries him to the lobby.

I check on Felicity who's sleeping peacefully on the couch, her little chest moving up and down with her shallow breathing. I look for my features, but she's a baby and doesn't look like anything but a baby with a hint of Brielle. Maybe she's mine, but I can't order a paternity test until this is over. It doesn't matter if she is or not. I'll still love her, as much as I want Claire to. More.

I move her to the crib in Claire's room and lie on the bed. The bed we shared as husband and wife. It's really fucking sad to admit that in my forty-eight years on this earth, only eleven months of them were happy.

She finds me in the bedroom and stands in the doorway, her skin flushed, her eyes sparkling.

I wish like hell I could trust what I see, but I've done that before and I won't let her break my heart again.

CHAPTER FOURTEEN

Claire

He watches me cautiously, and I begin to doubt. Doubt he loves me, doubt he'll forgive me for what I did to him, to our marriage, to our future. I begin to doubt we'll be able to build a family with Felicity and Daisy. Maybe I'm too late. Maybe what I put us through, the divorce, Brielle, Zeke, maybe all that was too much weight for the delicate relationship we have now.

"Roman," I say, his name like a prayer on my lips. It used to be mine. The faith. The love. The security.

"I'm sorry. I know you don't want us in your room," he says, sitting up. "I'll bring Felicity upstairs."

"No. Please don't." My voice is too loud and I don't want to wake her. "Please don't," I say again, my voice softer. "I want you here."

"You haven't wanted me since I asked you for children. Don't pretend things have changed."

"I don't have to pretend. Can we talk?" I want to make love, but Roman's too defensive, too hurt, to let me touch him. I've always shown him how I felt with actions, but I need to speak now or he'll never believe me.

His gaze rakes my face, searching for a sign I'm lying. He's always been able to read me. I taught him he needed to if he wanted to know how I was feeling. How miserable he must have been during our marriage.

He doesn't say anything, and I step over to the crib and rest my hand on Felicity's tummy. "I'm sorry for what I said. I would never hurt her."

Rolling off the side, he stands from the bed. "I know, but what you don't understand is there are many ways you can hurt someone. You can say you want her, say you love her, but if you don't mean it, she'll know. And she'll hurt. Just like I did."

I reach for his hand and urge him to come with me. He follows me down the hall and into the living room. Felicity's toys are everywhere. It used to be a nightmare for me, thinking about babies and how much they need. Not money, but time, love. I was always afraid I'd never be enough. No, not that I wouldn't be enough, but that they would somehow know and grow up only half the person they could have been.

We reach the middle of the room, and I squeeze his hand, try to smile. I love him so much and to have him here, to have this second chance, it's a miracle.

All I can do is stare.

"Where have you been?" he asks. He used to love me too, and he says he still does, but I don't know how. I haven't given him anything to love.

"Do you mean that literally? Figuratively?" I try to lighten the mood.

"At all. Ever since the night we met, I've been trying to find you. You're like an enigma, a fucking ghost. I think I finally understand, even a little part of you, and you disappear. Where have you been?"

I brace myself. I have to learn to share. I have to learn to communicate with words or I'll bottle up all my emotions and explode like I did in Dad's living room. Roman needs me to speak. Our children will need me to speak.

I take a deep breath and lick my lips. "You know my mother left me and Jack when we were small. I never told you why or where she went mostly because I didn't know, not because I didn't want to. My father thought she was cheating. She wasn't. Around that time, abortion was legal but state government over-turned it and the clinic in Bridgeport closed. Women were desperate and went underground. My mother was an obstetric nurse and she started treating women who were hurt. To protect her patients, herself, and the people working with her, she kept it a secret. My dad had her followed and he brought back evidence."

Roman nods, listening intently. He knows some of it. I shouldn't be surprised. Someone told him something. Maybe Jack. Maybe Raff. I know he's been coming here to update Roman on the case.

"He kicked her out. A year later he learned the truth, and he asked her to take him back. She said no. As punishment, he kept us from her, and we grew up without her."

"That must have been difficult for everyone," he says, watching me. Always watching me.

"You don't know how much something like that affects you until it stops you from living your life. I grew up thinking my mother didn't love me, that she didn't want to be my mom and I blamed myself. So did Jack. You spend your whole life convincing yourself you're unlovable, and it's impossible to get past that, you know?"

"Why didn't you talk to me? I knew you loved me. You

might not have said it often, but I could feel it, and that's why giving you the divorce you wanted was so damned hard. I didn't know why you wanted it, and you wouldn't tell me. You blamed it on me wanting kids, but that wasn't it, was it? It was only an excuse."

I pick up a stuffed teddy bear off a chair near the balcony doors, his head flopping on a loose neck, his butt filled with beads. "It wasn't an excuse. I was terrified to be a mother. I didn't grow up with one, didn't know how to be one. Didn't know if I could love a baby the way a mother should, and I'm scared as hell that one day Felicity will look me straight in the eye and tell me I'm not her mother. It's going to break my heart, I know it will."

"She *will* tell you that."

Shocked, I whip my gaze to Roman's face. He's tired, the investigation running him ragged. "Why would you say that?"

"Because it's true. You're not her mother, and when she's a teen and needs to rebel and lash out because that's what teens do, that will be the first thing out of her mouth to try to hurt you. Her mother was *murdered,* and that's not something she'll ever be able to forget. That little girl in there is going to live with a helluva burden. Just like you. And you're right. If you choose to have children, that's what you sign up for, but the pain is worth the love, isn't it?"

"I don't know. I never had the love to go with the pain."

Roman approaches me, slowly, waiting for me to flinch or back away. I want him close to me, need him near me, and I wait, unblinking. He frames my face in his hands. "Yes, you did. For the short time you allowed me to, I loved you with everything I had."

"It's not the same."

He drops his hands. "No, I guess it's not. I can't pretend to know what growing up without parents is like. My parents have always had my back, and our divorce crushed them. They knew how happy you made me, and the year I spent with them after it went through, my mother couldn't stop asking me if I was okay. They adored you."

"I hurt a lot of people, and I'm sorry for that." I like Roman's parents, too, and the honeymoon we had in Florida was one of the happiest times in my life.

"Where were you this morning? You're always running off. I appreciate the text you sent me last night—even if Emma made you do it."

"Yeah, she did. She told me Raff sent me your number. After I said those nasty things to you about Felicity, I went to my father's and this morning, Jack and I went to see Mom."

He sags in disappointment. "Why do you insist on doing things like that alone? I wish you would talk to me. That must have been extremely hard on you. Are you okay?"

"Last night I didn't think I would be. Jack was there, having a drink with Dad like the past forty years never happened. I was so angry and hurt. I hated Jack for being able to put it away. But why wouldn't he? In the end, he got Emma. No hard feelings, right?" I ask, still bitter he's had it easier than me.

"I think Emma had more to do with that than Jack or your dad," Roman says, brushing his finger down my cheek. "If she were a different kind of person, Jack might not have been so lucky. Did you have a fight?"

"Yeah. I said some horrible things and he said some smart ones. It wasn't all Emma. He's been able to let a lot of it go. I should have, too, when I found you, but Mom leaving me behind was too deep inside me for you to fix. I hated him for that, for how easily he set the past aside."

"Maybe not so easily. Jack has never been a sharer—he's like you. Keeps things to himself and suffers in silence. I'm willing to bet Emma forced him to open up. I didn't play hardball with you. Maybe it's been my fault all along, trying to make you happy and doing whatever it took, no matter how much it hurt me. I didn't want you to leave me, but it's what you wanted and I didn't fight for you. Was that a mistake?"

Helplessly, I shake my head. "I don't know. I married Zeke hoping you'd come to my rescue, tell me you loved me, and that you wouldn't sit by while I married someone else. But you didn't, and at our reception, I sat in the bathroom and cried, wondering if I'd made the biggest mistake of my life. No, second biggest. I should never have asked you for a divorce."

"You broke my heart," he whispers, his hand lingering near my face.

"And it breaks mine hearing it," I say, stepping closer. "Will you kiss me?"

"Why? I wanted this with you yesterday, but like you always do, you ran off instead of talking things through. It might have been a mistake to let you have your way, but it's not about us anymore. I have Felicity now and everything I do will affect her. If you can't promise both of us forever, I don't want anything to do with it. That's the way it has to be."

"I understand," I say, and I do. Everything I do, *we* do, from this point forward will affect Daisy, too.

Frustrated, he runs his fingers through his hair. "I don't think you do. Your whole life has been about you and how your dad hurt you kicking out your mom, and you spread that hurt everywhere. You can't control it and haven't bothered to try. I don't want you hurting Felicity, and I refuse to let you turn me into the villain. She's going to grow up looking up to you and loving you, because if I tell you right now that I love you and want us to remarry and you say yes, you will be her mother—in every way. So you need to think really carefully about how you want the next fifty years to play out."

"You want us to remarry?" I ask faintly. I thought we were

talking about dating, getting to know each other. Possibly moving in together and raising Felicity and Daisy as a family, and in a few years, tentatively talk about remarrying after I earn back his trust.

"Jesus Christ," he says, pulling me to him, his dress shirt crisp, the wrinkles not quite smoothed out from the shipping. "Where did you think all this was headed? All or nothing, Claire. It's always been all or nothing, and if all you're going to keep giving me is nothing, I don't want it anymore."

"I didn't think you'd risk it again."

"I'm not. You're not listening to me. If we remarry, that's it. I won't give you another divorce. I know how to tie one up in court for years. *Years*, Claire. If we remarry, and you want out, I will make the rest of your life a living hell. Just so we're clear. I won't let you leave me again."

Tears fill my eyes, and I bury my face against his chest. I love him so much, and I need him more than I ever let myself believe. "I'm so sorry, Roman. I'm so sorry for everything."

"The last four years have had some good stuff in them," he says, wrapping his arms around me. "I won't regret the tiny bit of happiness I found with Brielle, or the daughter she gave me when Felicity was born. Maybe you learned something marrying Zeke, maybe you didn't, but I'm not going to live with guilt and I'm not going to live with your guilt, either. Clean slate. If you can promise me that, then *you* kiss *me*."

A clean slate. A clean slate means no more secrets.

I couldn't tell Roman what my father did to my mother. I didn't know and I can't consider it a secret, but there are things I didn't tell him when I should have and there are things he doesn't know now.

"Then there's something I have to tell you," I say.

He drops his arms and steps away, and I didn't think I could hurt any more than I already have.

"Of course there is, because nothing can ever be simple. Should you have told me five years ago? Before we got married the first time? Fuck knows you kept enough from me. Christ. What is it, Claire?"

He's so angry, and if he doesn't want me after I tell him, so be it. I didn't come this far to turn into a coward.

"I had my tubes tied before Zeke and I got married. He had his own kids and didn't care about having more, or so I thought. I'm old now and I'm not interested in trying to get pregnant. If you were still hoping for that, then I apologize. It *is* something we should have talked about before we married the first time."

"I gathered as much, but thank you for telling me. I was so in love with you, I wanted everything a man can have from a woman. That included children. But we're different people now, in a different situation. As much as I'd love Felicity to have siblings, I would rather have you. I told you before, and I need you to start listening. I never would have chosen children over our marriage. That was your choice, not mine."

"Okay. I'm listening. But this is hard for me. Can we have a drink? Is Felicity okay? I really need a drink."

"I'll go check on her and meet you in the kitchen."

I hurry through the living room toward a brief moment of salvation. Two glasses are already on the island near a bottle of good whiskey. Raff must have been here earlier—he favors the label. I pour some into a glass, Roman's and my wedding date etched into the side. I down the two inches, the alcohol blazing down my throat and settling in a warm pool in my belly. God, do I need this. I do it again and lean against the island, pressing the glass to my cheek. Roman walks in holding Felicity who's bright-eyed and smiling. He must have changed her diaper— she smells like baby powder.

"Can I hold her?" I don't have the right to ask. Not after I told Roman I couldn't love her enough to be her mother. I don't know why I said it except at the time I thought it was true. "I won't hurt her. I promise."

"I wouldn't ask you to remarry me if I ever thought that. You're too hard yourself. You've shouldered your mother's leaving all on your own, but she didn't leave because of you. You know that now, don't you?" He positions Felicity against my shoulder, and I hold her to me, an arm under her butt and my hand caressing the back of her head. She snuggles into me.

"I know, but she didn't come back, and I blamed myself for that, too."

"She didn't take your dad back because he was an asshole, and he proved it in his very next breath. I'm sorry if you're going to get mad at me for saying it, but he had no right to do what he did. Cutting her out of your lives was despicable, and it had nothing to do with you as a person. You have a lot of love to give, and I hope you give it to me and Felicity. It's all I ever wanted, you know. It's all I ever wanted."

As he speaks, I cry into the delicate curve of her neck. This little baby depends on us to keep her safe. I want to be part of that.

He wraps both of us in his arms, and I wish we could stay here forever, but there's more he needs to know. Gently, I move away, and Roman releases me, sits on a barstool, and pours more whiskey into the glass I just used. "I know how your body speaks to me. You have more to say, and I know you don't want to say it. It's better to do it now, and if you don't feel safe holding her while we talk, you can put her in the swing."

"No. I can hold her. It's . . . how did you feel when you asked me to raise a child who wasn't mine?"

He downs the contents in the glass and frowns. "Should I have felt something? Hesitancy, maybe? I know not all women jump at the chance to raise children who aren't biologically theirs. I thought you were different. Are you telling me you won't love Felicity like you would if she was yours? That's really low, Claire. I wanted to give you kids. *She could have been yours.*"

"No, that's not what I'm saying. What if, what if I asked you to be a father to a child who wasn't yours?"

"Jesus Christ," Roman roars, and I jolt, tightening my hold on Felicity. He jumps from the barstool, his face red. Shaking, he gently lifts her out of my arms and straps her in the baby swing Zoey purchased, a bar of little stuff animals latched in front of her. He rounds on me once Felicity is settled, backing me up against the fridge, trapping me with his hands on either side of my head. His eyes hold so much anguish I turn away. "Are you telling me that between our divorce and you getting your tubes tied, you had a baby? Goddammit. Why would you destroy our marriage over something you went ahead and did anyway? Every time I think you can't hurt me more than you already have, you do it again."

"Zeke—"

"You and Zeke? *Fuck.* At least you married him, but God, Claire. Why? And where is she? Or he? What did you have?"

I push on his chest needing space, but it's like trying to move a brick wall. His eyes blaze, and his lips tremble with rage. He's never looked like this, not even when I asked for a divorce. Then it was sadness, guilt, and blame. This is fury, jealousy, and resentment. "Calm down. I told you I got my tubes tied and that wasn't a lie. I've always told you the truth. I didn't want children. That didn't change, it didn't matter who I was with." In an attempt to soothe, I rub my thumb along his jaw, the stubble scratching my skin.

"Then what? You don't throw a hypothetical out there like that for nothing."

"No, I didn't. While we were married, Zeke was dating somebody. I didn't know, and if I had, I might not have cared, either. I think, from the way his mother spoke about her, he married me to hide her, hide their relationship. They had a baby, and after our divorce, she moved in with him."

His eyes widen. "The woman he was with at the hotel, the night of the fire."

"Yes. I went to his attorney's office yesterday. He left me something in his will."

"The country house."

"What? What are you talking about?"

He huffs a laugh. "Nothing. Are you telling me he left you a baby? Can you do that?"

"Guardianship. I told his attorney I didn't want her—"

"Claire." His voice is full of disapproval.

"I know. Emma was there, and she said she and Jack would take her, and it's all a big mess."

"How old is she? Where has she been since her parents died?"

His anger recedes, and I relax. He still has me trapped against the fridge, but he's listening and I explain what I know about Lacey's family, my conversation with Jill, and not wanting her until this morning after Jack and I spoke to our mother. "It took me too long to figure it out and you can hate me for that, but I want her. I really do. And if you meant it, and you want to marry me again, the girls could grow up together."

He releases me and sinks to the floor, his back braced by cabinets hiding crackers and pasta sauce. "You have to be fucking careful what you're offering me. I want it all, and if you're going to rip it away in a moment of indecision, you better damned well tell me."

I sit between his legs, missing this man so much. From the second he drove away from me in the attorney's parking lot, all I ever wanted was this. "Do you still love me?" I whisper.

"God, Claire. I love you so much I can't breathe. These past four years, I haven't been living. I've been surviving day by day, dying little by little. Nothing could replace what we had. Not Brielle, not Felicity. I love Felicity and I will do whatever I need to keep her safe and give her a happy childhood, but that's not the same as holding you, whispering our dreams in the dark, though you never did. Everything I learned was through you showing me. Every kiss with your trembling lips, every touch with your shaking hands. What you said and what you showed me were two different things, and I knew you were lying to me when you told me you wanted a divorce. I'm sorry I listened to the wrong thing."

I straddle his thighs and he wraps his arms around me. If I had let him be strong for me four years ago, none of this would have happened.

"Kiss me, Claire," he murmurs, his lips pressed against my cheek. "I'll listen to the right thing now. Kiss me." He's hard beneath the thin layer of my panties, my skirt in a pouf over my thighs, bunching around my hips. I glance briefly at Felicity, and Roman chuckles low and smooth. "I'll only need five minutes if you promise me the rest of your life."

"You've always had it," I say and push my fingers through his hair in the way I know he loves.

"Ah, Claire, I may teach you to use your words yet," he says, and he doesn't wait for me to kiss him, yanking my body against his chest and fusing his mouth to mine.

His lips are firm, yet soft, and his whiskers scrape deliciously against my skin. I let out a sob, so grateful he can forgive me, so grateful for this second chance.

"You've always been so needy," he mumbles, his fingers searching under the material of my skirt, finding my panties. "I tried to give you what you needed, but no matter how much I gave you, it never seemed to be enough."

"It never was. I was trying to fill a space in my heart with your love that wasn't yours to fill." I lean back, my breath shuddering. "My mother still loves me, and she always has. She kept up with me and Jack. She has pictures of us and went to our graduation ceremonies. She knew Jack is engaged, knew I've been divorced. She never forgot about us, and after our visit with her this morning, I finally feel like a whole person. Do you know what I mean?"

"Yeah, I do, and I'm happy for you," he says, finding my slit. I raise slightly onto my knees, giving him space to slide his finger into me. I'm wet, and I bear down, needing him to fill me in a different way now.

"She wants to meet you and the girls," I whisper against his lips. "It would mean a lot to me if you met her, if she could be part of our lives."

"I think our daughters need a grandma."

"Our daughters," I echo in awe. That's what Felicity and Daisy will be. They'll grow up as sisters and our daughters. Tears run down my cheeks. "Roman—"

"Shh. Claire, I'm glad you found your words, but not now. Lie on the floor. I want to make love to you."

I do as he asks and wiggle from his lap and onto the tile already missing his touch. "We've never made love on the floor in here."

"We're starting a new tradition," he says and unbuckles his belt and unzips his pants. His cock springs free, and he strokes himself, pre-cum beading at the tip. "Yeah. I missed this. Take your panties off."

I do and scrunch the skirt of my dress around my waist. I know what he sees—I'm wet and swollen, my thighs trembling. I missed him so much, and before, whenever we made love, I was asking him to give me something that wasn't his to give. Now I can enjoy this and appreciate him for what we're showing each other.

He slides two fingers into me, and my muscles clench greedily.

"When was the last time you had sex?" he asks, his thumb finding my clit.

I arch my back, increasing the pressure. "When Zeke and I were married."

Surprised, he pauses. "It's been that long? The *Bridgeport Beat* was always reporting how you were going home with this guy or that guy, and every time I read a post like that, I would sink a little further into despair thinking we would never find each other again."

"It's what I wanted people to think. I didn't want anyone to know how much I was hurting inside."

"Claire, sweetheart," he says, positioning himself over my body, the tip of his cock ready to push inside me, "you don't know how happy I am to hear that."

"It's always been you," I say. He slides into me, filling me in a way I knew I would never find without him. I whimper, pressing my face against his arm. "Roman."

"Shh." He slants his mouth over mine, his tongue teasing my lips, asking me to open. I'll do whatever he wants, whenever he wants. He spent our marriage trying to give me anything he could to make me happy, and now it's my turn. "Christ, I missed this. Nothing compares to making love with someone you truly love. Nothing," he says as he moves, the tip of his cock hitting my center, sending shivers up and down my skin. He pulls out halfway and his fingers find my clit. "I want you to come for me. I want to hear you moan. You always sounded so cute."

I laugh weakly, an orgasm building in my belly. "Roman, I need you deep inside me when I do."

"Then you need to do some of the work."

I reach between our bodies, and briefly, our fingers meet

over my clit. His dark eyes smolder with arousal, and love, possession, and determination are set in his strong features. He braces his hands on the floor on either side of my head and begins to pump, my hips desperately matching the rhythm of his thrusts. He's buried as deeply inside me as he can be, and I come, relief and happiness coursing through my body.

Roman uses my orgasm, his cock slicking in and out of me, and tears escape from my eyes and run down my temples. He buries himself to the hilt and comes, filling me with hot gushes of cum. He'll never get me pregnant and that will be another regret I'll need to let go of. We're past that now, and there's no point in being sad whenever we make love. It was a decision I made, and like so many other things in my life, I have to let go to move forward.

He lowers himself on top of me and kisses away my tears. "The kitchen floor is less than romantic, but I hope it was good for you."

I press my face against his neck, his scent as intoxicating as it is comforting. "I know you don't want to keep hearing it, and I'll stop saying it, but I'm sorry."

"Claire, look at me."

I rest my head on the floor, his fingers tangled in my hair. "What?"

"Do you love me?"

"Yeah, I do."

"Then the rest has been, and always will be, a bonus. All I have ever wanted is you. From the moment we met at that masquerade ball, the only thing I have ever wanted is your heart. Give it to me, Claire. Be my wife again and give us the life we should have had the first time we married."

"I wanted to ask you that," I say softly, feeling his cock stiffen inside me. I tilt my hips, asking him to move. He does, and sensitive from my orgasm, I shudder.

"Then ask."

I swallow. "I know things have been rough, and it's my fault. In the past four years we've been apart, I haven't done much growing, but what I have managed has changed my life in a way I never thought possible. I'm ready now, to give you what you need, to be the kind of person you need in a wife who will love you and stand by your side no matter what. I want you to marry me, and I promise I will never shut you out, never suffer in silence. I promise to love Felicity as if she were my own and be there for both her and Daisy in whatever way they need me to be. Marry me, Roman, and I'll give you the life we should have had when we first married."

"Yes," he says, "yes," and we make love, promising each other forever, only this time, it truly will be forever. I know what my life is like without him, and I don't want to live that way again.

We lie on the floor, spent and sticky, until Felicity cries. She's hungry and tired of swinging.

"I'll feed her," I say, sitting up.

"No, I will. You told Zeke's attorney you'd get in touch with him today and it's almost five o'clock."

"Shit." I scramble to my knees and search for my panties. Roman's cum leaks out of me, wetting the insides of my thighs.

"Hey," he says, grabbing a fistful of my hair.

I pause. "What?"

"I love you."

Felicity lets out another wail.

"I love you too," I say, and kiss him hard, tightly hooking my arm around his neck. "But your daughter needs you."

"Yeah, okay."

I put on my panties. I need a quick trip to the bathroom and I have to call Emma. I need her with me when I go to Mr. St. John's office and to Zeke's penthouse.

"Claire," he says, squeezing my arm.

"What?"

"The investigation, Brielle's murder. It's not over. There might be some rocky days ahead of us, and if you don't want—"

"I want. You didn't do it, and we need to find out who did. She deserves to rest in peace. After they release her body, we'll give her a memorial service and we'll make sure Felicity never forgets who her mother was."

He lets out a breath. "Thank you."

"Roman, I know I wasn't who you needed me to be. I'm not going to pretend we had eleven months of wedded bliss. I was mean, and I was hurt, and I made you work for every second of happiness you found with me. I know I did that to you, to us, and I'm learning I don't have to be like that. Things will be different, I promise."

Felicity cries, her little body wiggling in discomfort.

"Feed your daughter," I say, resting my hand against Roman's cheek. "She's hungry, just like I was."

He presses a kiss to my mouth, and he lifts Felicity out of her swing, his pants riding low on his hips.

I run to the bathroom, clean up, and mist myself with a spray of perfume. I don't want to smell like sex. I brush my hair and take a deep breath. My life is changing today, in a way I won't be able to undo.

But I don't want to wind the clock back a single second. For the first time in forty-one years, the woman smiling back at me is happy.

I walk into the kitchen, and Roman's feeding Felicity. She's sucking greedily, her eyes fastened on her daddy's face. I'll need to learn to share his time and attention, but her gaze shifts to me and she smiles around the bottle's nipple, and I know it won't be so hard. I let her wrap her hand around my finger. "I'm going to call Emma to go with me. I don't know when I'll be back. A nanny's been taking care of Daisy all this time, but we can't have her here, even if Daisy's transition would be smoother."

"She'll be scared, and we'll need a lot of time to adjust. Things aren't going to be easy," he says, watching me.

I lift my chin. "I'm done running."

"Good." He pauses, his eyes boring into mine. "Come home, Claire."

I gently pull my finger from Felicity's grasp and brush a kiss over his lips. "I promise."

———

We glide to a stop in front of Variant's building, and Emma's waiting at the curb. It's past five o'clock and the sidewalk is full of people heading home. I don't see Jack, and I expected him to be waiting with his fiancée, full of questions. I didn't say anything on the way home from Lilyvale, our hearts full of our mother and the past. It wasn't the right time to divulge what Zeke left me in his will, and I thought Emma would fill in the gaps.

She gets into the truck without waiting for the driver's help, and he frowns at her in the rearview mirror. "We're in a hurry," she defends herself, laughing, and his frown melts into a reluctant smile. No one can stay mad at Emma.

"Where's Jack? I thought he'd be with you."

"He and Ron are going to a business dinner. Did you want him with us?"

"No, it's okay."

She nods and looks out the window at the passing buildings.

I'm trying to get better at speaking, voicing my thoughts and opinions. My real ones. Over the years, I developed a loud and abrasive personality, pushing people away and hiding what I truly felt. If I'm turning a corner with Roman, I need to turn a corner with everyone. Emma's played an important part in Jack's life, and, in turn, mine. She deserves the honesty a sister-in-law should give her.

"Emma." Sweat trickles down my ribs from underneath my boob. I'm nervous. I'll need a lot of practice until I'm comfortable putting myself out there. Not having the knee-jerk reaction that no one cares about me will also require a lot of getting used to, but the good things that can come from it are too great not to try.

"Hmm?" she asks, focusing her attention onto me.

"I want to thank you for knowing when to say something and knowing when to stay quiet. I haven't told Jack about Daisy because I wasn't sure what I was going to do, and I wanted to keep it to myself, think it through for myself. I didn't want to be pressured into doing something I wasn't ready to do. I spoke with Roman, and we're getting remarried. Thank you for that space."

"Staying quiet has rewards and consequences. I think we're both aware of the consequences. Daisy wasn't any of my business. She will always be between you and Roman, but please, if you need help—a babysitter or someone to talk to while you walk her to the park, anything—tell me. You have friends, good friends. I don't mean just me, but Zoey, and Mia and Haisley. Veronica. We're all here for you. And I am so happy you and Roman found your way back to each other. I could tell how much he still loves you."

"Yeah, he does. I'm lucky. My whole family is . . . because of you. You've done so much for my brother. He wasn't truly happy until he admitted he was in love with you. I apologized to him for what I said to you at the house. I don't want there to be bad feelings between us."

"Meeting your mom this morning gave him such peace. He said he wouldn't have if it hadn't been for you, but I think he would have circled around to it in his own time. He invited me to meet her, and I'm honored, really. Two months ago I thought being a part of your family was impossible. I'll treasure the time, Claire, and I know you will too."

The car pulls up to Mr. St. John's office building. "Shall we add another member?" I ask, gripping the door's handle. Anticipation settles in a huge pit in my stomach.

"I think there will always be room in our hearts for more love and laughter," she says.

The driver opens the door for us, and on trembling legs, I step onto the sidewalk.

In the elevator, I blow out a breath.

"You're doing the right thing," she says.

"I know. It's a big step for me."

"You're not in this alone."

The doors slide open and I don't have a chance to respond, but I don't know what I would have said. I know I'm not alone —I have never been truly alone, I just haven't accepted the love when I should have.

Mr. St. John is waiting with the papers I need to sign. "I'll contact your family's attorney, Miss Durand. There's still the matter of the stipend and trust."

"Don't bother with the stipend," I say, scrawling my name across the bottom of one of the forms. "I spoke with Jill. She said she would fight it, and that's fine. I don't need the money, and I don't know why Zeke said he would pay it out. The trust belongs to Daisy. I'll see to it she has access when the time comes."

Mr. St. John stands from his desk and rounds the corner. He waits until I look at him and then says, "Miss Durand, the stipend, in total, is fifty million dollars. I told you what I know of Miss Lawton's family, and you've spoken to his mother. Mr. Kavanaugh loved his daughter very much. He couldn't have known he and Miss Lawton would have their lives ended so tragically and prematurely, but he loved Daisy and he wanted Miss Lawton to know he did the only thing he could. He thought a healthy stipend would encourage you to accept guardianship."

"He was paying me to take her," I say faintly, dropping into a chair in front of his desk. "Oh, what a horrible person he must have thought I am." I cover my face with my hands, shame warming my cheeks.

"On the contrary, Mr. Kavanaugh thought highly of you, Miss Durand. He also understood your reluctance to have children, and in choosing you, took that into great consideration. The generous stipend was only meant as a persuasion. He didn't trust anyone else to raise his daughter. And due to the legalities, I'm afraid I must see to it that it's paid out appropriately and in full."

"What if I adopt her?" I ask, my throat closing with tears. It feels exactly right, and exactly what Zeke would want me to do.

"Claire, that's wonderful," Emma says, squeezing my hand in a show of support I appreciate and know I'll depend on over and over again.

Mr. St. John laughs. "In that circumstance, yes, the stipend would be null and void."

"Then you can expect to hear from my attorney within the next few weeks. Things will be a bit busy for me as we adjust, and I'll contact him as soon as I can."

"Thank you. I'll have Daisy's social worker meet you at Mr. Kavanaugh's penthouse. She'll have papers for you to sign that she'll need to file with the court. Her nanny will also be terminated, is that my understanding from our discussion yesterday?"

"Yes. Unfortunately, personal circumstances prevent me from keeping her on, though I do understand it would be easier on Daisy."

"Children are resilient. Once you establish a routine and she learns she can depend on you, I believe things will fall into place. Please reach out if you need. There are resources available."

"Thank you, Mr. St. John. I appreciate your patience."

"I think Mr. Kavanaugh is breathing a sigh of relief, may he and Miss Lawton rest in peace."

"Yes," I say, wishing I hadn't needed so much time. "I'm sure he is."

"It was nice to see you again," Emma says, standing from her chair and holding out her hand.

"And you, Miss Cox."

Emma follows me out of the office, and we stand in the empty elevator. Everyone has already gone home for the day, and it's a relief to be alone. The wall holds me up—my legs are trembling as if I just finished a day of shopping in five inch heels.

The truck and driver are waiting for us near the curb, and we settle into the backseat.

Emma says in awe, "Fifty million dollars."

I relay the address Mr. St. John gave me to the driver, and he slowly joins the traffic on the street.

"Love is supposed to be free," I say.

"Yeah, it is, but can you imagine having a child and knowing how your parents felt about her? Knowing they didn't want to be a part of her life? Don't you think that would be heartbreaking?"

"It is heartbreaking. That's what I thought about my own mother."

"I think Zeke knew that, and that's why he chose you. He

knew you would give Daisy a better life than you had. He knew you would have empathy and compassion."

"Then why the money? He knew how much he gave me in our divorce settlement. I didn't ask for that, either. He paid me off thanking me for asking for a divorce so he could be with Lacey."

"He had to put something in place in case you didn't do it. Had he discussed it with you before he changed his will, you would've told him you would and that he didn't need to make any other arrangements."

I glare. "You're too kind. I'd have told him to fuck off."

She laughs. "You would not have, and you know it."

I wilt. "You're right. Zeke and I shouldn't have married, but that's not Daisy's fault."

"She'll benefit."

"Somebody should," I mumble.

The truck glides to a stop in front of Zeke's building.

She laughs again and throws herself against me, pressing a hard kiss to my cheek. "Let's go. I want to meet my niece."

Emma scrambles out of the idling vehicle and onto the sidewalk, but I can't move a muscle. Her niece. Her easy acceptance of a stranger's child brings tears to my eyes. She gestures for me to hurry, and climbing out of the truck, I wipe my cheeks.

She turns on a heel toward the building, but I stop her. "Wait. Emma." I can't say more.

"Claire. I told you. I love your brother so much, being a part of your family is a dream come true. You don't have to thank me or cry. Just be there for me and Jack like we'll be there for you and Roman, okay?"

Sniffling, I say, "Yeah. Thanks."

"Come on," she urges, walking through the door the doorman is holding open for her. She thanks him with a squeeze to his arm, but she passes by him and doesn't see the adoration written all over his face.

Inside the elegant lobby, I relay my name to the concierge, and he calls up to the nanny to tell her to expect us. The social worker has already arrived, he said, and she's upstairs with the nanny.

My stomach is doing somersaults, and I swallow back the bitter taste of the whiskey I drank with Roman. The elevator carries us up, one excruciating floor at a time, and Emma says, "She'll love you. It might be tough as we all get to know each other, but she'll love you the way we all do."

"You must be psychic."

"I would have the same fears."

It doesn't seem right to waltz into Zeke's penthouse and take a baby home, but that's what I do. I introduce myself and Emma to Bonnie Hartman, the social worker, and she and the nanny, whose name is Catherine, give us time alone with Daisy. There's a picture of the three of them in Daisy's nursery, and she looks like her mother: shining reddish-orange hair, pale skin, and bright blue eyes. After three marriages, Zeke found what he was looking for in Lacey and their daughter, and the utter love on his face is more than I can bear. He used me to be with her, but our divorce pushed him toward the relationship he was meant to be in.

"I'm so sorry," Emma says, standing next to me, seeing the same thing I do in the picture of their happy little family.

"I am, too. He shouldn't have died so young. He left behind so much."

"He'll rest in peace now that he knows his daughter will be cared for," Emma says, holding Daisy and offering her to me.

She's a lot bigger than Felicity, but equally fragile. She doesn't know who I am, and huge tears drip down her cheeks.

I need all the willpower I have not to cry with her.

"Ah, sweetheart," Emma murmurs, and I don't know if she's talking to Daisy or me. Probably both of us.

I rock Daisy and she twists her chubby little fingers in my hair. She squirmed for a moment, wanting down, but she gave up in sadness and confusion and rested her head against my shoulder uttering a heart-shattering sigh.

Emma leaves us alone and sits in the kitchen with Bonnie and Catherine writing lists and discussing arrangements for us to retrieve Daisy's things. She has closets full of clothes, her crib, changing table, playpen, and much more that will need to be packed and moved. It's not that I don't want to buy her new things, but they're hers and I want her around familiar belongings. At one point we sit on the floor, and she crawls around the room, offering me stuffed animals and huge wooden puzzle pieces.

I want to linger, but the social worker is eager to go home, and the nanny is excited to see something other than the rooms of Zeke and Lacey's penthouse, even if they are beautiful and spacious. Emma helps me pack a suitcase I find in their suite, and I stuff it full of clothes, diapers, bottles, and formula—she eats a different brand than Felicity. "This is all I can do for tonight," I say, holding a blanket Catherine says Daisy can't sleep without and feeling woefully ill-equipped.

"I can help you tomorrow," Emma says, carrying a car seat from the closet in the foyer. "I can either be here with the movers, or I can help Roman take care of the girls while you're here. Whatever you need."

"Thank you. Will you come home with me now? Text Jack and have him meet us there?"

"Sure. He'll leave dinner early if he has to," she says, pulling her phone out of her purse.

While Daisy explores a living room she's never going to see again, Bonnie fills out forms and I sign them. She copies my driver's license and social security number and stores every-thing in her briefcase. Sliding her card across the table and says, "If there's anything I can do, call. I can put you in touch with a family therapist if you need help adapting to changes."

"I appreciate that."

"Here's her pediatrician's information, as well," Catherine says, also holding out a card that I tuck into my purse. "She's due for a well-check soon, but she passed the last with flying colors and there were no concerns. Mr. Kavanaugh's attorney will forward the guardianship information to the doctor's office, and you'll have access to her medical history."

I forgot all about pediatrician visits, and I swallow back panic. Suddenly, I sag in my seat, spent. Today has been too much, and I skipped dinner. I miss Roman, the few hours away from him leaving me despondent and sad. I want to go home.

Emma picks Daisy up off the floor, and reading my mood, says, "We should go. It may be a late night, and Jack will be at your house by now."

"I'll miss this little one," Catherine says and kisses Daisy's forehead, "but I'm so glad she has a new family. Mr. Kavanaugh and Miss Lawton were good people, and Daisy couldn't have asked for better parents."

"I'll do my best to fill in," I say, following everyone to the elevator, Daisy's fleece blanket draped over my arm. Daisy's suitcase is sitting in the foyer, and I put that and her carseat into the elevator, the weight and bulk of the huge seat unfamiliar.

Catherine apprises me and says, "I don't think you'll have to try too hard."

I lift my lips in a tired smile. "Thank you for that."

We go down to the lobby together, Daisy clutched comfort-ably in Emma's arms. I'm tired, and all I want is to see Roman, for him to tell me I'm doing the right thing, that what happened between us this afternoon wasn't a dream. He *did* ask me to remarry him, and I said yes. There's so much we need to do before we can, but I want to be his wife again as soon as possible.

Catherine shows me how to strap the carseat into the back of our vehicle, looping the safety belt through the base and giving it a good tug. She settles Daisy into the seat and demonstrates how to buckle her into the harness. "I can recommend a few baby care books if you're interested," she says, waving goodbye to Daisy. "You don't have to know it all overnight, but they are good references to have."

Roman will know more about babies than I do, having the nine months of Brielle's pregnancy to prepare. "Thanks. It will be a huge learning curve, but I have a lot of help."

Catherine nods at Emma. "You do, and that can make all the difference in the world. I'll miss her. Good luck to you, Miss Durand. You're doing a good thing."

"I think so, too, thank you." I pause. "Perhaps, after I deal with my personal situation, I can get in touch. I'll need someone to care for Daisy while I go to work and it would be nice if it were you."

Emma's eyes widen in surprise. I haven't spoken about getting a job, but Roman will need more than to sit in a penthouse playing with the babies during the day and making love to me at night. I'll love Felicity and Daisy with everything I have, but I'll need more, too.

"That would be wonderful, Miss Durand. I'll forward my agency information to Mr. Kavanaugh's attorney, and you can give them a call when you're ready."

"Thank you."

Emma and I stand on the sidewalk, and we watch Bonnie and Catherine share a taxi and ride away.

The drive to the penthouse is quiet, Daisy's eyelids drooping. She's too wary to let her guard down enough to fall asleep, and she stares at me, fighting against her fatigue. I'm as tired as she is, and I hope with a bottle and some snuggles, our first night together won't be too hard.

We reach my building, and the truck double parks and idles in the street. Emma helps me unload Daisy's suitcase and unbuckles her carseat. I don't think Daisy will be going anywhere anytime soon, but we leave her carseat at the concierge's desk instead of bringing it up.

I hold Daisy, wanting to be the one who carries her into the penthouse. Emma seems to recognize my intention, the symbolism of what the action will mean to me and Roman, and she lags behind in the elevator.

Tentatively, I step into the new life that Roman and I will create for our makeshift family.

CHAPTER FIFTEEN

Roman

The elevator arrives on our floor, and my heart leaps. I rush into the foyer as the doors slide open. They reveal Jack standing there, dressed in a sharp business suit, and I scowl. I should have expected him, Emma texting me an hour ago saying she and Claire would be home soon, and could I fix something to eat as Claire was looking tired and rundown.

"This isn't going to be one of those nights, is it?" I ask, but I'm only kidding. Because it was Emma who texted and not Claire, I made enough lasagna to feed an entire neighborhood. I'm slowly learning that if one person is involved, everyone's included.

He grins. "Every night is one of those nights."

"You can't be serious. I heard you and Emma are trying for a baby. How do you do that if you don't have any time alone?"

Comfortable in his sister's space, he walks through to the kitchen and snags a glass of the whiskey Raff left here earlier.

"In the middle of the night between the hours of midnight and three." He says it so seriously, I freeze. "I'm joking. It's not so bad. It's only when something's going on that you can't find a minute to yourself. After spending my life alone without anyone but Heath and Claire, it's a blessing and a curse. I love Emma's friends, I love you're back in my sister's life, but yeah, it will be nice when Emma and I are married and we go on a honeymoon. I need her all to myself for a bit." He drops to his haunches in front of Felicity. "Can I hold her?"

"Sure," I say, but I don't move to help. If he wants to hold her, he can figure out the buckle keeping her in place and lift her out of the baby swing himself. I stand near them, in case he needs a hand, but he supports her head, and with a little fumbling she tolerates, he cradles her against his chest. "Speaking of honeymoons, I asked Claire to remarry me and she said yes. What with Brielle's murder and now Daisy, I don't know how long we'll have to wait, but I wanted you to know."

"I'm happy for you. I always liked you and I truly felt when you and Claire divorced, I lost a brother." He holds out his hand and I grip it firmly. I missed Jack, too. "The past four years have been hard on her, but I'm hoping that Dad's confession and meeting Mom—did she tell you about that?"

"Yeah, this afternoon. We still have a lot to work through, but that was a turning point for her, and that's why I asked."

He lets Felicity wrap her hand around one of his fingers. "Good. We might not be able to put what Dad did to Mom away, and maybe we shouldn't, but I think we can finally move forward. The mystery of it has been dragging us down, and learning Mom didn't forget about us helped Claire understand that when someone says they love her, they aren't lying." He pauses. "Who's Daisy?"

I clear my throat. "She didn't tell you?"

"No."

"She'll be back soon. Why don't we wait? Why are you here? Not that it's not great to see you."

"Emma asked me to stop by. I was at a dinner with Dad, but you know women. I don't ask questions, I just do what they say."

I laugh. It's good to be back.

It's not long after that the elevator doors glide open for a second time. This time it's Claire standing there, holding a baby about nine or ten months old, her hair a gorgeous copper color. She's tired, well, both of them are, and Daisy's resting her head against Claire's shoulder. Claire's steps are heavy, and shadows rest beneath her eyes.

She meets my gaze, and hesitantly, she steps forward. "Was it all a dream?" she whispers.

"No. It can't be. I wouldn't survive the rest of my life if you're not in it." I kiss her trembling lips and smooth my hand down Daisy's back. She peeks at me with blue eyes, another stranger in a long line who will eventually become her family.

"I was so afraid . . . ." She trails off, ending on an exhausted sigh.

"You don't have to be anymore. I'll always be here, and you promised me the same."

"Yeah, I did. Meet Daisy."

"She's perfect."

We stand in the foyer, Claire leaning into me, not only for strength in this moment, but learning that I will give her strength for a lifetime. Emma skirts around us carrying a suitcase. She sets it down quietly near the closet and finds Jack in the living room giving us time to ourselves.

"I told Zeke's attorney I'm going to adopt her," she says, her voice barely a breath. She's waiting for me to object, for me to, I don't know, reject her and Daisy, maybe, but all I can do is stare at her in awe.

"Can I, too?" I want to ask about Felicity so badly. Brielle would have been an amazing mother to our daughter. She had so much light and love in her heart. I will never think Claire could replace what Felicity would have had with her, but I want Felicity's future secure and having two legal parents would do that.

"If, after Brielle is peacefully laid to rest and we're married and things settle, you'll let me adopt Felicity. I want us to be a family in all ways, Roman. I don't know if that's something that Brielle would have wanted, but I think Zeke and Lacey would be happy for us and for Daisy."

"That's what I want, too."

I kiss her, sealing our fate, but I didn't know how hard I would have to fight to keep my end of the promises we made to each other.

———

We walk into the living room, and Jack and Emma are cuddling Felicity. Holidays and other get-togethers will be filled with chaos when they have their own children, but it's something I'm looking forward to.

"Claire, what are you doing with a baby?" he asks, his mouth dropping open. "Is that what Zeke left you?"

"Yeah. I needed time to sort through a lot of feelings, and I didn't know if I wanted her until we spoke to Mom this morning. That's why I didn't tell you. I hope you don't think I'm a horrible person."

Gently, Jack transfers Felicity into Emma's arms and approaches his sister. Framing her face in his hands, he says, "Claire, I would never judge you. Not for doing what you thought you needed to do for yourself. I'm so proud that you can admit that things don't have to be the way they were.

You've been so unhappy, and with Roman and Felicity and now Daisy in your life, you can find the joy you've been missing. I'm happy for you, I really am."

"You've always been there for me, and I don't know how to thank you for that. My life would have been even more miserable if you hadn't shielded me from Dad and what he did. I'll never be able to thank you."

"You're my sister, and I love you. I would do it all over again." He lets out a shuddery sigh. "Christ, it's been quite the couple of months, hasn't it?"

"It's been crazy, but I think things are finally turning around." She glances at me, and for the first time since I met Claire Durand, there's nothing in her eyes but love and possibilities of a future that's wide open waiting for us to explore.

Daisy lets out a whimper, and instead of panicking or handing her off, she asks me, "I packed bottles, formula, diapers, and some of her clothes. Emma volunteered to help get Daisy's things moved over tomorrow, but for tonight, she's living out of her suitcase. Can you make her a bottle? I don't know how much . . . I have a lot to learn."

"I bet she's sucking down a full one. We'll go from there." I kiss them both, and Claire leans in like I wish she would have a long time ago.

It's difficult to tear myself away, but I know the signs of a hungry female, infant and adult, and I fix Daisy's bottle.

The elevator doors glide open, and I push back a sigh. Of course it wouldn't be simply the four of us, ah, the six of us, spending a quiet evening together. I'm thankful for the friendship, but Claire isn't the only one who's had a long day. I'm looking forward to getting some sleep, too. I have never slept well when Claire and I are at odds, and tonight I'm going to fall into a damn near coma.

Raff and Veronica bypass the kitchen and I hear him say,

"Jesus Christ, they're multiplying. Dollface, don't drink the water. We need to stop coming over here."

"Why?" Veronica asks. "Someone can cook better than we can. There's food, and it smells delicious."

I glance at the oven's clock. Daisy will have enough time to eat before it's our turn.

"Not good enough," Raff says, sounding more than a little panicked at the thought.

I join the group, and Emma's laughing, still holding Felicity. I catch Raff brushing his thumb over the baby's cheek, and I pass Daisy's bottle to Claire.

He's carrying a folder in his hands, and he says, "Got a second?"

Reality bursts my happy bubble. "Yeah."

We break away and sit at the island in the kitchen. I want to pour a glass of whiskey to dull whatever news he's going to throw at me, but having two babies in the penthouse now, I can't drink, or smoke, as freely as I once did.

"I talked to Preston tonight," Raff starts, looking up from the folder.

Claire joins us, and from behind, she rests her arms on my shoulders and her hands roam my chest. Somehow, she always knew when I was tense and stressed out, and this was her way of calming me down. I breathe, and she curls her body around mine.

"You two good now?" Raff asks.

"Yeah, yeah we are." I can't put into words how grateful I am that we *are* good. For four years, I never thought I'd see her again.

"Okay. I talked to Preston earlier. I caught him just as he was finishing up for the night. I asked him about his relationship with Brielle, but I can tell you right now, he's not our killer."

"Shit. Are you sure?"

"Yeah. I brought up Brielle's name and he started bawling like a baby, no pun intended," he says, tilting his head toward the living room. "He didn't do it. He loved her too much."

"But—" Love is exactly why someone kills.

"Nope. There's not an ounce of rage in his body. If he'd gotten mad at her, he would have fucked her, not killed her."

I know exactly what he's talking about. Claire and I had angry sex more times than I can count. Mostly because I'd be frustrated she wasn't talking to me, and she'd be frustrated because I was frustrated. Sex was the only way we could communicate, but in the morning, the issues would never be resolved. That required words, and I don't think up until Claire talked with her mother this morning, she had any to spare.

"So, we're back to square one," I say bitterly. I don't know what to do short of turning myself in and hiring an attorney. They don't have anything to hold me, but I can't hide forever.

"I don't think we are. I confronted him about the pictures, and Preston had no choice but to admit he was with Brielle and her friends at The Dugout. I asked what they did afterward, and he said they went into the alley to talk. One thing led to another, and they had sex. I asked him if he'd been with her like that the whole time she was seeing you, and he said no. I believe him. Felicity's yours."

"Well, that's some good news, at least. When did they start sleeping together?"

"After she started hooking up with you, you mean? Because they were before she met you, and he was really clear about that. He said she was about five months along, and her bump turned him on. That was more than what I wanted to know, and I steered him away from the subject."

Claire stiffens. We'll never make love while she's pregnant. I'll never run my hands over our baby growing inside her. It's something I've accepted, and I kiss her palm. We'll always have regrets, but it's what we do with them now that matters.

"Did he know why she started seeing me if they were so close?"

"They had a rough patch. She wanted more, and unlike Lulu, he doesn't have much going on upstairs. She wanted more, and he knew there was no way in hell he could give that to her. He fell through the cracks of the educational system when he was a kid, and he can barely read. He could have a learning disability that no one cared to ferret out. Whatever it was, Brielle was in love but wanted more out of her man. I would imagine she thought she struck it rich, again, pardon the pun, not only because you have money, but you're highly educated and ran your own firm. It wasn't your money that turned her on, it was your brains."

"That couldn't have been a pleasant realization for him."

Raff sighs. "It's what he knows."

"You gave him your card, didn't you?"

He scowls. "Let's stay on task."

"Yeah, yeah," I say, liking Raff more with every passing second.

"The other girls reluctantly went on to another bar down the street. Preston said they wanted to wait for Brielle. She'd been picking up the tab all night, and they wanted her to keep doing it. They weren't in the alley for long, a couple of minutes—long enough for him to shove it in and pull it out and tell her he loved her a million times. He said he walked with her to the front of The Dugout, and that's when a car pulled up. She got in and they drove away."

I straighten. "Did he know who it was?"

"No, but being a car guy, he tagged it as a Caddy, early 2000s, black, cracked back window. No plates, so don't ask."

"Shit. He wasn't with her when she withdrew that money, then."

"Nope. She didn't do it for him."

"She didn't tell her friends she wasn't meeting up with them?"

"No. From what Preston told me, they thought she blew them off to go somewhere with him. They didn't know anything was wrong until the guy with the dog found her body."

The oven's timer dings, and reluctantly, I pull away from Claire's touch to turn it off. "So where does that leave us?" I ask, donning oven mitts to pull out huge pans of lasagna.

"I still have some of her family to talk to, but the key is finding that car. Preston didn't catch the plates because it didn't have any. A paper from a dealership was taped to the driver's side back window. Someone had recently bought it. I have a feeling that was the car that transported her to Cavern Lake."

"That doesn't sound promising."

"We're getting closer. Brielle didn't have that many people in her life. I've already talked to the boyfriend, her closest friends, and some of her family. I have to be getting near the end of the list of people she would hop into a car with. I still have to talk to the bank teller. Maybe whoever it was went inside with her too. If this was a crime of passion like you say, maybe killing her was an impulsive thing and keeping his identity a secret wasn't part of his plan."

I shove a cookie sheet full of garlic bread into the oven to toast. "I can look through her social media some more and I never did get around to looking into her phone records. I've been busy dealing with other stuff."

Claire wraps her arms around my waist. "We've got that figured out now. We won't stop until this is done."

"You sticking with me means a lot, it really does," I say with a sigh, my forehead pressed to her temple. "I'm tired."

"I know. Let's eat and kick everybody out."

"Sounds good."

"I'll set the table in the dining room. We'll have more space."

"I'll go check on the girls."

Claire smiles. "Jack was feeding Daisy when I came in here. Having Felicity and Daisy around will give Jack and Emma practice until they have their own."

"I better go rescue him. We've been in here for a while, and Jack could probably use a drink by now."

Claire leans away from me, kisses my cheek, and pulls a stack of plates from the cabinet.

I follow Raff into the living room, and Veronica's sitting on the floor reading Daisy a book.

"No," Raff says.

Veronica crinkles her eyes at him in amusement. "I didn't say anything."

"You didn't need to."

Daisy doesn't have a playpen or a highchair, and I carry her and a handful of toys into the dining room. Hopefully she'll sit and play while we eat. Felicity isn't mobile yet, and she'll doze in the bouncy chair next to the table.

I have some wine with dinner, and soak up the presence of my friends. I enjoy the food and the easy company. Raff is a natural storyteller, gossip from *Talk of the Town* easy fuel.

After a meal that loosens some of the stress I've carried all day, Claire and Emma clean up the kitchen. They talk quietly about tomorrow, and I'm on board with moving Daisy's things here as soon as possible. I don't intend to cage her in a playpen, but until we babyproof the living room and block off the stairs to the den and bedrooms upstairs, it's safer to confine her. She's crawling, and once she's familiar with the penthouse, she'll want to explore every corner. Claire and I will also need to turn one of the bedrooms near the master suite into a nursery. The girls can share for a couple of years, and I want to sleep in bed with my wife, alone.

Emma hugs me goodbye and says she'll see me tomorrow. They decided she would stay here and help me watch the girls, and Claire would meet the movers at Zeke and Lacey's. I don't know what things she has the authority to take, but if I know Claire, she'll claim what she can for Daisy. Everything in that penthouse belonged to her parents, and Claire will do her best to see that Daisy has access to all of it. I don't need the help—I think I can handle the two girls alone—but it will be pleasant getting to know my sister-in-law and I don't object. I like what I know of her, and admire what she did for Jack and Claire.

Everyone says goodbye, and Claire wilts against me. Raff promises to touch base tomorrow after he talks to the bank manager and to some more of Brielle's family.

I wanted to thank him again for all his time, but there's no use thanking him for something he's obviously enjoying. It might even boost his campaign, not that he needs any help with the election. He and Veronica will be the Ken and Barbie of Bridgeport. I don't know how anyone would choose to run against him and think they could win.

"I like your friends," I say, holding Daisy. She's exhausted, but she hasn't succumbed to tears. I don't let myself think the transition will be smooth. While we were on the road, Felicity cried her fair share, missing Brielle.

"That's good. I don't think we could shake them off. They're like fleas," she says, laughing a little. "But I wouldn't trade them for anything. Emma's an angel. I have what I have because of her."

"I thought the same thing when we were saying goodbye."

"What should we do with the sleeping arrangements? I wasn't thinking clearly at Zeke's. Daisy doesn't have a crib."

I lead Claire to the bedroom. I'm eager to put the girls down for the night. After an evening with a full penthouse, they need the quiet, and I need time alone with Claire. This afternoon on the floor in the kitchen wasn't enough, and I stiffen in anticipation. She's using her words more than she ever has before, but I need her body, her lips on mine. It's the only way I know she's telling me the truth: that the four of us will be something I've always wanted.

"I'll lower the mattress in Felicity's, and she'll be fine. Felicity's used to sleeping on the bed, isn't she? It will be big enough for one night." I cast her an amused glance, and she blushes. No matter how hard she tried to keep from falling for the baby, Claire couldn't stay away from her.

All my clothes are upstairs—Daisy isn't the only one who will be moving things tomorrow. I retrieve a pair of pajamas I don't plan on wearing long, and Claire trades her dress for a nightgown that she definitely won't be wearing long. We're not settled into a nightly routine yet, and we change Felicity's and Daisy's diapers and dress them a fresh pajamas. They both ate not long ago, and we put them down without bottles. "Does Daisy sleep through the night?"

Claire lifts her shoulders. "I have no idea. Speaking to the nanny was like a dream. It felt wrong, somehow, to be able to walk into Zeke's emptyhanded and come out with a baby. Surreal, but I think all the paperwork is done for now. Until I start adoption proceedings. I asked for Catherine's card and told her I would be in touch. I thought it would be nice for Daisy when we need someone."

"When we need someone?" I echo, confused. Why would we need a nanny? I sigh. Maybe my future isn't as bright as I thought it was. "Let's pour a drink and go out onto the balcony." My dick shrinks. This isn't going to be the romantic evening I hoped it would be.

"Okay," she says, gripping my hand, knowing that's where I like to make love.

I pour a double into a lowball glass for us to share, and we stand on the balcony, the city's lights sparking around us. I used to love sitting out here with her, letting the energy fill up my soul as her love did for my heart. Married to Claire, I had everything.

A soft breeze floats over the stone balcony, and she leans against the balustrade.

I pass her the glass and she sips.

"Claire. Why would we need a nanny?" I ask, my heart thudding dully in my chest. Every time I think I have it all, she rips it away.

"I've been doing a lot of thinking," she says. "You quit your job after we divorced, and your firm is gone. Don't you want to work again?"

Her question brings me up short. This isn't the conversation I expected we'd have. I thought she'd say she wasn't ready to spend so much time taking care of the girls, or that she wasn't sure this is what she signed up for. I'm used to her backing away like a scared little kitten. "I don't know. I never thought about . . . well, that's not true. I talked to Raff a bit, and I don't want to go back to being a divorce attorney." I force a smile. "After we remarry, I don't want to be around divorce ever again."

"I'm sorry." She sips and passes the glass off to me.

I sip, too, and let the warmth travel through me. "You don't have to be sorry. What's done is done. I'm not even sure what prompted me to specialize in it. We were lucky. Maybe we didn't split as friends, but we were civil. Not all couples are. I don't have it in me to do the cut-throat cases anymore."

"When you were seeing Brielle, is that what you thought? That you would be home with her and Felicity all the time?"

I flash back to Brielle's apartment. I didn't feel trapped, but I hadn't been there long enough to feel that way. "I don't know. I wasn't thinking like that. You still have no idea how much you hurt me. Trying to live after our divorce was impossible. Brielle gave me something I needed, and Felicity added to that, but I knew I wasn't going to find what would keep me alive in her tiny apartment. I told you that before she was murdered, I mentioned splitting up. I was so confused."

"I don't think you'll find what you're looking for here, either," she says.

I want to throw my glass over the balustrade in frustration. Why can't she give me what I want? Why does everything have to be so fucking hard?

"You'll need more," she continues. "One day, I don't know how long it will take, six months, a year, all you'll have done is play with the girls, and you're going to look up from a puzzle and want to leave. You've always needed more, Roman, don't pretend you haven't."

I grip her shoulders, a dread so great gathering in my belly I fight back bile threatening to spew from my mouth. "Tell me this conversation is you trying to add to my life, not take anything away. I love you. Don't leave me again."

She snuggles into my chest. "I'm not leaving. This is me talking to you about things before we get married again. I want you to be happy, here and at work. Wherever that may be."

"You said we'd need a nanny. You won't need help taking care of the girls. This is for you too, isn't it?" I went to work, Monday through Friday, put in overtime on the weekends, but I never knew what Claire did with her time. She was already wealthy before she married me, coming into a trust her grandfather left her on her twenty-fifth birthday. I didn't care what she did as long as she was home waiting for me when I left the office every night.

She looks up at me, the light from a nearby skyscraper glowing in her eyes. "Maybe. Part of the reason I haven't been happy with any aspect of my life is because I didn't take control where I could have. I went to school but didn't do anything with it. I decided to fuck around instead, thinking if my mother didn't love me, why should I love myself? I'm going to be honest and tell you I think I'll need more than staying home with the girls, too. Maybe not at first, but eventually. Emma will work after her babies are born, and Zoey works, too. Veronica will be happy supporting Raff without kids. I need to find something that will give me purpose, satisfaction, too."

"What were you thinking?" Claire has a degree in journalism, but I've never seen her write a single thing. Not even a blogpost. I never would have guessed she even liked to write, except I saw her transcript and she graduated with a 4.0— straight As across the board.

"I don't know. That's why I'm talking to you, trying to puzzle this out. What you'll need, what I'll need. If Catherine would need to move in? I don't think I want that. Would you?"

"No. We have enough space, but if we're not at work, I want to be here, alone with you and the girls. Present in our lives, not with a nanny hovering in the background. Are you considering supporting Emma and Jack and working at Variant?"

She shakes her head, and I'm glad. I don't want her working for her father's company. Whatever we end up doing, it will be together. "No. Emma enjoys the work, and she and Jack are a good team, at home and at the office. Maybe once Emma finds her footing, my dad will actually retire. But I don't think I would be a good fit. I never cared about what we do."

"Can you tell me what you do?" I tease, brushing a piece of hair away from her eyes.

"No." She laughs and nudges my jaw with her nose. "You're right. Talking is better."

"I'm glad you weren't trying to figure out how to run. It will be a big commitment, raising two girls, and I know you'll be scared. I am. But I don't want you to run anymore. I don't want you to feel like the ring I put on your finger is a noose around your neck. I love you, but you divorced me and taught me I wasn't good enough. You'll have to give me time to unlearn it."

She guides my hand to her breast, and I caress it through the silk. "We never had a hard time in bed, and sex now won't convince you, but I've changed since that day in the parking lot. I want to be a mother to Felicity and to Daisy, but more than anything, I want to be your wife. Will you make love to me, the way you used to?"

I grip her hair and force her to look at me. "You would never say it. Like it was poison, and if you said it, you would die. Tell me, Claire."

"I love you," she says, her green eyes shimmering. "I love you so much. I never stopped." Her words end with a sob, and I crush my mouth to hers. She jams her fingers into my hair, tugging, and our teeth gnash together. Our bodies are plastered against each other, and I know she can feel how hard I am. The second she told me she loved me, I stiffened, ready to feel how much she does.

Dragging my lips away from hers, I suck in a breath. "We should do this inside, in case one of the girls needs us," I say reluctantly. There's nothing more I want to do than make love on the balcony the way we used to, but we didn't bring the baby monitor out here and we wouldn't be able to hear the cries of a hungry baby.

"You're right," she says and finishes off the whiskey in the glass sitting on the rail. "Hurry." She turns toward the doors.

I catch her arm. "Claire."

This time I'm the one who can't get the words out. Humility, gratefulness, love, they're all knotted around in my heart. Brielle's murder is turning my life upside down, and I'm so thankful that she's standing by me.

"I have a lot to make up for," she says over the silence, "but I promise things will be different. I can't expect you to believe it, but I'll spend the rest of my life showing you. Not only showing you," she says, blushing. "I'm learning you need to hear the things I have in my heart. Not just the good, but the bad, the doubts and fears. I'll never forget that."

"Well, let's not go crazy," I say, opening the door and pushing her through. "I was never so sure you loved me than in the middle of the night when you would reach for me. That was when I truly knew, and the night we made love before you told me you wanted a divorce, you can say whatever you want, but remember, what you show me, I'll believe first."

I walk with her to the couch where we made love hundreds of times during our short marriage. Quickly, I tug my t-shirt over my head and toss it onto the floor. She slides off her robe, and it joins my shirt in a puddle of silk. My lounging pants are next, along with my boxers, and I stand naked, her gaze raking me from head to toe. I haven't changed much since our divorce, working out one of the only ways I could push through the grief.

Claire slides her nightgown's straps from her shoulders, and it falls down her body like a waterfall, fluid and smooth. I already know she wasn't wearing a bra, and I could snap the lace of her panties without much effort, but she disposes of them without the destruction of material and stands in front of me, her breasts heavy with arousal, her stomach quivering in anticipation. She's gained a few pounds, her breasts heavier, her hips curvier, giving her an hourglass figure she didn't have during our marriage. Sometimes we would go for a run together through the park, but evenings like that were more for spending time together than exercise. We'll take the girls on a lot of walks to the playground, and nights like this will be all the workout I'll need.

"You're still beautiful," I say, holding her to me, my hand skimming her back, down her spine. She would always shiver, and she still does, my hand stopping right above the gentle slope of her ass.

"You were so strong," she whispers against my chest. "I felt so safe when you were holding me."

I pause, surprised. I never would have expected she felt like that, but then, how could I? "Really?"

"Yeah. That's why I liked having sex with you so much. Why whenever we were together, I had to be in your lap or in your arms. I spent my entire life feeling like I was somehow in danger. Afraid of losing my father, though he was never really a part of my life, or losing Jack. I was always standing on the precipice of my whole existence crumbling away, and then I met you, and in your arms, I was always safe."

"Ah, Claire," I say, the pad of my thumb playing with her nipple. It hardens under my touch. "I wish you would have told me that a long time ago. I should have fought harder to keep you. I'm sorry."

"You gave me what I wanted, and I stopped hating you for that." She cups her hand around my cock, and I bite back a moan.

"Lie with me," I murmur.

The cushions are barely wide enough for us, and we lie on our sides, her head resting on my arm. She wiggles as close as she can, and that's another thing I have always loved about her.

The desperation, the urgency, but now I know why. She props her leg over my hip, and I find her slit and sink my fingers into her.

"More," she murmurs.

"This is all the more I can give you," I say, nudging her onto her back and pushing my cock inside her. I stare into her eyes. "I love you."

Wrapping her arms around my neck and tilting her hips to help me slide all the way in, she says, "I love you, too. I love our family, those little girls in there who need us. We belong to you."

Emotion carries me away. I lose my ability for words and ravage her mouth instead. One arm is still under her head, and I use my other hand to hold her ass in place as I thrust. She'll need more to come, but for now, I need to find my release, and I do, my cock buried deep. "Jesus Christ, I missed this," I rasp, finally able to speak.

She laughs, and it sounds free, no hint of sadness weighing down the notes. Before, even if she laughed, she never *really* laughed. It never sounded full of joy like it does now. Her fingers rake my scruff and I kiss the tip of her nose. "I missed you, too," she says.

"I know, but it's more than that. I miss you when you're running errands. I miss you if we're not in the same room together. You wouldn't let me in, and I *missed you*." I pull out, my cock deflated, but never satisfied. I could make love with Claire every day for the rest of my life, and it still wouldn't be enough. Settling next to her, I pull her to me, her tapered legs tangling with mine.

"I never wanted you to see how incomplete I felt. If you didn't see it, you couldn't love me less," she says.

I meet her gaze in the soft light wavering in through the balcony windows. "You've always been everything I needed.

Your mom and dad had a lot to do with how you felt about yourself, and I'm extremely grateful finding out the truth has made a positive impact on your life. I don't think we could have had this second chance if you hadn't found your mom, spoken with her, and heard her tell you she still loves you. The issues we divorced over wouldn't have been resolved."

"You're right," she says, reaching for my hand and guiding it between her legs. "Kiss me."

I do, and I push two fingers inside her. My thumb finds her clit. I know what gets her off, and I lazily circle the nub, my tongue licking the inside of her mouth. Her hips tilt upward increasing the pressure, and I nibble my way from her lips, down her neck, and to her nipple that I suck into my mouth.

She moans, and a light mist covers her skin. I know the exact moment she comes, a quiet mewing whining from the back of her throat, and I bite her nipple in the way I know she likes. Her muscles clench around my fingers, her cum and mine, mixing together.

Her eyes flutter open, and she rests her hand against my cheek. Her mind is working, her lips trembling with words wanting to burst from her mouth, but a delicate cry drifts into the living room from our suite. Felicity's hungry, but that isn't a surprise. I don't remember the last time she ate.

"I'll feed her," Claire says propping herself up onto her elbows.

"Are you sure?" I don't want her to feel obligated.

Kissing me, she mumbles against my lips, "Roman, she's mine, too."

She rolls off the couch, snagging her nightgown and robe. She hurries to the bedroom, but I can't call out to her.

My throat is too clogged with our future for me to make a sound.

———

We'll need time to establish any kind of routine, but for now, Claire picks up Felicity from our bed and I mix her a bottle. Knowing I'll feed her the next time she's hungry, I don't let myself feel guilty for succumbing to my exhaustion, and I go to bed. Claire rocks my daughter in her sitting room, cuddling Felicity to her, staring out the window.

Daisy wakes once, leaking out of her diaper. She falls back to sleep after I change her and the wet sleeper, and for having two babies under the age of one in our bedroom, I manage to get enough sleep to feel human the next morning.

I want to shower with Claire, but Felicity needs a bottle and a fresh diaper, and Daisy looks uncertain, searching for Catherine, perhaps. I do my best to see to the girls and let Claire shower, unfortunately, alone. We need Daisy's things as soon as possible.

"Can you bring her highchair home with you, and a playpen if she has one? They should both fold up and fit in whatever vehicle you use. We can wait for her other things, but she's eating solid food and she needs a safe place to sit."

"Yes, I will. The movers said they could do it same day, so she'll have her own crib tonight. Emma texted me and said she would be here soon. What are you going to do while I'm gone?" She loops her arms around my neck.

Daisy's crawling through the living room, and Felicity's curiously watching from her bouncy seat. I don't have but a minute. The living room isn't babyproofed and Daisy won't need long to find something she shouldn't have.

"Go through Brielle's phone records. Raff's going to the bank today to talk to the manager about her withdrawing money from a joint account we had. We're getting closer, but I think I'm going to have to turn myself in. I don't want to, but I can't keep hiding."

She swallows. "If that's what you have to do. They don't have any evidence. Not even circumstantial. All they could do is question you and let you go."

"That's my hope, but first, let's see what Raff can come up with. I don't know what the police have been digging up, if anything. Between him and the detective, maybe we know who did it."

We stand in the foyer for a few seconds, her face pressed to the side of my neck, my arms around her. This is the Claire I remember. Not the one on the couch last night, so full of words only my tongue in her mouth would silence her. This is how she would communicate, her body aligned with mine. She's scared. So am I, but about different things. If they arrest me, Claire doesn't have a claim on Felicity. I don't know Brielle's parents well—don't know if they would take good care of my daughter if they were ever awarded guardianship. I don't want to find out.

Reluctantly, she breaks away. "I better go. Emma should be here any minute."

"Okay. Come home, Claire." It was always my prayer, and not so easily answered.

"I will."

The elevator doors hide her, but it's only a few minutes later Emma arrives, dressed to play in denim shorts and a pink tank top. I didn't think I would need her, but I should do the research I told Raff I would do, and she'll be helpful keeping the girls occupied.

"Thanks for helping out," I say.

She slides off her sandals and drops her purse onto the floor. "It's no problem," she says, tentatively walking into the living room. The moment Emma sees Daisy using the couch to pull herself up, she lowers onto the carpet next to her. Felicity's still in the bouncy seat and she brightens, already pegging Emma as a trusted friend.

I unlatch Felicity and hold her out to Emma who immediately reaches for the baby. "Looking forward to your own?"

"Yeah," she says, letting Felicity snuggle into her shoulder. For two weeks she didn't have a woman to hold her, and she's enjoying the attention. "Jack especially. Felicity has given him terrible baby fever. Do you have something you need to do?"

"Raff asked me to look up a few things, and I want to have some answers when he stops by."

She smiles sympathetically. "Is there anything I can help with?"

"You're already doing it. They should both be good for a bit. We fed and diapered them right before Claire left. Did you know Claire while she was married to Zeke?"

"Not really. I was Jack's PA for the last three years, but your professional life doesn't always mix with the personal. She would come into the office to see Jack, but I never met Zeke. Why?"

"I wondered what you thought of him."

"I don't need to have met him to think he was smart. I think he saw Claire in a way she didn't expect, in a way maybe nobody expected, or in a way nobody does now for that matter. He knew she didn't want a baby, but he left her guardianship of his daughter anyway. Maybe he didn't know how deeply she was afraid of having kids, but if he had any awareness, intuition, he probably did. His attorney made it sound like Claire was his last resort, but there's always an aunt or an uncle, a third cousin twice removed who would be willing to step up, especially considering how much Zeke was willing to pay for her care. He left Daisy to Claire because he knew his daughter would be loved, and that's the bottom line. She might not have a lot of good things to say about their marriage, but I think that's extraordinary."

"Zeke knew her better than I did," I say, and I feel like shit knowing it's true. I sink onto the floor next to Emma. Letting go of the cushion, Daisy tries to step toward me but falls onto her butt. She's not sure if she wants to laugh or cry, but Emma steals her attention, waving a rattle in front of her, and the moment passes.

"You know Claire better than anyone, you read her with just a glance, but I think you're right, too. Zeke knew she was still in love with you and wouldn't hurt her if he married her to hide Lacey from his parents. I wonder why he went through all that though, instead of simply marrying Lacey? I guess we'll never know."

"I know why." There's only one reason why a man doesn't marry a woman he's in love with.

She frowns. "Why?"

"Zeke couldn't marry Lacey. She was already married to someone else."

"Oh," she says, her eyes widening. "Zeke's attorney never said anything."

"It could be Zeke didn't tell him. It wouldn't be his business he and Lacey were having an affair. Besides, it was responsible of him, but who could have known Zeke would need his will before Daisy turned eighteen?"

"I suppose. Claire talked to Zeke's mother about Daisy, and she said she and Zeke's father buried Lacey. I'm surprised her husband didn't claim her body."

"Maybe he couldn't. He could be incarcerated, or he couldn't afford to bury her, or it could be he didn't want to step up and admit his wife was cheating on him with a billionaire playboy. I really don't know, Emma. Raff could find out, but sometimes things are better left alone."

"Yeah, you're right. If you said you would do something for him, you better get to it. Brielle's murder is more important than Zeke and Lacey's affair."

"It's interesting to puzzle out," I say, standing. "Zeke used Claire and the attention from their marriage *and* divorce to live a double life with Lacey. I remember when their divorce hit social media. It was all anyone could talk about for months. Claire's lucky she didn't end up getting hurt."

"Zeke didn't want to hurt her, he was only tired of hiding."

I point at her. "And that is probably the closest we'll get to the truth. Thanks again for watching the girls. I'm going to sit in the kitchen. If you need anything, ask. Felicity still eats every two hours, so you've got about an hour before she starts squirming. Daisy lasts a little longer, but not by much."

"I will. We'll be fine."

On the way to the kitchen, I dodge toys scattered on the floor. I'm livid Zeke would use Claire that way, but everything Emma and I pieced together makes sense. I wonder who Lacey's husband was. I should ask Raff to check it out to be sure something ugly doesn't creep up behind us. Zeke's and Lacey's deaths should have ended all of that, but my luck isn't running too hot right now.

I wake up Claire's laptop and connect to the internet using the hotspot on the burner phone Raff gave me.

On my carrier's website, I log into my account. I don't have my cell phone to confirm the two-step verification, and I answer all my security questions and type in my date of birth and social security number. It's only then does the website grant me access. I click on Brielle's number and scroll down to her usage.

Fuck.

I don't know who any of her friends are, and without her contacts to compare, there's not much I can do. I carry Claire's laptop upstairs to the study, download the spreadsheet and click Print, hoping her laptop is wirelessly connected to the printer. It is, and the list of numbers Brielle called and received calls from spits out on pristine white paper.

One thing that occurs to me is that she was on her phone—a lot. Not texting, as those are a separate list, but she liked to talk on the phone. I never realized that about her.

I print out the numbers she texted to and from as well and carry everything back downstairs in case Emma needs me.

Using different colored highlighters I find in a junk drawer that's still a junk drawer, I begin to assign each number with a color. I cross out the number that's mine using a black marker. We didn't text or call as much because we were always together. After I do that, there are eight repeated numbers. I won't know who they belong to unless I call them. It could be with a burner phone no one will answer the unknown number, and maybe I can parse out who the numbers belong to listening to voicemail.

It might be safer for Raff to do this, but he assured me the cell can't be traced, and I have the time now. He's been doing the hard part.

I dial the first number, and like I thought, it goes to voicemail. "Hey, hey. You've reached Lulu. Leave a message and I'll hit you up later." I write her name by the number.

I do the same with the others, reaching a generic voicemail at one that doesn't give me a name. I call another, and a gruff-sounding kid answers with a "This is Pres. What can I do for ya?" I hang up. Preston probably can't afford not to answer his phone if he's hoping for mechanic jobs. I mark his name down along with Lulu's and the one that didn't give me anything to go on. I reach Courtney's voicemail, and the landline for the diner.

A woman answers the next number, her voice teary and sad. My throat burning, I hang up on Brielle's mom. That number is her parents' landline—her mother doesn't have a cell phone. I hold my head in my hands. I liked her family. Her mom wanted us to get married, and I never minded the nudges whenever we would visit. She wanted to see her daughter settled, and I want the same for mine.

There are three numbers left that Brielle called and received calls from constantly. An angry man answers the next number I dial, and he says, "You fucking asshole. Think you can harass us? Leave us the fuck alone." Brielle's father. They must be home together, and I called them one right after the next.

I clear my throat and tag the number on my list. I didn't intend to bother them.

The next number belongs to Ana, her voicemail telling me to leave a message after the beep and if I'm lucky, she'd get back to me.

I call the last number as Emma steps into the kitchen, Daisy on her hip. I hold up a finger. A man answers, and I stiffen. I know his voice. "Hello? Hello? Anyone there? Are you another goddamned snoop who thinks they can get a piece of me? Fuck off." He hangs up.

His voice is familiar—I've heard it several times before. I look at my phone records and search for the number, but I have never called it or received a call from it. That means I met him in person, and if that's true, the only people I've met in Brielle's life are her family. He's one of her uncles, or a cousin, though he sounded too old to be a cousin. The ones I met were all around Brielle's age.

I work through it, Emma standing patiently near the island, and her silence is very helpful. I can write down a list of Brielle's uncles later, and I look up from the paper. "Thanks for that. I was on to something that could have easily slipped away."

"You and Jack work similarly. I didn't mean to interrupt, but I think Daisy's hungry and she could use a diaper. I would have changed her myself, but I don't know where you and Claire put her things. I left Felicity in her bouncy seat."

"I'll change her first, and then give her something to eat. Maybe she'll fall asleep for a nap." Last night went smoother than I thought it would, but I think Daisy will like having her own crib again. Until we can figure out a nursery, the setup in our bedroom will be interesting. "If you could keep an eye on Felicity, that would be great. She'll need to be fed soon, too, so I might as well give you a bottle for her now. We keep all the diapers and clothes in Claire's, I mean, our room, but we should move some into the living room, too."

"It's so nice to see her happy," Emma says, bouncing Daisy and coaxing a smile out of her, showing us a flash of little white teeth.

"You're a good friend. She's said she wouldn't have anything if she didn't have you."

She shrugs. "Maybe. I don't feel like I did anything except fall in love with Jack."

"And changed everyone's lives in the process." I hold out my hand for Daisy and in exchange, pass a bottle to Emma for Felicity.

"Even yours?"

"Especially mine. Without you, I never would have met Raff, and I believe he's going to get me out of this."

"He will. He wanted to be a reporter, but he went into law to make his family happy. I think that's why he and Claire get along so well. He helped her find information about her mom, and they talked shop. I wish he didn't have to shut down his e-zine. I'm happy he has Veronica. When that goes offline, it's going to break his heart. I better feed Felicity."

She disappears into the living room unaware of the seed she planted.

Claire comes home a little while later, and the doorman and concierge carry in Daisy's highchair and playpen. Away from their posts, they quickly deposit the baby paraphernalia in the foyer and hurry back down to the lobby. We're alone, and I pull her to me, trapping her with one hand between her shoulder blades and one to the back of her head. I'm still angry Zeke used her, and not a little scared she could have been seriously hurt.

"Hey, are you okay?" she asks, leaning away.

"Yeah. Give me a minute."

"All right." She wraps her arms around my waist and rests her cheek against my shoulder. I breathe in and out, brushing my hand against her hair. I need this woman. Christ, do I need this woman.

The doors to the elevator slide open, and over Claire's shoulder, I watch Raff step into the foyer. He shakes his head, mumbling about fools in love, and darts around us to join Emma in the living room. Everyone knows everyone's business —I'm not surprised he knows she's here.

"Roman?" Claire asks after too many minutes go by.

I frame her face in my hands. "I love you so much. You know that, right?"

"I know. I love you too. Did something happen? Did you hear bad news?" She winces. Brielle's murder is about as bad as you can get.

"No. Not really. Emma and I were talking about Zeke. I'm sorry he's dead, but I'm not sorry you divorced him."

Amused, she says, "I didn't expect you to be. I'm sorry Brielle is gone, even if you're standing here right now because she is."

"I would have found my way back to you," I say, and I mean every word.

"No, you wouldn't have. I know you. You would have married her, and that's okay. Sometimes Fate has other plans."

I clench my jaw. "It's not okay."

She's patient, and she's talking to me, and what she says eases some of my guilt. "Yes, it is. It's my fault you would have been free to do so, but she's gone. There's no point in talking this way. Raff must have found out something. Let's go see what."

I can't argue with that and I let her pull away. I follow her into the living room.

Raff's holding Felicity, and Daisy's using his leg to pull herself up. Emma's not around. Claire covers her mouth and laughs.

"Shut up," he says, scowling. "She had to go to the bathroom."

"I didn't say anything," I say, too grateful Felicity and I have people who love us to give Raff a hard time because he enjoys holding a baby. "Did you go to the bank?"

"Yes. Were you able to pull up Brielle's phone records?"

"Yeah. I have a list of the numbers who frequently called her."

"Good. Let's take a look."

We settle in the dining room where we ate lasagna, and Raff looks around the table in confusion. Emma joins us holding a folder. She slides it onto the table and reaches for Felicity. "Something's missing," he says, handing her off.

"Only half of us are here," I point out.

Raff narrows his eyes, pauses, and then flips the file open. "I went to the bank's branch in the little grocery store near Brielle's apartment. She did withdraw the money that night in the form of a cashier's check."

I lean forward. "Made out to whom?"

"The manager wouldn't say. She insisted I would need a warrant, which, of course, I will never have. I tried to cajole her into telling me, but she was unimpressed with my natural good looks and glowing charisma. She'd tell you, since you're also on the account, but I don't think she would divulge something like that over the phone, and right now it's not safe for you to go out."

"Then what do we do?" I'm frustrated, and I push the file away. It slides in front of Claire, and she skims Raff's notes.

"The grocery store's manager was more cooperative after I bribed her with a free year of exclusive e-zine content, and she showed me security footage from the parking lot that night. Brielle was there with the same person who picked her up outside of The Dugout. I couldn't catch a look at the driver, but Preston wasn't lying. A rusted black Caddy was parked in the loading zone. They didn't plan to be there long."

Claire rubs my back through my shirt, my muscles rigid with stress.

"I wondered about her car," he continues, "and I back-tracked to talk to Preston again. He was rotating tires in his mother's garage, and surprisingly, that's not a euphemism for something dirty. Not pleased to see me, but it didn't stop him from talking. The morning after Brielle rode away in the Caddy, Preston walked to the bar and hotwired it. Her car's sitting in his mother's yard. I looked inside, but I didn't see anything of importance. He asked if I was going to turn him in for stealing it, but I said I didn't give a fuck who had it, I only wanted to know what happened to it." He looks at me for confirmation.

"I don't care."

"If you have a spare set of keys and the title, I think Preston would like to keep it. For the, ah," Raff coughs, "memories."

I pull a face. "Seriously?"

Raff lifts an eyebrow. "Are you telling me you *didn't* have sex with her there?" He flicks a glance at Claire. "Sorry, kid."

"It's obvious he had sex with her, Raff," she says drolly. "Sex in cars is a guy thing."

"Sex anywhere is a guy thing," he replies.

I huff a sad laugh. "I don't have them. They're in her apartment. Keys on a hook in the kitchen, and she kept a plastic box under the bed with paperwork like that. You said you could get in there."

"Yeah. I can go later today. Was it paid off, do you know?"

"I settled the bank loan when we started seeing each other and the lien is attached to the title. She didn't have any other debt."

Raff spins the notes around and scribbles a few things. "What did you find out?"

I tell him about the phone calls I made and upsetting her mom. I write out her uncles' names whom we saw regularly. Her father had two brothers and her mother had one, and they all live in Bridgeport.

"I'll see what I can find out today. We gotta get this going. If her uncles don't know anything. I'm going to have to suggest you lawyer up. I can call my brother if you think that's something you want, but the longer you hide and the longer we don't find anything, the worse it looks. Even if you have to give Felicity up for a couple of days, you'll never keep custody if you don't cooperate."

Emma hugs Felicity to her. "No. They can't have her unless they have a warrant."

"They will, baby girl," he says, the endearment slipping out with a sigh. "Brielle's parents haven't been quiet. The cops know Roman has her, and at the very least, they want to see her."

He's voicing my worst fears, but having his brother on my side is a perk I didn't consider. "A couple more days. Do you know what the police have found out? If anything?"

"They must have a lead somewhere. I asked Preston if the cops have been hassling him and he said no. He looked good for it, very good for it, especially since he was with her that night, so if they're not poking around him, they've got something, and that something probably has to do with you."

"Fuck."

"They don't have anything on you," Claire says, pressing a kiss to my shoulder.

"Be that as it may, innocent people do go to prison."

Raff *tsks*. "Not on my brother's watch. Hell, not even guilty people go to prison on my brother's watch. I'll give him a call. I don't think he's in the middle of a case. I'll at least get his advice, though I can tell you right now he's going to say get your ass to the police station and cooperate. Let me hunt up Brielle's uncles, and I'll run by Brielle's apartment complex for Preston. He was in love with her. A car won't do much, but it's all he has left."

It's sad that I wasn't in love with her, but I was the one who ended up with the very best of her.

We break out the booze and leftover lasagna, but Raff doesn't stay for long. I follow him to the elevator, leaving behind the girls and Daisy who woke up from her nap. After Emma leaves, we'll start on a nursery. I don't care if the walls are cream instead of pink, I want to sleep with Claire alone tonight. I need to wrap my body around hers, sink into her and let her tell me she loves me in her way. She might be opening up more with her words, but I need her bodytalk.

Raff steps into the elevator, but I hold the doors open. "Can I talk to you for a minute?"

"Yeah, what's up?"

"Earlier, Emma and I were talking about Zeke and his girlfriend."

"The woman who was with him in the fire? Daisy's mother?" He leans against the wall and crosses his ankles. He smells a story and he's already intrigued.

"Yeah. I did the math, and Zeke was seeing her the whole time he was married to Claire."

Raff flicks his gaze toward the living room. "Okay?"

"Emma asked me why he married Claire in the first place. Took me a second, but I haven't been a divorce attorney my whole life for nothing. She was already married, and he couldn't."

"You don't think it was because she didn't want to?"

Skeptically, I tilt my head. Who wouldn't want to marry a billionaire? Even if he was an asshole playboy.

"Maybe he didn't want to marry her," he suggests.

"Then why see her in the first place if he had Claire?"

"You don't know how often he was seeing her."

"True, but it doesn't sound right."

"He was a prick who thought he could play two women at the same time and he was successful until Claire wanted out. You want me to look into it?"

"Yeah. Would you? It's probably nothing, but I'm curious now." I pause. "What are you going to do with your 'zine?"

"Curiosity killed the cat, remember that. I'll see what I can dig up." His shoulders slump. Emma's right, he's going to miss the fuck out of his website. "Been putting it off. My mother knows how a campaign works and hasn't been giving me too much bullshit, though she's been ragging on me to fly up with Nic so they can meet her. We won't do that until this is over . . . there's no way I'm leaving you high and dry, but to answer your question, I'm not sure. I have a little more time to decide. Sniffing out buyers. I've had a couple of offers, but she's like a baby—I don't want to give her away. I'd rather hit Delete."

"What if you didn't take it down?"

"My mother would never go for it. Besides, I can't do both. I've gotten quite fond of Mayor Clark, and Nic said she won't, but I'm looking forward to blowjobs under my desk."

My lips twitch. He must keep Veronica very busy. "What if you let us run her?"

He straightens and jabs the lobby button, though it doesn't do much good with me standing in the way. "I'm open to negotiations, but first, Brielle's uncles and Miss Lawton's husband—if she had one."

I hold out my hand, and Raff grips it firmly. "Thanks."

"We have to find that car. That piece of shit belongs to someone around that area. I can sniff around Brielle's apartment building too. I'll keep in touch."

The doors slide shut and I'm left standing alone in the foyer. With each passing day, the odds stack higher against me, and the fact the cops want me for this is a big red flag. Every second they try to pin this on me, the real murderer thinks he got away with it.

I leave Claire and Emma playing with Felicity and Daisy and flop onto our bed.

Claire finds me a half an hour later with tears in my eyes and not an ounce of hope in my body.

CHAPTER SIXTEEN

Claire

I hate seeing him like this. In the past, I would blame myself for his unhappiness, never believing I was enough. Bad day at the office, my fault. Bad day in court, my fault. Bad day at home, definitely my fault. I didn't know how to cook, didn't want kids, and didn't know how to be a wife.

I would hide and suddenly I wasn't consoling him, he would be consoling me, and it would be another shitty thing to add to the list of why I wasn't good enough to be married to Roman Mansfield.

Emma's gone, and I leave the door open to listen for the babies. Daisy's playing in the playpen Emma helped me unfold and set up, and Felicity's sleeping in her bouncy seat. Daisy's been okay since I brought her home, quiet and a little scared. I'm prepared for her to one day blow like a volcano with stress, fear, and loneliness, like Roman is about to do now. He can tell me all he wants he wasn't in love with Brielle, and I believe him, but that doesn't mean he doesn't miss her. She gave him something I didn't, couldn't back then, and I can't replace her now. The mother of his child.

I unzip my green pencil skirt and tug it over my hips. I don't know why I dressed up today, except a sharp skirt and a blouse has always been my uniform, my armor, a warning for everyone to stay away.

Roman watches, not saying anything. Falling so quickly into the routine we used to have. Silence shredded him, but it comforted me.

I pull my cream silk blouse over my head, stand for only a moment in my bra and panties. I've gained a few pounds since we were married. He never commented on my fuller hips and thighs, the little belly fat that accumulated no matter how many carbs I cut from my diet, my breasts that went up a size. Old age, maybe, or sadness and loss.

Bitterness.

Pain.

Too much wine.

I crawl over him in my pretty lingerie, and he lies still, a hand tucked under his head, his watch shining in the light filtering in through the window. He always wore a watch, and I loved it, the metal and leather peeking from the cuff of his crisp white shirt, the glint and the gleam calling attention to his strong, masculine hands. Best of all was his wedding ring, the plain gold on his finger telling the whole world he belonged to me.

I raise his hand to my mouth. His fingers curl around mine like his daughter's, and I kiss his empty ring finger. He would have married her. He would have done the right thing and married her.

He parts his lips to speak, and I shake my head. We don't

need words right now. I don't want him to apologize for being the man I need him to be.

I unbutton his shirt and brush kisses over his chest speckled with hair turning grey. I never remember he's older than Jack, almost fifty, and I want him to be happy with me for fifty more. He wraps my hair around his fingers, tugging, until I understand what he wants, and instead of kisses to his chest, I press my lips to his. I settle my weight on top of him, and he's hard, my cleft cradling his cock.

Our mouths fused together, he rolls until we're both on our sides. His hand dips beneath my panties. I'm wet, and he feels it, his fingers skimming over my pussy. I feel like I'm suffocating, and I wrench away, sucking in a breath. The acrid odor of cigarette smoke fills my nose, the gritty, dirty smell not as unpleasant as it should have been. I never minded that he smoked, and I never minded when he stopped. He picked the habit up again, sneaking a cigarette when I'm not around. I try not to picture him standing on the balcony alone and unsure, trying to find something to calm his nerves, worried there's no way out.

He pushes two fingers inside me, and I whimper.

He might know my cues, but I know his too, and my body tightens in anticipation. He's priming me. He's going to take me hard and I'm going to let him. I don't have anything else that will show him that this time I mean every word I don't say.

I lift my head and he slants his mouth over mine in a violent kiss, bruising my lips. The heel of his hand is pressed against my clit, and I grind against him wanting more. He leans into me, angling his hips, his cock thick and hard, and I jerk away, my breath shuddering from my lungs with the loss of contact. I could have come right then, but it's too soon. I want to give him what he needs first. I unbuckle his belt and unzip his pants. He's breathing as hard as I am. I free his cock from his briefs, and he moans. I wiggle down the bed and cover the tip with my mouth, my hair hiding my face.

The pre-cum is salty, and I lick, the tip of my tongue finding the divot. He pushes my head down, and I take more of him into my mouth. I love getting him off, love the roaring that erupts from the depths of his chest, the feel of the hot semen sliding down my throat. His balls are heavy, and sucking greedily, I gently cup them. I want him to forget, just for a moment, all that's hanging over his head. I've never seen him so hopeless before, and it scares me. He used to be my rock until I wore him down and there was nothing he could do but be swept away in the current that was my misery.

He shudders, close to coming, and he yanks me away, tugging painfully at my hair. Without a word, he rolls off the bed and undresses until he's wearing nothing but his watch, leaving his clothing in a messy pile on the floor. His cock is straining, covered in my saliva.

I tremble and sit and wait.

He unclasps my bra, gently slides the straps down my arms, and throws it on top of his clothes.

Kneeling, he pulls me to the edge of the bed and licks at my nipples, holding my breasts in the palms of his hands. I lean in, threading my fingers through his hair. He nibbles at both until my panties are soaking wet and I'm close to coming from the stimulation alone. Roman knows my body, hasn't forgotten how I respond, and he stops, leaving me teetering on the precipice of an orgasm. My clit quivers and heat is threatening to explode in my belly. He nudges my shoulder, and I turn over and scoot up to the middle of the mattress. How many times has he taken me from behind on this bed? I remember each and every one, but there's too many to count.

Impatient now, he snaps the delicate lace of my panties, stinging my skin. I'm bare, open to him, and skims his fingers along my seam. He acts like he's in control, but he's not. His fingertips dig into my ass cheek, and I'll have bruises in the morning, marks he'll kiss and apologize for.

Without warning, he shoves his fingers inside me, and I yelp, the comforter muffling my cries. I'm wet and swollen, near the edge, about to fall over, but this is for him. I can't come until he's ready for me to do so, and not a second sooner.

This is my punishment for the past four years he's had to live without me.

I understood that when I found him after Emma left.

What he needed.

He pulls his fingers out, and I know what's coming, but knowing doesn't prepare me for the pain. He rams his cock into me with everything he has. A sob catches in my throat, and my heart slams in my chest. We've had sex twice since getting back together, but it wasn't anything like this. Last night was tender, getting to know each other all over again. A respite.

From this.

He thrusts into me, and I moan, the tip hitting my center. He grips my hips in a way that will leave more bruises, and the entire bed shakes with his anger. He comes with a fierce growl from deep in his throat, and I relax in relief. I know the kind of stamina he has, and he could have pounded on me for a lot longer than he did. He pulls out but he's still hard, and the friction hurts, the amount of cum he left behind doing nothing to soothe the burn. I squeeze my eyes shut, and I'm tensing for another vicious round of sex but he caresses my ass and presses on my thigh.

He wants me to turn over.

I do, my legs quivering, and he lowers his body over mine, protective now. He kisses me, his anger dissipating with his climax. He trails his lips down my breasts, lingering at my nipples, over my belly, to my cleft. I want to close my legs. I'm too sore for this, but if he wants to eat me out, then I'll let him.

He laps gently at his own essence, but even the silkiness of his tongue hurts. I arch my back, my body instinctively moving away from the source of the pain, and he stops me, anchoring an arm over my belly, pinning me in place.

He continues his ministrations, licking the sensitive skin where his cock had been moments before. I'm raw, and my heels dig into the mattress as he forces me to hold still.

Tears drip from my eyes, and a sob escapes from my lips. I don't want him to know he's hurting me, but Roman knows me like no one else has or ever will. He knows my every thought, my every feeling, before I do.

It doesn't stop him, and a plea is a whisper from my mouth, ignored. He licks at my clit, and I buck, but not from pain. I need more, and he gives it to me, in slow, lazy circles. He knows he hurt me despite me trying to hide it and doesn't slide his fingers inside me. He releases his hold over my stomach and widens my legs. I press my cleft into his face and come with a shattered cry, the pleasure mixing with the pain.

The punishment finished, he lets me go.

I melt into the comforter, sore and sated, and he cuddles me to him, his scruff scratching at my cheek.

"I'm sorry," he murmurs, our pact of silence broken.

"I want to give you whatever you need," I say, brushing his cheek with my fingers. I love him so much, and all I've done is make him miserable.

"That's always been you, Claire. You don't get it. It's always been you."

He sobs into my hair, and this is the first time in five years I've ever seen him cry.

———

Daisy's whimper interrupts us, and reluctantly, I scoot off the bed and snag my nightgown and robe I left on the bench this morning. "I've got her."

From behind, Roman wraps his body around mine, pressing his face into the side of my neck. "Marry me," he murmurs, his hand clutching the fabric of my nightgown.

"I already said I would."

"Not a big fancy thing like last time. Small, just our friends. Your mom and dad, mine. The girls. Ask Emma and Veronica to stand with you, and Jack and Raff will stand with me, and it will be just us. Next month. Raff's close, and we won't have to wait much longer. For a honeymoon, we'll go away with the girls where I can have you all to myself before the holidays start."

I pause. Next month. So soon, yet, marrying around the holidays would be difficult and my family would never let us skip Thanksgiving or Christmas to go on a honeymoon. Not now. And I want to see my mother for our first Christmas together.

"Don't say it if you don't mean it," he says gruffly, "because I meant what I said. You'll never get another divorce from me. Ever."

I twist in his arms. "Can we honeymoon with your family again?"

"I would really like that. They've missed you."

"I've missed them too. I better see to Daisy. She's probably hungry. Her highchair is set up, and I can mix her some cereal."

"I'll get dressed and help you." He kisses the tip of my nose, and I tilt my head, our lips meeting. He slips his tongue into my mouth, and my belly flutters as he softly licks.

Daisy's soft whimper turns into a frustrated cry.

Reluctantly, I break away. "Okay."

I bring a fresh diaper with me from the stack near my

dresser, and I change her before settling her into the highchair. She's excited she has my attention, and she bangs her chubby hands against the tray. I don't have a baby bowl or plastic spoon, and I make do using a regular bowl and soup spoon. I sit down to feed her, but Roman's burner phone vibrates. I don't know where he is—needing a few minutes to breathe. Raff's name on the screen and I answer. "Hey."

"Is Roman there?" he asks, his voice tense.

"In the bathroom, I think."

"Tell him to go down to the station—"

"What?" I drop the spoon and it clatters onto the floor.

"Now, Claire. One of my guys has a contact at the police department. They think they have enough for a judge to sign off on a warrant."

Roman walks into the kitchen, and I enable the phone's speaker.

"Tell him to turn himself in before they arrest him. Someone knows I've been sniffing around, and they followed me to your penthouse. They know he's there," Raff continues.

My eyes meet Roman's, and he wilts against the island.

"Do they have anything to charge me with?" he asks.

"They must if they think they have enough to ask a judge. I don't know what exactly. Something about your truck. But it's there, isn't it? At Claire's?"

"No, I abandoned it a few hours from here."

"Well, they found it, and there must be something inside it. I called my brother and he contacted an attorney who will meet you there. Don't say a goddamned word. Not to confirm or deny anything. Go there now before they look for you at the penthouse. I didn't hear anything about Felicity. Keep them away from her."

"Okay. Thanks for the heads up."

"His name is Will Kincaid. Don't speak without his say-so.

I'm at Brielle's apartment, and I'm talking to her uncles today. I'll keep at it. Claire, if you hear anything, keep me informed. I'll do the same."

Raff hangs up, and I drop the phone onto the island as if it were burning my hand.

Roman dressed in the pants and dress shirt he wore before we made love, and he shoves his wallet into his pocket. "I'll grab a taxi. Claire, I didn't do this. Please believe me."

"I know. We'll figure out who did, no matter what we have to do. I'll always be here for you. I'm never leaving you again."

"I love you. Take care of the girls, and I'll be home as soon as I can. They can hold me for seventy-two hours without charging me, but I have no idea what they found in my truck." He wraps me in his arms.

My lips brush the soft cotton of his shirt. "You better go. You have a head start. Don't waste it."

"Yeah. I love you, Claire. Please be here when I come back."

I rest my palms against his cheeks. "We are a family. We'll all be here when you come back."

Eking out every last second he can, he rests his forehead against mine, and for once, he's the one talking without words.

"Go," I say, pushing on his shoulder.

The elevator carries him away, and numb, I sit with Daisy and don't feel anything.

CHAPTER SEVENTEEN

Roman

I don't have to step two feet into the Bridgeport police department before a uniform escorts me to an interrogation room. I've been a person of interest for weeks, and everyone knows who I am. Claire's scent clings to me, the delicious way her pussy gripped my cock lingers, a phantom ache that won't go away. I took her rough and I hurt her, but remembering the way she came under my mouth and how she tastes will be the only things that get me through this.

Someone knocks on the door the moment I sink onto the metal chair, and a tall distinguished Black man strides into the room dressed in a sharp grey suit holding an expensive briefcase. "William Kincaid," he says, reaching out his hand. "Stepped in a pile, huh?"

I shrug. I'm not in the mood for small talk. After the conversation I had with Raff about his brother, I should have known the attorney he'd recommend would be just as slick. Doesn't care if I did it or not, it's his personal challenge to get me off, guilty or innocent. As long as he can do his fucking job, I don't care. I'm not going to prison for a murder I didn't commit.

We sit for over an hour, the cops thinking they can gain the upper hand forcing us to stew, and Kincaid asks for the rundown of Brielle's murder. I tell him everything I know, including the snooping Raff's been doing on my behalf. "Alibi?" he asks.

"No. I was home alone with my, our, daughter."

He writes everything down in meticulous print, pausing between sentences and clicking the pen in a focused habit. That could get old real fast, but I tighten my jaw and let him work.

Finally, a detective steps into the room, playing the game wearing a rumpled suit and a grey five o'clock shadow. A bored uniform follows behind him and positions himself in a corner, his face stoic, hands clasped behind his back. There's a camera bolted to the wall near the ceiling, its light glowing red, filming us.

"You're a hard man to pin down," he says, settling into a seat across from Kincaid and me. "Lawyered up fast. I'm Detective Shaw. I was assigned to the case when Brielle McIntosh's body washed up on one of Cavern Lake's beaches."

I know the drill, and I don't say anything. Shaw's older, fifteen years my senior give or take, looking forward to retirement, but he's sharp, his weariness part of a guise. This isn't his first homicide, and in a city the size of Bridgeport, more than likely it's his hundredth. Divorce and death—one happens every day. Job security of the darkest kind.

"Why'd you run?" he asks, resting his arm on the back of the chair next to him, tipping a pen back and forth between his fingers. It triggers my need for a cigarette, and I push it back. The expression on his face is interested, almost kind. He might actually be a detective who will listen, but he won't let me go so easily if there's no one else on their list of suspects.

I don't need Kincaid's approval to answer that. "I knew I'd end up here."

"Do you know why we want to talk to you?"

At this, Kincaid does nod, and I say, "I heard you found my truck."

"Curious why you'd dump it. 2020 Range Rover. Drive it off the lot for twice what I make in a year. You leave it at a Walmart in a shitty little town. Must be nice to have that kind of money you don't care what happens to it."

There's not a question there, and I don't reply.

I should have told Raff I abandoned my truck in favor of the rusted Toyota I drove to Claire's, that probably has gotten towed by now, too, since I left it on the street and there isn't parking on that side on Wednesdays. I wasn't thinking about anything but finding Brielle's killer, keeping Felicity safe . . . and Claire.

"There's no overnight parking in their lot, and Walmart had it towed. The city impound ran your plates and called us. We had our CSU team go over it, and the traces of blood in the front seat wasn't a big shock. She was still healing from having your baby, wasn't she? What did you do, fuck her before you killed her? The ME found semen when he performed the autopsy. Is it yours?"

I grit my teeth and tears fill my eyes. Yeah, she was still bleeding, and bile burns my throat. I didn't think she wasn't ready to have sex, and the thought of hurting her turns my stomach. What Claire and I did this afternoon was different. That kind of pain during sex takes intimacy to another level. I never would have hurt Brielle for my own satisfaction . . . or hers.

I check my emotions. I can't let Detective Shaw see me weak. He'll think I'm guilty.

"That kind of talk isn't necessary," Kincaid admonishes politely. "Explain the blood for the detective."

"She managed a diner, and she sometimes filled in if an employee called out sick. One of her cooks had the flu and she was doing the best she could in the kitchen. She was carving roast beef for their lunch special and she slipped and cut her hand. She called me and I picked her up. It was faster than waiting for an ambulance, and she was in too much pain to drive herself. She was bleeding pretty badly, and it dripped on the seat and onto the floor. They gave her ten stitches at an urgent care five blocks from the diner. You can check her medical records. It was last summer sometime."

"But you did have sex with her that night."

"No, and for the very reasons you just described. I would never have hurt her."

"Do you know who did?"

I pause. If he's asking, either he knows and wants to see if I know, or he didn't question Preston hard or long enough to find out he had a quickie with Brielle outside The Dugout the night she was killed. If they've looked through Brielle's social media, they already know she had a relationship with him prior to dating me, and I say, "Yes. Preston Nelson."

Detective Shaw scribbles a note, nodding. He won't waste time fighting me on it—a DNA test will prove I'm telling the truth. "Where have you been bunking all this time?"

I'm about to respond, but Kincaid holds up a hand. "That's not relevant."

Relieved, I close my mouth. I can't point them in Felicity's direction.

"Where were you that night?" Shaw asks.

Kincaid nods.

"At home with our daughter. She was only five weeks old and we didn't want to leave her with a sitter."

"Can anybody confirm that for you?"

"No. Maybe a neighbor. Brielle's walls are thin, and I watched TV while she was gone." That won't prove anything. Anyone can turn on a TV and leave, but it's the best I have.

"Did you know she was cheating on you?"

"No. I didn't find out she had a boyfriend until after her death."

"And how did you find out?"

I'd like to keep Raff out of this for as long as possible. "Her social media—like I'm sure how you found out."

"This doesn't look good for you, you know that, right? The mother of your child was having an affair, no one can corroborate you were home with your daughter, and if I recall, you told Miss McIntosh you weren't sure you wanted to remain in a relationship with her. Was she needy? Did she want your money? Did she threaten to keep your daughter away from you if you broke it off?"

Kincaid raises a hand, but I shake my head. I'll sound like a prick, but I tell Detective Shaw the truth. "I gave her money and never in our whole time together did she ask for more. She wasn't needy. She was independent when we met, and she stayed that way. It's what drew me to her in the first place. There was no chance she could have kept Felicity from me. I have the means to sue her ass off if she would have tried. I had the control in our relationship. I didn't need to kill her."

Shaw narrows his eyes at me and jots down a few notes. "We found a sweater in the backseat of your vehicle. Did it belong to Miss McIntosh?"

"Of course it did. We were practically living together and she rode in my truck often. Why wouldn't she have things in my vehicle?"

"We'll want to compare your DNA to what we found, and we'll check with the urgent care. You don't mind hanging out while we do that, do you?" he asks, closing the file laying on the table. "It shouldn't take long."

I scoff. He'll go out for a leisurely dinner and let me simmer, and then he'll tell me the labs are closed until tomorrow and it would be a big help if I spent the night in a holding cell until the tests came back.

I'm trapped until at least morning, and I stare at my hands. I miss Brielle, I really do, but my heart is with Claire and Felicity, and there is still a very small part of me that's afraid that no matter what Claire promised, she won't be there when they release me.

CHAPTER EIGHTEEN

Claire

Whether he wants to believe it or not, Raff is entangled in our group. Not a half an hour goes by before the elevator doors slide open and Jack and Emma step into the foyer. Raff must have called or texted them and said I shouldn't be alone.

It's nice to have help taking care of the babies, but I wouldn't have minded waiting for Roman by myself.

"We'll get him out of this," Jack says, hugging me. "Why are you in a nightgown?"

"Why do you think?" Emma asks, lifting Felicity out of her swing.

My brother's face turns red. "Oh. Well, go put some clothes on."

"Thanks. I'll be right back."

I steal more than a minute to wash my face and brush my hair, and Jack's in the living room holding Daisy when I'm done. I have nowhere to go and ended up dressing in a pair of black shorts and a tank top. Jack's also dressed down—he must have skipped work today.

Daisy, like every other female on the planet, is enthralled with Jack, patting his cheeks and giving him open-mouthed kisses. She squeals, and he laughs. If she has problems settling into our family, he's going to be my go-to for help.

I succumb to the pressure and pour a glass of wine. These last few days have been so stressful, and until we clear Roman's name and find out who really killed Brielle, things won't go back to normal.

Emma joins me, Felicity propped against her shoulder. I don't bother to ask if she's pregnant. She wouldn't be drinking if she was. We carry our wine into the living room, and she sinks onto the couch. Too agitated to sit still, I stand near Jack and hold out my free hand out to Daisy. I want her to get used to me, but I've done a poor job of giving her attention.

"Are you and Emma still getting married in November?"

Jack's eyes turn all gooey, and he looks at his fiancée. "Yeah. Is that going to be a problem? We'll push it back if it is."

"No, I'm only planning. Raff and Veronica aren't getting married anytime soon, are they?"

"Not that I'm aware," Emma says. "The last I heard from Veronica is that they're marrying in Boston next fall. They need to get the wedding out of the way before Raff hits the campaign trail, but his brother's fiancée is pregnant and they want to get married first."

"Okay. Good. Roman asked if we could get married next month, and I didn't want to be in anyone's way."

"Ah, Claire, that's great. I'm happy for you both," Jack says, leaning over and kissing my cheek.

"Thanks. He didn't say so, but I think if Raff can't find out who killed Brielle, he won't want to. This is going to taint anything we find together, as a couple and as a family. Felicity deserves to know what happened to her mother."

"Raff is getting closer," Raff says, stepping into the living room with a file in his hands. "Claire, can I speak to you for a moment?"

I shoot a questioning glance at Jack, but he nods and says, "We're good."

"Thanks."

Raff follows me into the kitchen and pours a glass of whiskey that seems to be a permanent fixture in the kitchen since Roman moved in. I add more wine to my glass.

He shoots the inch of whiskey and then asks, "How well did you know Lacey?"

I scowl. "Lacey? I didn't know her at all."

"Did you know *of* her?"

"No. Why would I have? The first I heard of her was when the news reported hers and Zeke's deaths."

"So, while you were married, Zeke didn't mention her, didn't spend long, unexplained amounts of time away from you?"

"He didn't mention her, but we weren't attached at the hip. Neither of us worked. He had an ex-wife and children, and I assumed he spent time with them without telling me. We partied a lot, sometimes together but mostly separately. Usually, if we were together, he was sleeping."

"Sleeping, or *sleeping*?" Raff asks.

"Sleeping. We only had sex a couple of times after our wedding day, but I didn't analyze it. I was relieved, really. I missed Roman and didn't want to have sex with anyone else. Zeke didn't want to have sex with me, either, obviously, and now I know it was because he was in love with Lacey."

"How often did you sleep together, but only sleep together?"

I shrug. "Once a month, maybe?"

Raff glares at me. "For fuck's sake. You were married to the guy and saw him once a month? And you didn't think that was odd?"

"Haven't you ever married someone you didn't want to marry?" There's no way I can defend myself. I used Zeke to draw out Roman, but by then he'd already met Brielle. No one saved me from myself.

He quirks his mouth. "No, I can't say that I have. So, once a month. How did you two meet?"

"At a party. He said he wanted to fuck, and I played along said I didn't screw strangers. He knew somebody at the court-house, threw a few thousand around to rush a marriage license, and we were married the next day. Then he screwed my brains out in the pastor's office against a bookshelf, that, ironically, had a copy of *Love and Respect, Building a Solid Marriage through God*. I banged my head on it a couple of times."

"Jesus Christ," Raff mutters.

"Yeah, I'm sure He watched."

He thrums his fingers against the marble island. "You didn't think it was strange, up and getting married like that?"

"We all do dumb shit, and I was still in love with Roman. It's not like I was thinking clearly. I was lonely and I missed him. I regretted it the second we said our vows."

"Where did you live?"

"His family owns a penthouse not far from here. I moved in, but it never felt like home. Jill and Teddy made it clear that it wasn't. They weren't impressed with our marriage, and I think they were both surprised we lasted as long as we did."

"They're his parents?"

"Yeah."

"They didn't know anything about Lacey?"

I trickle some whiskey into the glass Raff used and sip. The wine isn't cutting it. "I called Jill about Zeke's will, and she said she did. She said in no uncertain terms Daisy would be homeless if I didn't take her in."

"But she did know Zeke was seeing her."

"I guess so. She wasn't happy about it. Called her white trash. Why? Where is all this going?'

"Bear with me a moment. Pregnancy isn't my wheelhouse, but it's safe to say he was dating her the whole time you were married. Where did *she* live? I assume he had her tucked away somewhere, especially after she got pregnant."

"I don't know. I really don't. Maybe the penthouse where I picked up Daisy? We were strangers when we married, and we were strangers when we divorced."

"Did he give you a hard time about that? Did he beg you not to divorce him? Essentially, he was using your relationship as a cover, was he not? If he spent more time with Lacey than with you?"

"Yeah, I figured that out after talking to Jill, but I don't know where he spent his time. He asked me if I was sure I wanted out, and I said yes. He kissed me my cheek and told me goodbye, and that afternoon his attorney contacted mine. It went as smoothly as it could have."

"Okay, I walked you through all that because I want to know why he married you and not Lacey. If he loved her that much, why didn't he tell his parents to fuck off? Why go through all that trouble, and millions of dollars," he says, referring to the settlement Zeke paid me in the divorce, "to hide it? She would have been a rags to riches story in the media and it would have passed in a blip."

"Oh," I breathe and sit down heavy on a barstool. "I didn't think of it that way." Zeke was a mama's boy, but I don't think that would have stopped him from telling Jill to shove it if he had loved Lacey that much.

"Emma did, and she asked Roman about it. Roman knew right away."

"She was already married."

"Bingo. You and he think alike. He asked me to look into who it was just in case he turned up later to cause trouble."

"Is it anybody important?"

"First, I had a hell of a time finding him. Lawton isn't her husband's name, it's her mother's maiden name, and she's been dead for several years." Raff opens his file and pushes a piece of paper at me that turns out to be a copy of a marriage certificate. "Zeke and Lacey were in the process of pushing her divorce through court, but they died before anything was finalized. Her husband was stalling, accusing her of physical and emotional abuse and suing her for spousal support and for her to pay his attorney fees—his very expensive attorney's fees. She was fighting the abuse allegations, and she was right to do so. She wouldn't have wanted rumors and accusations like that tarnishing her character and casting doubt on the kind of mother she would have been to Daisy, or the kind of wife she would have been to Zeke, for that matter. She was also refusing to pay her husband a dime, something he didn't like very much. That held everything up."

Jack and Emma walk into the kitchen each holding a baby, and they freeze, noting the tension in the room.

Raff continues, "Zeke wasn't using you only to hide Lacey, he was using you to hide the scandal he would have caused had it gotten out he was dating, and knocked up, a married woman. Jack knows the kind of shitstorm that can happen if documents," he says, tapping the certificate in front of me, "like that are leaked to the press—"

Jack scoffs.

"—and Zeke's parents already hated Lacey. That would have made it a million times worse."

I skim the marriage certificate. "Who's Greg Olsen?"

"Lacey's husband."

"Yeah, I can see that, but should I know him?" The name doesn't sound familiar.

"No, but Roman will. He's Brielle's uncle."

I stare at the name.

"Why does that sound bad?" Emma asks.

"Because, baby girl, I think it's going to turn out to be very, very bad."

———

"There's no way Brielle's and Lacey's deaths aren't connected," Jack says, popping his lips at Daisy who wants his undivided attention.

Thoughtfully, Raff sips on the whiskey I poured but didn't finish. "Deaths, maybe not. No one could have known Blaise Barker would set the Bridgeport Hotel on fire, or that Zeke and Lacey would be at the bar that particular evening, but it's all connected somehow. I'm going to talk to this Olsen guy, see what he has to say."

I hop off the stool. "I'm going with you."

"Claire," Jack says, his voice full of warning.

"I have to go. His wife and niece are both dead, and whether they're connected or not, they're connected to *us*. It's my responsibility as Daisy's guardian, her *mother*, to keep her safe. And I don't like it, but this guy is related to Felicity. Roman would want me to go."

"I can go," Emma says, ready to hand Felicity to me.

Jack presses his lips together. He likes neither of those options, but he wouldn't stop Emma from going with Raff, and I give him big props for that.

Raff doesn't need anybody to go with him, but he's walking

into a potentially dangerous situation, and it's never a good idea to do something like that alone. "Claire, go change," he says, taking the decision out of our hands. "He'll talk if he thinks we're somebody important."

I hurry down the hallway, and in the bedroom, I put on the skirt and blouse I wore to Zeke and Lacey's penthouse. That was only this morning, but it feels like a thousand lifetimes ago. They're lying in a heap on the floor next to the bed, but they aren't too wrinkled and will do the job. I'm changed and shoving heels onto my feet in under five minutes.

Raff's waiting by the elevator.

"Do you know where he lives?" Jack asks.

"In a mobile home park in north Bridgeport, not too far from Brielle's apartment building." His eyes dart to me. "Ready?"

"Yeah." I unhook my purse from a knob in the front closet and step into the elevator with him.

No one tells us to be careful.

We have to be.

There's too much depending on it.

———

Raff drove himself, and he's parked around the corner. He holds the door open for me, and I slide in and latch my seatbelt.

We're quiet as he drives north, the skyscrapers giving way to shorter buildings, and those give way to strip malls, rundown grocery stores, and parking lots dotted with holes. The idea Roman regularly spent time in this part of the city isn't as puzzling as it could have been. He would fit in here, enjoy the simplicity of this kind of life. Where every day wasn't full of fake glitz and glamour, and again, I wonder if I can replace what he found in the narrow roads and tired houses. What fed his soul in the yards covered in weeds and the abandoned play-grounds?

Raff points out Brielle's apartment complex, broken-down cars rusting in the parking lot, the balconies sagging. Even in the bright sunlight, the chipped brick building doesn't appear cheerful. A tired woman pushes a stroller past the front steps, and a skinny stray dog watches her, hoping for food.

He liked it here because there was always more to Roman than money and social status. Brielle gave him a baby and a home in her little apartment, and I bet all *my* money he was content waking up to her every morning after a night of spinning dreams. He would still be with her if she hadn't been murdered.

"Are you going to be like Jack?" Raff asks, turning a corner. A mobile home park looms ahead, a maze of trailers that all look the same.

"What do you mean?"

"Always doubting the good? You and Brielle are different women. What he got out of his relationship with her is different than what he's getting from you, and the only reason he was looking for anything in the first place was because he missed you. As Nic likes to say, put some lipstick on and get your shit together. This isn't about you anymore."

"How did you know?"

"The way you stared at Brielle's apartment complex. You're jealous people could be happy living in that little box when you're miserable with millions and a penthouse so high in the sky a woman like Brielle would get a nosebleed. You should learn something from that." He navigates his truck over the gravel road, potholes filled with water from a rain I don't remember. The homes are a dilapidated mess, and I feel very out of place. He idles and tries to decipher which mobile home belongs to Greg Olsen. "Roman needed her happiness and was drawn to it. Are you happy, Claire?"

"I am when I'm with him."

"Then you need to find more. Happiness with the girls, happiness with your mom. You need more than Roman—you always have or you wouldn't have divorced him." He keeps going, gravel crunching under the tires, and turns onto a narrow path. A lone mobile home sits near a giant evergreen tree, an old black car with a cracked back window parked next to it. "There's Olsen's house and the car I've been searching for. He picked Brielle up the night she was murdered. I don't know what to expect, and I'd prefer if he didn't know we know about Lacey. Let's keep it about Brielle, where they went that night. He drove her to a bank and she withdrew ninety-five thousand from an account she and Roman shared. I don't know if it was for himself." He glances at me. "Okay? Follow my lead."

"Yeah."

There isn't a proper driveway, and Raff parks behind the black car on the gravel path leading up to the trailer house. He peers into the vehicle, cupping his hands around his eyes. Briefly, I peek in, too, but I don't see anything except empty cigarette cartons, an old coffeeshop cup, and a fast food bag thrown into the backseat. Nothing that would indicate he was the last to see Brielle alive.

The porch sags with age, and gingerly, I follow Raff as he mounts the wooden stairs. I don't want to break through the rotting planks.

He pushes the lit-up button to the doorbell, and inside the mobile home, it sounds like wind chimes.

An older man wearing jeans and a black t-shirt answers the door a second later. He studies us through the screen, and I study him in return, looking for the type of man a woman like Lacey would have married. I don't know how old Lacey was. In the photo I found in Daisy's nursery, she looked younger, sparkling with joy and the family she'd created with Zeke. Brielle's uncle looks older than Roman, lines dredged into his face, but that could be the smoking or the hard life he's been living. No matter what Raff said about finding happiness in Brielle's complex, struggling to make ends meet is difficult. I've struggled to make emotional ends meet all my life. I know it's not the same, but I still empathize.

"What do you want?" Olsen asks gruffly.

"I'm Rafferty Clark, and this is my assistant. I'm working on a story about Brielle McIntosh's death, and I was hoping you'd give me a few minutes of your time." Raff's voice is smooth, unruffled. "I'm willing to compensate you."

He glares at us, considering. I think he's going to turn us down, but he unlocks the screen door and pushes it open.

"Thank you." Raff holds it open for me, but he steps through first. We don't know what we're going to find, and I appreciate his caution.

I've never been inside a trailer house before, and the rectangle layout is interesting. The living room and kitchen are in the middle, bedrooms located at the ends. A long strip. Once I heard a country song about a double-wide trailer, but I doubt Mr. Olsen would appreciate me asking if that's what this is. I don't know the difference.

Olsen gestures to the living room area, and we sit on a couch that's in decent condition. The air is scented with eggs and pepper, and my stomach growls queasily. Booze wasn't the best option for lunch, but after Roman left to turn himself in, I didn't want to eat.

He sits in a matching chair to Raff's right.

"First," Raff begins, "I'd like to say I'm sorry for your loss. It must be devastating to lose a member of your family." He perches on the edge of the cushion, resting his elbows on his knees.

"Her mama and her father took it a lot harder than I did. Bri and I were close—her folks live down the road a bit—but she moved into her own apartment a few years ago and I didn't see her much after that."

"What did you think about her dating Roman Mansfield?" he asks.

I stiffen. I didn't think Raff would go there so soon.

"Son of a bitch. I know he killed her," Olsen says, his leg jiggling in agitation.

"Why would you say that?"

"I know those rich types. You're one of 'em. Think they can buy whatever they want, then when they don't want it anymore, they throw it away. Bri was in love with the fucking bastard, and he didn't give a shit. He got tired of her and did something about it."

"How are you related to Brielle?" Raff asks.

"I'm her mother's brother."

"You're not married, don't have any children?"

"No kids. My wife ran off, but in the end, she got what she deserved." Olsen purses his lips.

"I'm sorry. Women—can't live with 'em, can't live without 'em." Raff tries for camaraderie, but Olsen isn't impressed . . . or swayed. He glowers, and I have a feeling if Raff doesn't hurry up, Olsen is going to kick us out of here without the answers we want. Raff clears his throat. "When was the last time you saw your niece?"

"A few days before her body washed up on the beach. That prick she was seeing took up all her time, and after she had her baby, she never left her apartment. I think he locked her up. Wouldn't let her see anybody or go out. Too afraid of what she'd say."

I want to object. Roman would never be that way with anyone, but Raff touches my knee in warning, and I relax. Defending Roman would ruin this for us.

"That's interesting. I talked to someone who was with her at The Dugout the night she died, and he said he saw Brielle get into a car that looked like the one sitting outside."

Olsen's voice chills even colder than it was. "They must have been mistaken."

"Did the police ask you where you were the night Brielle disappeared?"

"No, they didn't. They didn't have any reason to. I was at my sister's playing cards with her, my brother-in-law, and some of their neighbors. You can ask her."

Raff nods, knowing Olsen is lying.

"Did Brielle ever give you any money when she was dating Mansfield? From what I know of him, he's rich as fuck."

Olsen sneers. "Richer than you? I'm not stupid. I see your fancy suit, and I saw your tricked out truck when I opened the door. Your assistant is carrying a purse that would feed me and my family for years if I sold it on eBay. My wife was like that. Always wanting the money. She bartended at the Bridgeport Country Club, schmoozed rich fucks like you every day hoping for big tips. Turned her head. Couldn't be happy with what I gave her, she always had to have more. Money is the root of all evil, and she's in hell where she belongs."

Aggression rolls off him, and the hairs on the back of my neck stand up. I don't want to be here anymore, and Raff also senses the atmosphere turning hostile.

Smoothly, Raff slides to his feet, and I can't scoot off the couch fast enough. I step toward the door, but Raff pauses and asks, "Brielle never gave you a dime. I've spoken with Mansfield, and he said he opened a joint account for Brielle and himself. She had access to some money. Not a lot, considering how much he's worth, but it would have been a significant amount to her . . . and to you."

Olsen stands as well and narrows his eyes. "What are you implying?"

"I'm not implying anything. I'm asking you what happened that night. Mansfield said Brielle drained that account the night she was murdered. Where did the money go, do you think?"

"What I think is that you need to leave." Olsen's sweating, perspiration trickling down his temples, and his lips are white with rage.

Raff wants answers and he's pressing our luck, but I want to do what Olsen says and go. We'll lean on the police and force them to do their jobs.

He walks with me to the door, a hand to my lower back. He turns and says, "I chatted with Preston Nelson. Brielle was in love with him. Why did she start dating Mansfield if she was already in love with someone else?"

Olsen snarls, and before I can blink, he's clutching a black handgun I didn't see hidden under an old newspaper laying on an end table, the metal dull and scarred. His hand shakes, his finger curled around the trigger.

Raff freezes.

"I had the perfect plan. She didn't want to go through with it, but I wasn't going to let her back out for that stupid moron. Sit down while I figure out what to do."

"Olsen—" Raff starts.

"I said, sit *the fuck down*. You know too much."

Raff sighs. "This won't bring your wife back."

"My whore of a wife is dead, and if you don't shut your mouth, in two minutes, you will be too."

CHAPTER NINETEEN

Roman

Kincaid and the uniform follow Detective Shaw, and I'm left alone in the interrogation room with a terse "I'll be in touch" from the attorney. Curiosity gets the better of me, and I try the door's handle. It's not locked, but I doubt I would get very far if I tried to leave. I don't have the burner phone Raff gave me and all I can do to keep myself occupied is daydream about Claire and what I want to do to her the next time we have a few minutes alone. I love her so much, and it will be bittersweet to raise Felicity and see Brielle in her features as Claire and I build our lives into the future I wanted with her in the first place.

A clock on the wall clicks away the seconds, and no one bothers to ask if I want even a cup of coffee.

Two agonizing hours after Shaw walked out, the door squeaks open. Maybe I was wrong and he requested Brielle's medical records tonight instead of waiting for morning. Between the scar on her hand and the medical report, that should be enough to explain the reason why there are traces of blood in my truck. I doubt Shaw would have bothered to track Preston down and ask for a sample of his DNA, but because of his record, maybe they already had something on file. They didn't ask for mine.

I look up from the table expecting Shaw or Kincaid, maybe even a uniform wanting to know if I'm hungry, but it's Brielle's mother. Short and curvy, her greying hair is pulled into a sloppy ponytail, and her face is etched with pain. She hesitates in the doorway but realizing she could be seen, lets it close silently behind her.

"Mrs. McIntosh," I say, my voice thick.

"You couldn't do the right thing, could you?" she asks, clutching her purse tightly to her side. "You knocked her up and moved in with her, for God's sake. Why didn't you marry her?"

"Mrs. McIntosh, Brielle was a sweet girl, and I liked spending time with her, but I didn't love her." It's a hard truth to tell the mother of the woman I dated for two years.

She curls her lip. "So what? You think everyone marries for love? You got her pregnant. You loved her enough to sleep in her bed, and you asked her to open her legs for you. And she did it, didn't she? Every time. Is that how you repaid her, telling her she wasn't good enough to give her your name?"

I sit up, wary. This is the second time someone has told me Brielle didn't want to have sex with me. What was she saying behind my back? "I was always going to take care of her and Felicity."

"A shitty child support payment wasn't part of the plan."

"Plan?" I stand up, not liking this at all. "What plan, Mrs. McIntosh?"

She scoffs, the pain on her face turning into something

uglier than grief. "You think it was just a coincidence she was outside that bar the night you met?"

I flash back to that evening. I'm not drunk, but I'm not sober, losing at '80s trivia and muttering about the side bets we placed that I lost. I missed Claire, looked for her everywhere I went, though by then news she'd married Ezekiel Kavanaugh hit the newspapers and social media. In a tizzy, no one could stop talking about the handsome bad boy billionaire and the richest socialite in Bridgeport tying the knot one day after they met. My heart broke for her, the lost, unhappy woman I kissed goodbye in her attorney's office's parking lot, and I was needing something.

Anything.

I stepped out into the cool evening, and a slim brunette was leaning against the building, tears on her cheeks and a broken shoe in her hand. I asked if she needed help, and she tried to smile. In a watery voice she told me her heel snapped off her sandal and she twisted her ankle.

"Of course it was a coincidence. She sprained her ankle that night. Her shoe broke."

"You're such a fool, but that's what we counted on. She sprained her ankle at work the day before. One of the dumbass waitresses was mopping up a spill, and she slipped and fell."

"I don't understand. Why would she trick me?"

"To make you fall in love with her, why the hell do you think? We knew how rich you are, we knew if she married you we'd all be set for life. That ninety-five thousand was just a taste of what we could have had. I told her, you leave Preston alone. Give that rich asshole whatever he wants. She didn't want your baby, she wanted your money."

"Ninety-five thousand?" I repeat. "How do you know about that?"

Ignoring me, she continues, "You should have just married

her, but no, you told her you were thinking about dumping her and she ran right back to Preston. She didn't give a fuck you wanted to leave her. She was happy, the stupid girl. She wouldn't listen to reason. Didn't want to see how much we needed the money she could have gotten her hands on if she married you."

"It was a setup? But how did you know about me? There are thousands of rich men in Bridgeport. Brielle was beautiful and had such a kind soul. She could have dated anybody. Why me?"

"After Greg's wife left him, he thought of the whole thing. Convinced Brielle it was the only way if we wanted out of the trailer park. She could do better than Preston, dumber than a box of rocks, he's not going nowhere, and he dragged Brielle down with him." Her face is white, tears of rage, bitterness, and resignation in her eyes.

Christ, it would be great if someone was on the other side of the two-way mirror, but I doubt anyone is watching this. Even the red light on the camera is gone.

"Greg? Your brother? I didn't know him before I met Brielle. What does he have to do with this?"

"Greg's wife left him, and he was devastated. I've never seen him so beaten down. He loved Lacey so much, and the only thing she did was cheat on him. He wanted someone to pay, and he chose you. All you had to do was marry my sweet Brielle, instead you led her around, forcing her to pick up pennies."

I don't hear anything past Lacey's name, and I'm only more confused. "Lacey Lawton? Zeke Kavanaugh's girlfriend?"

"That skank. Greg searched online and found out who he was, and we found out he had a wife. Your ex-wife, and that's where Greg got the idea. The night Brielle met you, she said you were a sucker, but we never imagined it would be that easy.

She might have hung in there if you hadn't needed to fuck her every night."

That evening becomes clearer now. How many men did she ignore waiting for me to come out of the bar? The way she snuggled into my side in the taxi. She was shy when she asked me to help her upstairs, and I took that as hesitancy. It's not safe to have a stranger in your home. It wasn't caution. She was coyly baiting me. Brielle played me and I fell for it. I was heartbroken and missing Claire. Maybe Greg couldn't have known that, but Brielle was pretty and he counted on me wanting her.

Shame burns my cheeks because I did.

But I thought she wanted me, too.

In the middle of the night, was I waking her up or was she steeling herself for another round of sex she didn't want?

I push back saliva that pools in my mouth and a sick queasiness that rolls in my stomach. I never would have hurt her, yet I did. Every time I was with her. But none of this answers the question I've had since they found her body. "Do you know who killed your daughter, Mrs. McIntosh?"

"We couldn't let her change her mind. You told her you didn't want to be with her anymore and she should have convinced you to marry her. Promised you anything. But she was in love with Preston. Greg was livid. All that planning, all that work, only for her to run off with that loser. They fought. He didn't mean to. I can't let him go to prison."

"Greg killed Brielle." Static fills my ears.

"He didn't mean to," she repeats. "I don't blame him. She should have stuck to the plan. We were so close."

"You need to tell the police," I say, but she won't. She cares more about keeping her brother out of prison than her own daughter's death.

"Nobody's telling anybody anything. Greg has two reporters at his house right now, thinking they can get him to confess. He won't let anyone send him to prison, and he'll kill them too before that happens. He's already done time, and he doesn't want to go back to that hellhole."

"He should have thought of that before he strangled Brielle and dumped her body into the lake. He thought he wouldn't get caught?"

"No one would have known if that busybody from *Talk of the Town* hadn't stuck his nose into our business. Another rich asshole thinking he has the right to do what he wants because he has money."

Raff's at Greg's house. I've never been inside his trailer, though I know where it is. I picked Brielle up there on several occasions during the two years we were together. I'm close with my own family, and I never thought anything of it. But now I know she wasn't simply visiting—he was checking in with her and our relationship. "You said two people." My voice shakes.

Mrs. McIntosh smiles, and the woman who doesn't care her daughter is dead comes out, satisfaction and hate flashing in her eyes. "Oh, we know who Claire Durand is, and if you think for one minute we're going to let her raise Felicity, you're dumber than Preston. That woman won't get another day with my grandchild. Tell her goodbye."

CHAPTER TWENTY

Claire

Raff rolls his eyes. "Seriously? We told people we were coming here. If you're trying to avoid going to prison, killing us won't help."

I part my lips to say, what? I don't know. He shouldn't be so cavalier about this.

He shoves his hands into his pockets and pulls out a roll of mints. "Want one?" he asks me, holding out the roll.

I shake my head. What the hell is he doing? He offers the package of mints to Olsen, and his hand trembles in response.

"Suit yourself," Raff says, thumbing one off and popping it into his mouth. "Can we at least get the story straight?" He ambles around the living room, not concerned in the least Olsen is pointing a gun at him.

A large portrait of a couple hangs over the couch, and Raff studies it. I do too, now that my attention is on it, and the woman's appearance is what Daisy will look like in her thirties. Bright red hair, clear pale skin. It's no wonder Olsen took her leaving so hard. She's beautiful, and at the time of the photo, maybe she wasn't in love with her husband, but she held a fondness for him. It's evident in the way Olsen holds her close and she leans in. Daisy will be beautiful, too, and I don't think Zeke gave his baby one gene. At any other time, I would be amused that a man who had to claim everything he touched had a daughter who wouldn't look like him in the slightest.

"What story?" Olsen asks, his voice shaking as much as his hand.

"The story of that night," Raff says, strolling away from me.

Olsen doesn't know where to keep his aim, but Raff 's the one who's talking, and Olsen reluctantly turns toward him, his focus off me. I know what Raff is trying to do, and I slowly dip my hand into my purse. I wake up my cell with a touch to the screen, and I try desperately to open my phone app without looking.

"What night?" Olsen asks, glancing back at me, but he's too nervous to keep his eyes off Raff for long.

"The night you killed Brielle. You said you didn't do it, but, come on. We can be honest here, can't we? Walk me through it, for my own morbid curiosity. She *did* give you the money, didn't she? I went to the bank and watched the parking lot security footage from the camera attached to the building. You picked her up at The Dugout and drove her to the grocery store. When she had the cashier's check made out, did it have your name on it? There's so much evidence stacked against you, Olsen, it doesn't matter if you kill us."

Olsen's back is facing me, and I open my recent call list. Jack's name is there, Emma's more recent, but I connect to my brother. Emma might have her phone in her purse, but Jack keeps his in his pants pocket.

The call connects. Jack answers and I cough, covering up the sound of his voice.

"I picked her up," Olsen says.

Raff wanders around the living room, his hands tucked casually into his pockets. He moves the mint from one side of his mouth to the other.

Olsen continues, "She was standing on the sidewalk with that fucking dumbass and he was drooling all over her. Fucking idiot. She got in the car, and I could smell the sex on her. I needed the cash to pay off a loan, and I drove her to the bank. She withdrew the money, and after that, I parked at an empty playground just to talk some sense into her, but she wanted to go back to the bar and find Preston. I didn't mean to hurt her," he says pathetically, and I almost feel sorry for him.

"But you did," Raff says, keeping his eyes on Olsen's face, and Olsen's eyes off me.

"She didn't want to marry Mansfield, couldn't stand his hands on her. She wanted to run away with Preston. We were so close. All the planning, all the time we put into tricking him. She wanted to throw it all away for some scumbag who's only good for changing the oil in my car. She threatened to tell Mansfield everything, and I lost control. I choked her. I didn't mean to for so long or so hard, but all his millions were just *right there* and she was going to ruin everything."

"You drove her out to the lake?" Raff asks, leaning against the breakfast bar that separates the kitchen area from the living room. Three stools are pushed under the counter, and Raff rests his elbow on it and crosses his ankles. He pulls the roll of mints from his pocket and plays with the foil wrapper.

"I had to get rid of her body. I didn't think the current would wash her onto the beach, or that someone would find her."

Raff tilts his head and quirks his mouth. "That might have worked, but you keep forgetting that love is very powerful. As a man who recently found the love of his life, I can vouch for that. Roman might not have loved Brielle, but you know what? Preston did. He wanted to know what happened to her, and he was a big help putting the pieces together. But there're different kinds of love, Olsen. Roman's my friend, and I've seen the way he is with Felicity. He loves that baby. He'd do anything to protect her, and he wanted to know what happened to her mother. He wasn't going to let Felicity grow up with that uncertainty. I'm sorry Lacey fell in love with Zeke. You say she was after his money, but hmmm. I've held their daughter. There was love in their relationship, and they named her Daisy."

Raff's speech brings tears to my eyes. I blink to clear my watery vision and glance at my purse. The call is still connected.

I have proof Jack heard everything when police cruisers screech to a halt in the gravel outside Olsen's mobile home.

Olsen hears it too, and in a panic, pulls the trigger.

CHAPTER TWENTY-ONE

Roman

Brielle's mother beams at me, knowing I'm right where she and Olsen want me, and I stand frozen in horror. The fluorescent lights are too bright, and the air is too stale to fill my lungs. Heat prickles my skin, and sweat slides down my back. If Greg Olsen killed his niece, he would have no qualms killing Raff and Claire to get them out of the way.

Shaw steps into the interrogation room, and Mrs. McIntosh heaves a dramatic sigh of relief. "Detective, Roman confessed everything."

His gaze flicks to me, an eyebrow raised. "Did he?"

"Yes. He killed my Brielle. You have to arrest him."

Shaw nods thoughtfully, and my heart sinks. I need to call my attorney. If Shaw arrests me, they'll hold me until my arraignment, and the judge could turn down my bail request. I can't leave Claire and the girls alone while Olsen and Brielle's mother are free.

"Right. You should stay here and tell this officer everything you know. Mansfield, with me," he says, and jerks a thumb over his shoulder. He opens the door wider, and the same uniform who was with us earlier enters the interrogation room.

Mrs. McIntosh is pleased and settles onto a metal chair, hugging her purse to her chest. The officer stands stoically in the corner and stares straight ahead.

I don't have time to ask if he's actually going to question Brielle's mother. Shaw strides away and I have no choice but to follow. I'm not in cuffs, and he didn't read me my rights. Am I under arrest for Brielle's murder or not? I follow him down a hallway and no one looks concerned.

"We had a call come in from Jack Durand. We have what appears to be a hostage situation. You know Rafferty Clark and Claire Durand?"

I swallow hard. "Yeah. Raff's a friend and Claire's my fiancée."

"Helping you out, huh?" he asks, pushing through a door that lets out into the police department's parking lot. He unlocks an unmarked police car and gestures for me to get into the front with him.

"Raff's been investigating on my behalf," I admit, settling into the sedan and latching my seatbelt.

"Got a lot further than I did. Never would have suspected Greg Olsen. I liked you, especially after you dropped off the grid and we found your truck."

"If you believe that, why did you ask Mrs. McIntosh to give her statement?"

"Didn't want her disappearing on me. I'm charging her with obstruction. She didn't turn him in, and she knew from the second he did it."

Shaw speeds down the street, and I stare out the window, the flashing lights and wailing siren clearing our way through the city. It's past rush hour, and the streets aren't clogged like they would have been an hour ago. He makes good time following the GPS directions to the north side of town, and we're close to the mobile home park where Brielle's family lives in under twenty minutes.

We turn onto the narrow gravel road that leads to Olsen's trailer. Three police cruisers skid to a stop behind a black truck that I assume is Raff's and the beat-up black car Preston said Brielle got into the night she disappeared. Jack and Veronica are already standing in the grass waiting, and I don't give Shaw a chance to stop the car. I unlatch my seatbelt, open the door, and leap out.

Veronica's face is hidden against Jack's chest, and her shoulders shake.

My heart pounds. Veronica's steady. If she's crying, something bad happened.

"What's going on?" I ask.

"Emma called 911 as soon as I answered Claire's call. We knew where they were headed, and she wouldn't call unless she needed help. We just got here. Olsen has a gun, that's all I know," Jack says, his hand resting against Veronica's back.

"Are Felicity and Daisy okay?"

"Emma's there with Zoey and Heath and their girls."

A gunshot blasts from inside Olsen's house, and I need all my strength not to run inside. I can't lose Claire. I just found her again. She owes me, goddammit. She owes me a future, a life raising our children. She owes me a honeymoon and waking up in bed with her, laughing about the day we have ahead of us, family vacations, and birthdays, and holidays. She owes me for the four years she was too scared to love me.

Veronica jumps, and Jack's hold on her tightens.

Shaw rushes into the trailer, his weapon clutched in his

hand. Three uniformed officers are behind him, their weapons also drawn.

A moment later Claire steps onto the sagging porch. Our eyes meet across the cop cars, dirt, and desperation, and she runs toward me.

CHAPTER TWENTY-TWO

Claire

Wood splinters behind Raff, and a framed painting hanging on the wall near a round kitchen table falls to the floor.

"You shoot like a girl," Raff says, striding unruffled toward Olsen who's desperately aiming to get another shot off, his hand slick with sweat. He grips the gun and squeezes the trigger, but Raff smashes his fist into the man's face. Olsen drops to the floor, moaning, and the gun skids across the carpet. Flexing his hand, Raff kicks it under a chair. "No offense, kid."

"None taken," I say faintly.

He presses his foot to the center of Olsen's back, pinning him in place. Olsen doesn't say anything, only closes his eyes against the sound of heavy footfalls thundering up the wooden steps to the door. Blood trickles from his cut lip.

Police swarm inside, and a plainclothes detective Raff seems to know cuffs Olsen and yanks him off the floor. Olsen spits blood onto the linoleum and glares.

Raff adjusts his suitcoat and tie and swipes a hand through his hair. "Let's get out of here."

An officer holds the door open for me, and I step into the bright sunlight. Roman is standing next to Jack and Veronica. I weave around the officers standing in the narrow driveway and launch myself into his arms.

"Ah, dollface," I hear Raff say, and I peek from Roman's chest. Raff's wiping the tears off her cheeks. "He wasn't dangerous. Not with a gun, at least."

Roman pulls back and grips my shoulders. "Are you okay?"

"Yeah, thanks to Raff. He had it under control."

"I'm glad you thought so. Crazies can be unpredictable." He tightly holds Veronica and kisses the top of her head.

"I wasn't scared." I was, but I would never tell anyone.

"You did good, calling Jack. Exactly what I wanted you to do."

Shaw pushes Olsen out of his trailer, blood running down his chin, his hands secured behind his back.

"I don't suppose we can go home." I want to see the girls. "Are Felicity and Daisy okay?"

"I asked Jack the same thing. Emma's at the penthouse with Heath, Zoey, and their girls," Roman says.

Jack pulls his phone out of his pocket and hooks an arm around my neck the way he used to do when we were kids. "I better call her, tell her everything turned out."

"Thanks," Roman says, reluctantly giving my brother room to hug me. "We can't leave yet. It will be a long night piecing this all together for the cops. This started a long time ago."

Jack releases me and moves away to have a private moment with Emma. She would have been here if it hadn't been for the babies. I'm grateful people I trust are there to keep them safe.

"Lacey was Greg Olsen's wife," I say.

Roman nods and cuddles me to him. "I found out earlier.

They're holding Brielle's mother at the station. She was in on it."

I blanch. "She knew Olsen killed her."

"Yeah, she did. The money was more important. All they wanted was money."

"What do you mean? Zeke's money?"

A shadow crosses over his eyes. "No. Brielle. Her meeting me, us dating. It was a setup, and Olsen planned it. She was supposed to get me to marry her so her family could have access to my money."

"Oh, Roman, no." My heart sinks.

"She never loved me, didn't even like me touching her. Every time we had sex, she hated every second of it. It was all a lie. All a waste. Fuck." He turns away.

"It wasn't a waste," I say to his back.

He whips around, his eyes flashing with fury. "How can you say that? The past two years were a sham. She didn't love me, Claire. She let me get her pregnant to reel me in, but after Felicity was born, she realized her mistake. It's why Olsen killed her. She wanted to leave me and go back to her boyfriend."

Raff, Veronica, and Jack are quiet, listening.

"The past two years were for nothing. A waste."

He scowls. "That's what I just said."

"Then you should give Felicity to Preston. He loved her—I think he would appreciate having a piece of his girlfriend back. Give her to him and forget this ever happened." I lift my chin.

Roman staggers backward like I slapped him, and behind me, Jack sucks in a breath.

"Is that what you want? You said you love her," Roman chokes out.

"It's not what I want. It's what you want. Brielle used you, and I get that. But you used her, too. I was stupid and scared and put you in that position. *None* of this would have happened if I had talked to you like you begged me to. Instead, I ran away, and you found something with her. Maybe it was fake, but Felicity came out of that. If there's no good in it, then give her away."

The policemen watching are silent, and the birds have stopped singing. There's nothing but the howl of a dog across the trailer park and the cracking of Roman's heart.

Tears run down his cheeks. "I can't. She's my daughter, and I love her."

He might have a difficult time coming to terms with the idea Brielle and her family used him, but in some way, don't we all use each other? I used Zeke to try to forget about Roman. Zeke used me to hide Lacey.

"Then we'll keep her. Will you hug me?" I ask him, stepping closer. He wraps me in his arms, his face sticky and covered with stubble against my cheek. "I love you, Roman. And my love was never fake. I just didn't know how to give it to you."

He kisses me, and his lips taste of salt. "I love you, too. And I'm sorry I dragged you into this."

"It wasn't you. It didn't start with you. It started with Lacey and Zeke falling in love, and maybe that can be a good thing too. Now we have Daisy."

Roman shakes his head, brushing my hair out of my face. "You've come a long way from the woman who divorced me."

I reach my hand out, and Jack clasps it. "I had a lot of help. Let's finish this."

The detective who arrested Olsen is leaning against a car, his ankles crossed, waiting for us. In Jack's truck, we follow him to the police station where we sit until well past midnight, Roman and Raff going over everything they found during their own investigation. Pieces fall into place, a scheme so clever in its simplicity I can't help but be impressed. Greg Olsen was cunning and desperate and the only thing that thwarted his plan was love.

After the last I is dotted and the last T is crossed, we spill out into the parking lot, the crickets chirping, the lot lights bleeding a milky white across the pavement. Roman won't face charges for running or abandoning his truck, and a weight drops from his shoulders.

It's over.

We step into the penthouse I'll share with Roman for the rest of my life. Emma, Zoey, and Heath are waiting for us and Graciela is also awake, waiting for Veronica who hugs the little girl and sits with her on the couch.

Daisy and Felicity are sleeping in Zoey's and Emma's arms, and Roman thanks them for babysitting.

I kiss the girls' cheeks wanting to hold them, but I don't want to wake them. I have the rest of my life for snuggles.

Jack settles into a chair, and Emma cuddles into his lap with Felicity. One day they'll have their own, adding to my family.

"It feels good, doesn't it?" Roman says, his hand cupping the back of my neck. "Thank you for giving this back to me."

"Thank you for not giving up." I brush a kiss over his cheek.

Raff steps next to us, a glass of whiskey in his hand. "Are you ready to negotiate?"

"Can we do that in the morning?" Roman asks, stifling a yawn.

"Negotiate what?" I ask at the same time.

Roman nuzzles my ear. "The last piece of our future."

I know exactly what he's talking about, and I smile at Raff. "Perfect."

CHAPTER TWENTY-THREE

Roman

We don't meet Raff for over a week.

Zoey, Heath, and their girls ended up spending the night since Paige and Hilary were already asleep upstairs. With Veronica's urging and a promise to see her in the morning, Graciela went to bed, too. I helped Claire put Felicity and Daisy down in our room, and the adults lingered, sipping whiskey and enjoying each other's company. Claire and I didn't stumble into the bedroom until close to three in the morning, and we fell asleep, Felicity between us.

We used the days to spend time together without the pressure of a murder charge hanging over my head. We put the nursery together, two cribs against the wall and a rocking chair under the window that will go unused—Claire and I prefer to feed the girls in her sitting room. When the girls are older, they'll need a playroom too, but for now the nursery near our suite if full of toys and will be enough.

Without Felicity in our bed, I make love to Claire whenever I can. The first time I woke up in the middle of the night and kissed her awake, I was hesitant. She knew what I was feeling, and she said, "I'll always want you, I'll always need you," and she slanted her lips over mine and spread her legs in invitation. It will be a long time before the sting of knowing Brielle didn't want me that way fades. I feel dirty, my palms gliding over Claire's skin, but she reads me better than she ever has and never fails to have a gentle word of love to whisper in my ear in the middle of the darkest hours of the night. Our second chance at marriage will be a different experience for both of us.

Claire reached out to Catherine, and we hired Daisy's nanny to watch the girls Monday through Friday, perhaps with some weekend hours thrown in. We have plenty of people willing to babysit, but everyone is planning weddings and we don't want to impose. Catherine arrived at the penthouse excited and not a little teary-eyed thinking she may never see Daisy again. The little girl brightened when she saw her, too, and Claire and I shared a smile. We did the right thing.

The morning we meet Raff is cool, a brief reprieve from the summer heat. I hold Claire's hand, and we walk down the sidewalk to Raff's office. "Are you sure this is okay?"

I apologized for not asking her if this was something she wanted to do, but she said, "It's the perfect solution. He doesn't want to shut it down or sell it to someone he's not sure he can trust, and we need more than the girls. I couldn't think of a better fit."

She pushes me against the building and presses her body against mine. I love how her body talks, but it's when she speaks, her voice low and raspy, that's when I know she's telling me the truth. "As long as you're okay not having your own firm. Are you sure you don't want to be an attorney again?"

"Nothing will be able to compare to working with you every day," I say, my hands rubbing her back.

"Then you don't need to ask me again." She pauses. "I know you're not used to me talking, but I promise that if I need you to hear something, I *will* speak, so long as you always promise to listen."

"I'll need time to shake off those two years with Brielle. I know it's not fair to hurt. I admit I wasn't as invested as I thought she was, but we shared a lot of what I thought were good times. To find out it was all a scheme . . . I feel like a dirty old man who coerced her into sex and a pregnancy."

"I can't speak for her," Claire says, pedestrians walking by, traffic congesting the road, "but you were with her for a long time. Deep down, if she would have had a real problem with you, you would have known. Roman, you are so kind, warm, and generous. She liked being with you regardless of how or why you met, but like isn't love and in the end, she wanted Preston." She kisses me, her lips warm and soft. "I love you, and I'm sorry she's gone."

I bury my face in her hair and hold back a sob. Brielle didn't love me, and I didn't love her, and that's the crux of it. "I love you, too. You will never know how much."

"I think I do, but I'll let you show me," she says, smiling, her dimple winking, and like old times, I press a kiss to it and she laughs.

Upstairs in his office, Veronica's waiting with Raff and he has a breakfast spread out on a table between two leather couches. The bullpen is full of bloggers typing their posts for the e-zine, and for the first time since Claire divorced me, I'm looking forward to the future.

"Not many things work out," he says, gesturing for us to sit. We do, and he and Veronica do the same. "But you asked me if

I would sell, and something clicked. I wouldn't give *Talk of the Town* to just anyone, but you and Claire? I like it."

"We do too," I say, holding Claire's hand. "We need something more than Daisy and Felicity, but I'm not interested in going back to divorce law and Claire's had a difficult time finding something that would satisfy her professionally. She's done fishing." I say it jokingly, but I've never been more serious. Her days of trolling for a husband are over.

She blushes.

"There are a few things I'd like to go over with you," he says, pushing a file toward me. "I handpicked all my bloggers. I'd hate to see anyone go."

"Claire and I will need a few days to get to know your staff, but I doubt keeping everyone will be a problem. The e-zine obviously brings in enough to pay their salaries and then some. They'll also know a lot more than us, and until Claire and I figure things out, we'll depend on them."

Raff nods. "I still have time before campaigning pulls me away for good, and until then, I can train you in, so to speak. You'll need to learn the back end of the site, who posts what when, and the topics they write about. You're going to create content, too, I assume."

Claire nods. "Of course. We've consumed your content for years, so we know what your readers like. We may add to it, a fashion segment perhaps. An advice column in the way of Dear Abby, but we know gossip is what your audience likes most, and we don't plan to change that."

"Good. People like spilled tea, the more the better, and pouring whiskey in it has paid my bills, but we add the real stuff to lend a sense of legitimacy and professionalism. That piece my guy did on Variant went viral—in business circles. It was a big win for us, but scandals . . ."

"We all like dirt," Claire says wryly, knowing she's been the subject of her fair share of mudpies.

"Of course we do, no point in lying about it. You have the connections to keep that part of it going, so remember to check in with it every so often. We don't think of it because we live it, but readers want to know what we're doing."

I nod. "We can start with me. I'll give you the exclusive—what happened between Brielle and me. It can be your last big piece."

"Might as well go out with a bang," he says. "Now, we haven't talked price. I pulled the numbers—what you can expect yearly from subscriptions for the premium content and ads."

I glance at Claire. We didn't talk about what we'd pay Raff. Between us, we can afford any price he names. "I don't want to buy it from you."

Raff laughs. "I don't need the money, but I put a lot of work into this 'zine, and I'm not giving it away."

"What, exactly, did your mother say when she forced you to get rid of it?"

Veronica winces, and Raff catches it out of the corner of his eye. He twists on the couch and cups her cheeks in his hands. "Stop. I love you. I'd do it again in a heartbeat."

She swallows. "I know."

Raff turns back to me, his arm around his fiancée. "We didn't go into details. She doesn't want me running it or writing for it. That's about as far as it got. She was more interested in me being Bridgeport's mayor and knowing I can't do both. Lately, she's been all about meeting Nic, and we're scheduled to fly out tonight now that things have calmed down. You don't have to worry about the 'zine—Justin can handle things while Nic and I are gone for a couple of days, and when we get back, we can dig in. Why?"

"Because I was thinking, if you don't want to sell it, don't. Claire and I will take it over, write for it, manage it, draw a salary from it, but the whole thing can stay in your name, legally, and say, in five years, we revisit and revise. Maybe you want it back after your stint, maybe we don't want to keep it. Maybe you like being mayor and want to sell it, and we love running it and want to buy it. Who will know by then? But what I know now is *Talk of the Town* is your baby, and Claire and I need more than our babies. It's a good compromise. Claire? We didn't talk about this part of it. Are you on board with not buying it outright?"

She leans forward. "We know how much it means to you, Raff. Let us babysit her and see where we are in a few years, after your first term."

"You'd still have all the say. To compare notes, we could have a meeting every quarter. What do you think?" I ask.

Raff stares at the table, and Veronica rubs his back. He's emotional, and I get up to give him space. At the little bar near the window, I pour him a drink. It's too early for it, but he accepts it gratefully and drains it before he can speak. "Are you sure?"

"Yeah, we're sure."

"Then you have a deal. My mother won't look too closely at it. In her mind, she won, and that's all she cares about. Thank you." He holds out his hand, and I give it a brisk shake. Claire does the same. "I have a few things to amend, then, if that's the way we're going."

"Don't rush. This is between friends, and we're good without signatures for now."

Claire and I stay for another hour, nibbling on the pastries Raff served and drinking his booze we pour into orange juice so we don't feel bad about drinking so early in the morning. I can savor his whiskey now, sipping to enjoy rather than drinking to numb the pain, and my need for a cigarette is gone.

"Have a safe flight," Claire says, hugging Veronica goodbye.

Raff brushes his lips over Claire's temple. "You got this, kid."

"For the first time in years, I think you're right."

I think he is, too.

That night, after we've had dinner and the girls are bathed, the four of us sit on the bed in our bedroom. I'm feeding Felicity, my back propped against the headboard, and I look into her sweet little face. It doesn't matter how she came to be, if Brielle wanted to have a baby or only did to manipulate me. Because Greg Olsen confessed and dragged Brielle's mother down with him, they don't have any rights to Felicity. Her father claims he didn't know what his wife was doing, but he hasn't asked to see his granddaughter and if he's not asking, I'm not offering. Maybe it's selfish of me, but avoiding her family feels right.

Claire reads Daisy a book and the baby grins, her hands patting at the picture book filled with textured squares. So far her transition has been smooth, and we have Jack to thank. Her eyes glow when he gives her attention, and he can rock her to sleep like no one else can.

I can't say my whole life is in this room. Claire has given me the children I craved, the love I needed from her from the second we met, but I also realize how important family is. Jack and Emma will be imperative parts of our lives, and I'm looking forward to meeting Claire's mother and reconnecting with her father. Raff and Veronica are good friends, and I missed Heath and Zoey and their little ones.

It was right that I came here, to the place I once considered home, and will again because finally, damned her stubbornness, Claire has finally given me what I want.

We lay the babies in their cribs, and I tug on her hand,

urging her to follow me to the balcony. The city is bright with lights and life. She leans against the balustrade, the wind teasing her hair, playing with the hem of her nightgown.

There aren't any words, but her body still speaks to mine.

Wrapping my arms around her, I press my chest to her back.

And listen.

CHAPTER TWENTY-FOUR

Jack

If someone would have told me regular meals at Rafferty Clark's house would be a thing, I would have said they were fucking crazy.

It's funny how life has a way of showing us who's boss.

In Raff's kitchen, I open a much-needed bottle of wine. He's hosting another dinner party, something we do twice a month, somewhere. It's not always here, but Heath and Zoey's girls like his renovated factory building the best. Graciela, especially, since she knows she'll definitely see Veronica when we all meet for dinner. At first we were concerned with her attachment, but as the weeks went by and Veronica attended therapy sessions with her, their relationship turned into a mutual respect between females. When they go for a girls' night out, sometimes Zoey allows Gracie to join them. It's nice to see.

My sister has come a long way, and she's never been happier. She chats with Mia and Haisley and Zoey and Heath about *Talk of the Town*, sitting next to Roman, his arm around her. The 'zine is such a great fit for her, and working alongside Roman has opened her up even more. Daisy and Felicity round her out in a way I never thought possible, and I love those little stinkers with all my heart. She visits our mother once a week, driving to Lilyvale with Roman and the girls.

They were married in a little church not far from Mom's house, and it meant a lot to Claire she was there. So was our father, but unfortunately, Mom and Dad don't speak. There are some things that can never be repaired, and their relationship is one of them. They don't let that interfere, and I'm grateful they can set it aside and enjoy time with us.

I drive out, though not as often. Mom loves Emma and she's attending our wedding, too. In a few weeks, we're getting married in the same church as Claire and Roman, and they can't go by fast enough. Especially for Paige who reminds me every chance she can I asked her to be our flower girl. Raff is less excited to be a groomsman, but he's already had practice as Roman's best man.

Everyone is looking forward to Raff and Veronica's ceremony in Boston next fall, and Veronica asked me to give her away, an honor I humbly accepted with tears in my eyes.

Sometimes people will still ask if I resent Raff and Veronica their relationship, but how could I? Veronica is where she belongs, Raff whispering something into her ear, his hand resting on her thigh, making her laugh. I've loosened up, not gritting my teeth whenever he calls Emma "baby girl." It's his way of showing affection, and I could never keep away the people who love her. I've loved her from the very beginning, so who am I to blame anyone?

"You always get sad when you're thinking about the past," Emma says. I grip the corkscrew and she covers my hand with hers.

"I'm not sad. I think those days are finally behind me," I say, brushing her cheek with my fingers.

"I'm not pregnant yet," she says softly.

No one is paying us any attention, and I rest my forehead against hers. "I don't care. Emma, I love you so much. I look at you, what our relationship has given to me, to us, and it doesn't matter. As long as you can stand here, look me in the eyes, and tell me you love me, that's all I need."

"I do love you. From the moment we met."

"Then I'm happy."

She reaches onto her toes to kiss me, and I press my lips to hers.

Carrying the wine, I hold her hand and lead her to the table where she sits in my lap.

I used to think I needed a baby to create a family, but I've learned over the past few months that family is what you make it, and mine is perfect, just the way it is.

If you like trilogies, I have another one available! The Ghost Town Trilogy about three damaged rockstars is available on Kindle, in Kindle Unlimited, and Paperback. Fall in love with Sheppard, Eddie, and Brock . . .

Lust, forbidden love, and betrayal haunts rock bands, and Ghost Town is no exception.

When one of our bandmates dies in a tragic accident, our lead singer, Sheppard, falls into a spiral of depression. Out of desperation, our manager hires a life coach to get him back onto his feet and into the recording studio.

Sheppard looks into Derrick's death and finds out people will die, but their secrets don't.

https://www.amazon.com/dp/B0CDQJ28SB

I hope you enjoyed the *Lost & Found* trilogy! If you did and want to keep up with news, special sales, and giveaways, sign up for my newsletter and have exclusive access to that and a free full-length ugly-duckling billionaire romance novel, *My Biggest Mistake*. Sign up here: https://vmrheault.com/subscribe/

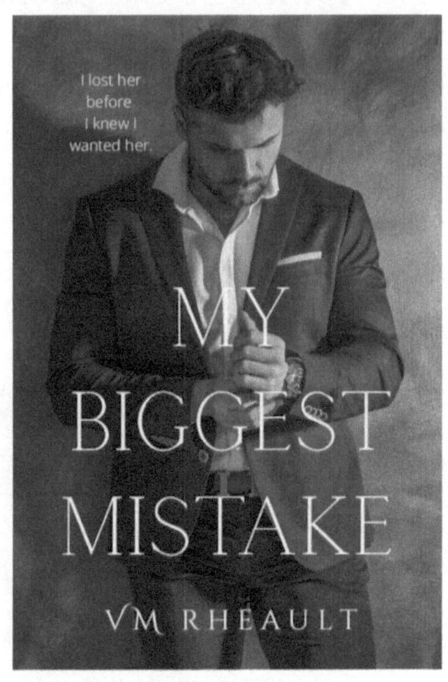

ALSO BY VM RHEAULT

Captivated by Her (Cedar Hill Duet Book One)

Addicted to Her (Cedar Hill Duet Book Two)

————

Rescue Me

————

Give & Take (The Lost & Found Trilogy Book One)

Lost & Found (The Lost & Found Trilogy Book Two)

Safe & Sound (The Lost & Found Trilogy Book Three)

————

Faking Forever

————

Twisted Alibis (Ghost Town Trilogy Book One)

Twisted Lullabies (Ghost Town Trilogy Book Two)

Twisted Lies (Ghost Town Trilogy Book Three)

————

A Heartache for Christmas

ABOUT THE AUTHOR

VM Rheault writes billionaire romance and contemporary romance under Vania Rheault.

She lives in Minnesota with her two children. When she's not writing, she's working her day job, sleeping, or enjoying the four seasons with a hot cup of coffee in hand.

Find her at vmrheault.com.